# Ghosts of
# Sackett Lake

By

Phil Sills

International Standard Book Number 13: 978-1-60452-029-3
International Standard Book Number 10: 1-60452-029-9

Library of Congress Control Number: 2009935131

BluewaterPress LLC
52 Tuscan Way Ste 202-309
Saint Augustine FL 32092

http://www.bluewaterpress.com

This book may be purchased online at -

http://www.bluewaterpress.com/ghosts
or through
amazon.com

You can take the boy out of Brooklyn...
but you can never take Brooklyn out of the boy

# Dedication

To my wife and life partner Jackie, my sons Mike and Chris, and my daughters June, Bonnie, and Lisa

# Acknowledgements

The author wishes to extend his sincere appreciation and thanks to his dear friends, Irene and Mike Toomey for their support and encouragement.

The author also wishes to thank his publisher, Joe and Ardis Clark of BluewaterPress LLC, for their skillful and intuitive editing of my manuscript.

# Prologue

*7:27 AM, Monday, June 24, 1999*
*Far Rockaway, New York*

Slowly and painfully I sat up to the sounds of vertebra cracking as I arched my back and rubbed my eyelids trying get the circulation in my body going. I felt like one of those cartoon characters who has just been run over by a Mack truck and has to peal himself off the pavement. After fumbling around for a few seconds, I finally found my elusive reading glasses perched on top of my head. 'How did they get there?' I thought.

It's 7:27 AM, I said to myself as I adjusted my glasses and peered down my nose at the Mickey Mouse watch on my wrist. My wife, Vicky, got it for me at Disney World. It had to be eight, nine years ago. I think I had one as a kid. Well anyway, I told her that I did and she surprised me with it. Naturally, the next time we went back, I got her the ladies version. Those were nice times. The boys were little then. I took a deep breath, closed my eyes and thought how happy, how simple and uncomplicated life was then and how things can suddenly change.

Let's see its now 7:28 AM, that meant that I've been scrunched down, sleeping on and off in my car for over six hours. I was so stiff that I wasn't even sure my legs would work anymore. And trying to kick my shoes off didn't help either when it caused a sharp cramping pain in my right calf. To make matters worse, when I reached down to rub my leg, I banged my head on the steering wheel. As I fingered a little lump forming on my forehead, all I could think of was, 'what else could go wrong?'

Looking around the car, I noticed that the windows were all covered with condensation except for a couple of small circular spots I'd made with my knuckles. When my boys were little, I used to play a game with them to keep them occupied. I'd rub the frost off my windshield with a finger and say to the oncoming traffic, "peek-a-boo." They'd giggle and strain in their car seats to imitate me by rubbing on their windows and screaming, "peek-a-boo, peek-a-boo."

On the seat next to me were the crinkled, ketchup stained food wrappers of last night's dinner, a Whopper with fries, and in the cup holder, a plastic cup holding the watery remains of a Diet Coke. I fidgeted around and found the lever that adjusted the seat back and brought it to an upright position bringing me face to face with the reflection of a tired, gray haired, 60 year old man in the rearview mirror. That confirmed it, not only did I feel like I was hit by a truck, I looked like it too. And try as I might to rub the wrinkles away, they just sprung back every time. It wasn't fair. Nor was life, I thought. You reach that magical age of 60 on life's odometer and it seems as if your body's warranty has run out. Your motor doesn't start well on cold mornings and when it does, it looks for any excuse to stop and rest. And if that's not bad enough, when I go to see my trusted doctor, he tells me I've got to lose twenty pounds and exercise knowing full well that I'll probably stop off on the way home to pick up a pint of Ben & Jerry's Coffee Heath Bar Crunch ice cream. I feel so guilty about my lack of resolve that I've put off my annual physical exams with him because I don't want to hear what organ or body part is defective or wearing out because of my weight. The way I see it, when you reach 60, you should be allowed to eat whatever you wish, sleep on the couch as long as you wish, and if you want stimulation, have long metaphysical discussions about life and death with your dog.

I rolled my window down to get a whiff of some fresh air and a better look at the street where I'd been parked. It was a quiet residential street with single family homes. You know, mostly little two bedroom capes and ranches about twenty five feet apart with manicured shrubs and well cared for postage stamp sized lawns. Some sporting birdbaths, bird feeders, and others, "For Sale," signs. My guess was that the place was rife with retirees looking to sell so that they could migrate south to escape the cold.

And as I sat there daydreaming, I thought, 'how could something as innocent as wanting to visit a place you might have worked one summer, 44 odd years ago, turn into such a nightmare?' Then, I noticed a car slowly turn onto the street. At first, I was temporarily blinded by its headlights but then, as he got closer, the unmistakable array of lights mounted on his roof became visible. It was a police car. With an adrenaline rush, I realized it was too late to run and that there was no place to hide. Frantically I rolled up the window and yanked the seat adjustment lever as hard as I could propelling me backwards almost through the floor. There I stayed motionless, praying he'd go away.

# ONE

It all started a little over a week ago, June 12th, 1999. After herding my twins, Randy and Kenny, into the back seat of our ancient Volvo wagon with promises that this would be "a trip they'd never forget," I stopped at my local Mobil gas station to "fill'er up." While Phil, the co-owner of the gas station, was pumping fifteen or so gallons of premium into my almost empty tank, I walked around the car to check out the tires. They looked O.K., but what did I know about tires anyway? The car was twelve years old and had; I'm almost embarrassed to say, one hundred and sixty seven thousand miles on it. I knew it was time to trade it in because of how much gas it drank. It seemed to get thirsty every time we passed a gas station. I'm not kiddin', it seemed to cough as I approached the Mobil gas station and if I didn't pull in to give it a sip, it would start making these funny growling noises like, 'stall, I'm going to stall.' It got so bad I debated whether or not to carry a can of gas in the trunk of my car.

Over the years, I've had lots of cars . . . seven, ten, fifteen . . . I forget how many. Yet of all the various makes and models, one stands out . . . that Caddy convertible. I remember that one, it was a pisser. I was going to the University of Miami back in the 60's and working at a ritzy clothing store on 'Miracle Mile' in Coral Gables. I usually took the bus to work but one day a college buddy, Pat, offered me a lift to work on the condition that he could use my employee discount for a sports jacket he wanted to buy.

"Sure," I said, "Pick out what you want and I'll buy it later."

Well, on our way there, I was telling Pat that I'd love to buy a car and . . . whammo, like Yogi Berra's déjà vu, there it was! Parked right out in front of, 'Honest Ed's Used Car Lot,' was the most beautiful car I'd ever seen. It literally took my breath away. It had these sensuous curves and spoke of, pickup power. It was a 1951 steel grey Cadillac convertible. The top was down, tucked neatly under a black canvas cover exposing a rich looking, buttery brown leather upholstery.

Noticing my interest, Pat came to an abrupt stop. "Go try it out," he demanded.

"Oh, I ... I can't afford it," I said.

"Bullshit. Just see how it feels," he said.

I remember running my hand over the hot metal hood and opening the massive door and sliding into the driver's seat. It had a genuine leather steering wheel and a rich polished wooden dashboard. As I sat there imagining I was driving my Cadillac under a moonlit Miami night, Pat closed the door and as he did I could swear the car said to me, ever so quietly, "take me home big boy."

"It's you," Pat said, with a broad toothy smile.

I remember the leather seat was burning hot but all I could feel was the excitement of sitting in that luxurious car. The rest is sort of fuzzy. But, by hook or crook, I did finagle a loan and did we have fun cruising Miami Beach at night in that convertible.

There was nothing like it. Pat was working his way through college singing weekends in a band at a couple of the big hotels on Collins Ave on Miami Beach. He had put together a makeshift trio; piano, drums, and he sang while pretending to be playing the bass. He said the clubs paid more if there were three instruments. Come Friday night, we'd throw the bass in the back seat of the Cadillac, stuff the drums in the trunk, and pile everyone in to head out for that night's gig. It was a blast! I used to just love sitting in the back of a lounge munching on warm Rum Rolls while drinking Pina Coladas watching women throw their rooms keys at Pat as he sang those romantic ballads.

Ah, that was a lifetime ago. Today I'm tooling down the Massachusetts Turnpike doing 75 mph heading for the Catskill Mountains in upstate New York with my 12 year old twin boys in tow. We left our home in Hull, which is a coastal community approximately 30 miles south of Boston this morning after packing enough stuff for a trip to the moon; clothes, games, books, and more games. The idea for the trip started innocently enough when I returned from my mother's funeral in Florida. I had to close up her home and in the process found a cigar box tucked in a corner of her closet, it was labeled, 'Max's Memorabilia.' Inside it were some old black and white photos and a color postcard of The Laurels Hotel and Country Club in Sackett Lake, New York. The postcard was one I had sent to my dad in 1955, over forty years ago, saying I was working as busboy. There were also clumps of water logged papers, which had fused together. It looked like a Journal made up of cryptic, indecipherable notes.

Well, I had mentioned it to my wife Vicky, about . . . you know, how nice it would be to take the kids with me down memory lane and revisit some of the places of my youth. The trip would be an opportunity for me to bond with my boys. Yet, what I didn't tell her and what really troubled me was that I drew a complete blank about ever working at The Laurels. I knew it was a long time ago, over forty years ago . . . but no matter how hard I tried, nothing. I studied the postcard, an aerial view of The Laurels Hotel for clues, nothing. One of the photos was of a guy in his 20's, wearing a Temple University Athletic Dept. T-shirt. On the back it said, "Sam Bergman." The other photo was of a pretty girl, maybe 15 or 16. Scribbled on its back was, "My Daisy Mae."

Just thinking about it was driving me nuts. In fact, the night I brought the box back from Florida, I had a strange dream. I dreamt I was running wildly through the woods at night. I'm not sure if anyone was chasing me but I just couldn't stop. I remember waking in a cold sweat. The odd thing about it is that, I usually never remember my dreams.

What's also constantly nagging me is that some things in my past are so vivid, while others are just a blur and it's getting worse. I can't seem to remember the most mundane things lately, like where I put my keys or where I parked my car or what I had gone to the supermarket to buy. Deep down in my psyche something was telling me that I needed to take this trip before some door in my mind closes for good.

To help me remember that period, I even purchased music that was popular during the 1950's with the thought that it might help me recall the past. I put one of the cassettes into the car stereo and pushed back in my seat to let the music carry me back to that time:

*"Heavenly shades of night are falling, it's twilight time."*

I smiled and allowed myself a deep breath as an old ballad by the Platters softly poured from the car's stereo speakers. And as I sat there, staring out at nothing but highway, I thought to myself, just relax and let the music ... Bang!

A kick, with the force of a black belt in Karate, hit me at the base of my spine bringing me instantly back to reality. Kenny, defending himself from his brother Randy's attack, had inadvertently shot his foot into the rear of my seat with jarring results. Kenny, now 12 years old, was not the skinny, frail little boy he had once been. Now, fondly referred to as "the hulk," he was a five foot five and one hundred twenty five pounds of muscle. His constant protagonist and twin brother Randy was about the same height but ten pounds lighter. Their battle, at this moment in time, was over a Nintendo Gameboy cartridge.

"Boys, boys, boys ... stop that," I shouted. "If you can't behave, I'm going to have to put one of you in the front seat." I said, as I shot a glance at the boy's expressions through the rearview mirror to assess what impact, if any, my words might have on their future behavior.

"But he had it for over an hour," clamored Randy, straining on his seatbelt to grab Kenny's arm. Kenny, his dark brown eyes glued to the games tiny screen, deftly switched hands keeping the Nintendo just out of Randy's reach.

"Dad, tell him to let me have it," protested Randy.

I thought that this seemingly antagonistic behavior on their part was merely nonverbal expressions of their affection for one another. I was convinced that they acted the same way in the womb, pushing and shoving each other until birth and that they'll probably continue to do so all their lives. I had never been exposed to the mysteries of twins before and as I watched my sons develop, I realized that my boys shared some type of special, inexplicable bond and that their fighting was probably some ritualistic play acting.

"O.K., let me have the Nintendo," I demanded reaching my arm back over the seat.

"But I'm in the middle of a game," pleaded Kenny. "And I've only had it for a few minutes."

"That's a lotta bull," barked Randy. "He . . . ."

"That's enough," I said firmly interrupting him.

I reached over to lower the music so that I could make a point, saying, "You know, I ... I thought that you were both old enough to come with me on this trip. We're going to a special place you've never been to. A place dad once worked when he was just a little older than you are today. I wanted to share it with you," I said.

"Well, how long will it take?" chirped Randy while Kenny continued clicking the Nintendo controls to Randy's dismay.

"I thought we went over this the other day. I showed you where we were going and the route we're taking. We'll be stopping for lunch as soon as we get off the turnpike," I said.

Let's do this," I pleaded. "Kenny, you can use the Nintendo for another ten minutes then give it to Randy. O.K.?" I said.

"And, Randy, put on your headset and listen to some music until then, O.K.?" I suggested.

When I didn't hear any further discussion, I figured that my suggestions were accepted and resumed listening to my tape just in time to hear:

*"They asked how I knew,*
*My true love was true.*
*Ohhhhhhh, I of course replied,*
*Something here inside,*
*Cannot be denied."*

The music, like a masseurs touch, slowly relaxed the muscles in my neck and back and as I gazed out at the road ahead, I wondered what I hoped to accomplish by taking the kids with me and why was it so important now. What was the urgency of the trip? Was it a last desperate attempt to relive something in the past? Something I did or didn't do those many years ago? Did what happened in that place so far in the past set in motion events that I had no control over and in returning, could I, in retrospect, change things and their consequences? And if I found whatever it was I was looking for, would I recognize it now some forty years later? The more I pondered the trips rationale, the more ludicrous the whole idea seemed.

The boys were becoming restless again and I decided it was probably time for a pit stop at the next highway oasis. "We're going to stop at the next rest stop, O.K.," I announced.

"We'd better stop soon . . . or I'll pee in my pants!" advised Kenny.

I smiled at him through the rearview mirror and reassured him that the rest stop was only a few miles ahead.

"Can we call Mom?" Kenny asked.

"Sure," I replied. I thought of telling them to wait until we got to the rest stop to use the phone but decided the distraction now might be a better idea. I unclipped the cell phone from the cigarette lighter and handed it over my shoulder saying, "Just a quick one, O.K.?"

Kenny grabbed the phone before Randy could and pressing himself against his side of the backseat, as far away from his brother as he could and hit the #1 speed dial to call the house. It connected almost instantly.

Funny, I said to myself, that never happens when I use it.

"Mom, it's Kenny," he said, as he looked over at Randy with a big smile on his face as if he won some type of contest. "Yes, yes, we're alright," he said shaking his head and listening intently to his mother on the other end of the phone. Occasionally whispering some tidbits to her about how long the trip was and about having a lack of things to do and see, this undoubtedly was meant for me to hear as well.

"Can I speak to her now?" commanded Randy, reaching over to grab away the prize.

"Let me speak to Mom next, please," I requested.

Kenny, oblivious to our requests, continued unabated about how boring the darn ride was and how cramped he was in the back seat and on and on to his delight and our frustration.

"Just give me the ... phone," I caught myself before I said, "goddamned phone," knowing that they would use that outburst as a bargaining chip against me. I could hear them saying, "we're going to tell Mom what you said."

"I've got to tell Mom something . . . then it's all yours," I said, this time softly.

Kenny reluctantly passed the phone to me but not before giving it a few, "I love you too, Mom's and . . . kisses."

"Hi, honey," I said as a tractor-trailer thundered past me.

"What did you say?" said Vicky.

"This truck just went by at 100 mph and . . ." I started to say.

"Are you O.K.? I told you that this was a busy weekend and the traffic would be heavy," she continued, "I don't know why it was so important to take the kids with you on such a long trip. I mean what are they supposed to do?"

"Listen, we're pulling into a rest stop. Everything is O.K. I'll call you tonight," I said and pushed the end button disconnecting the call.

"But you promised I could talk to Mom," said Randy in dismay.

"Let's use the bathroom and I promise, you're the next one to use the phone ... O.K.?" I said pulling off the highway and stopping in front of the Burger King.

After collecting our bags of burgers, fries, and shakes we retired to one of those uncomfortable molded orange plastic booths that were not designed for the adult posterior. As I watched them inhaling their burgers and fries, I passed out napkins and attempted to open those little packets of ketchup without spraying the contents all over myself. I once had an embarrassing incident with one of those innocent looking ketchup packets. Unable to rip it open with my fingernails, I resorted to biting it open with my teeth only to have the contents explode into my mustache. The kids were little then and didn't know what to make of their Daddy with the red mustache. Even now, years later, they ask me to open their ketchup packets with my teeth hoping it will happen again.

"I'm still hungry," exclaimed Randy begging for another burger. I placated him with a couple of dollars saying, "See what you can get with his." Only to have him return a few moments later advising me that, "It doesn't buy anything!" Eager to start off our trip on a positive note, I found a five-dollar bill in my pocket and gave it to him. He snatched it from me like a frog catching a fly and was off. After all, I said to myself, 'keep 'em happy, we're on an adventure.'

# TWO

Around 7 PM I pulled off the highway at the first sign for Monticello and started looking for a place to spend the night. After passing a few motels reminiscent of, "The Bates Motel" of "Psycho" fame, I found a half decent looking motel on the outskirts of Monticello. The woman in the office was most likely the owner since she had a number of "rules" she wanted me to know about. "You pay in advance. You break it, you pay for it. Check-out time is 11 AM and don't go taking any of my towels either." I gave her my credit card and she told me where to find a rollaway cot for one of the boys.

The room was small and smelled of stale tobacco smoke. The knotty pine walls had a skim coat of polyurethane which had turned yellow and the low ceiling showed blotches of rusty water stains. The room had two twin beds which occupied most of the floor space and after setting up the rollaway; I had to literally walk on the beds to get into the bathroom. While I unpacked, the boys began their customary bickering as to who would sleep on, 'the thing,' referring to the cot and how it would be decided, one toss or three. When the contest was one each, the third and deciding toss accidentally rolled under the bed, whereupon each dove, head first, to discover who had won the prized twin bed.

"It was tails," cried Kenny straining his head under the bed." He cheated."

"Did not, you're a sore loser," replied Randy holding the nickel up for Kenny to see.

As Kenny made a grab for the nickel, Randy pulled it away only for it to become airborne, flying clear across the room and hitting a mirror that was resting on the dresser with a loud, CRAAACK.

"What's going on out there?" I protested while setting up the toiletries on the bathroom sink for the morning.

"Can't the two of you stop fighting for one freakin' ..." Oh, now I've done it, I thought as both boys stared at me from the bathroom doorway.

"I didn't mean to use that word. Daddy was just angry, I mean tired. It was a long ride and my back is killing me and . . . I'm sorry, O.K."

The decision on who was going to sleep here or there was put on hold pending one of more importance, where to eat dinner. Pizza was always an option, I thought and the ad for Mama Mia's in the thin Monticello phonebook looked inviting. So, I packed the boys back into the wagon for the short journey to town.

As I drove around looking for the pizza joint, I scanned the now empty streets hoping that we'd passed something familiar, something that I might remember. But the town looked like so many other old neglected towns that saw their businesses flee to the burbs where the Wal-Marts' and Safeways' had sprung up. It wasn't until we were almost out of town that I spotted Mama Mia's little red neon sign down a narrow side street.

The place was kind of Norman Rockwellian, with high school students fiddling with miniature jukeboxes mounted to their tables and assorted families crammed into booths. From the look of the place, had I not known that we were in upstate New York, we could have been in Kansas. We waited a few minutes until one of the booths were wiped down and were perusing the menu when this cute waitress came over to the table holding a pencil and a small order pad. Glancing at the boys, she smiled and asked them if they wanted a drink. Naturally, Randy puffing out his chest, and giving her one of his Charles Boyer smiles asked, "What brands of imported beers do you serve?"

With that, the waitress smiling from ear to ear recited 6-8 brands of beer staccato style ending with, "That's if you're old enough to drink?"

Bemused, Randy continued the fantasy and remarked, "How old do you think I am?"

The waitress, probably all of 17 herself, put the pencil to her lips and cocking her head to one side remarked matter-of-factly, "15."

Randy, poking his brother in the ribs, smiled at the waitress and said, "You're way off the mark."

"O.K." she said, "How old are you?"

Anxious to get an order in before the kitchen closed, I cut off the histrionics with, "We'll have two cokes, a Michelob and one large cheese pizza."

"Half pepperoni," blurted out Kenny looking at the waitress with far away eyes.

"The beer's for me," Randy said shaking his head and poking his thumb to his chest.

"Yeah, right," replied the waitress over her shoulder as she walked away scribbling on her pad.

"Did you ever come here?" asked Randy.

"No, I don't think I remember this place," I said.

"Dad, how come you don't remember if you've been here?" Kenny asked.

Hmm, I thought to myself, how much have I actually told the boys about our trip? It's an adventure I told them. They love adventures; their movies, their video games, their action hero toys . . . theirs is a world of adventure and fantasy. The actual violence they witness on TV is filtered through their prism of make-believe. Maybe that's true of all of us. We've become desensitized by movies and TV.

Luckily, I was able to dodge their questions as the waitress approached with our drinks. She put a coke in front of Kenny and one coke in front of me, then nonchalantly, placed the bottle of Michelob with the glass inverted over the top, in front of Randy. Randy deftly removed the glass from the Michelob and placed it in front of himself. Then with big smile on his face began the ritual of pouring it slowly into the glass as he'd seen me do countless times before.

"Let me have that, son," I said quietly.

"Oh just one sip, it can't hurt," pleaded Randy grasping the glass.

"No, they can lose their license," I said reaching for the glass.

Randy pretended to drink from the glass until seeing the waitress was out of eye shot, then handed the glass back to me and said, "You see, she thought I was 18."

"Where are we going for breakfast?" Asked Kenny.

"Don't you every think of anything else but food?" asked Randy sarcastically.

Frowning at his brother, he retaliated by poking him with an elbow in the ribs almost spilling the cokes.

"STOP IT!" I said sharply. Then, in a lower voice, I said, "If you can't behave, the two of you will eat all your meals in the motel room."

"But he ...," started Randy, until I cut him off, raising my hand signifying that it was enough.

"How was the beer? Can I get you another one?" asked the waitress, as she slung an arm over the back of Randy's chair with a coquettish grin on her face.

"Oh, ah, not right now," replied Randy, with an embarrassed look on his face. She smiled, and headed for another table with a noticeable wiggle in her walk.

"I think Randy's got a girlfriend," teased Kenny. "He always gets the girls," he mulled sullenly.

"Humm, I think you're right," I said to Kenny smiling.

I sat back in the booth looking at my 12-year-old boys, amazed at how quickly they had grown from a pair of butterballs that I once juggled in my arms to two strapping young men, who were already wearing some of my clothes. They were already taller than their mother and I expected them soon to tower over me, and I was 6'2". But thankfully they were still my babies, if only for a little while longer. They still slept with a night light, played with miniature Star War action figures and got into bed with me and my wife each morning to enjoy different parts of the newspaper; the Sports section for Randy, the Arts and Entertainment section for Kenny, before going down for breakfast and school. As babes, they were identical, but not so twelve years later as they now had begun to look different. Not completely, but enough that most people could now tell them apart. A far cry from the surreptitious techniques we used to tell them apart when they were newborns by painting a toenail with nail polish to tell who was who. It was a treat to watch them grow into manhood. I often thought that I had missed my own childhood growing up in Brooklyn and didn't want to push them too quickly into the modern pressures of manhood. I'd seen too many examples of parents who lived vicariously through their children and put them through so much pressure to excel, that the kids were often candidates for an early burn out. They'll have plenty of time to grow up, I thought. Now, let them enjoy just being children.

# THREE

The boys awoke early and switched on the TV to the ESPN channel to catch up on their favorite WWF wrestlers. No matter how many discussions I had with them about the fact that professional wrestling was choreographed down to the last flip-flop, the boys pretended that it was real. Each had their own heroes; Randy had a poster of 'The Rock' in his room and Kenny sported a poster of 'Hulk Hogan.' They dutifully followed each of their favorite wrestler's careers on TV, as well as on the Internet, even to the point of receiving e-mails from some of their heroes. I assumed that most of the e-mails from fans were actually answered by PR agencies under contract with the WWF. However, all this didn't stop the boys from following the day to day machinations of their action heroes. But in a way, I couldn't begrudge them this innocent diversion from reality, when in fact I listened intently at their age with the same enthusiasm to episodes of the 'Green Hornet' and the 'Lone Ranger' and his trusted friend, 'Tonto' on the radio. I guess if there were similar heroes and electronic marvels available during my day, I would have been hooked also.

After wolfing down an artery clogging breakfast at a McDonald's just outside of town, I checked the map to find the way to Sackett Lake. It didn't look too far from Monticello and as we drove along winding country roads, I noticed what looked like old bungalow colonies converted into summer camps by orthodox Jews. Some of their signs were in both English and Hebrew. It reminded me of some of the shops that had Yiddish lettering on their windows in Brooklyn where I grew up. One was a bakery around the corner from my building. In the morning, my mother would give me a list and some coins to bring to the bakery. I'd race down three flights of stairs, out the front door, past the tailor shop, the fishmonger, the drug store, to Edith's Bakery. I'd give the note and the fistful of change to the lady behind the counter.

She'd smile at me and hand me a cookie to eat while she threw my order into a white paper bag. She always said something to me in Yiddish as she handed me the bag, which I didn't understand but was smart enough to smile and nod my head in agreement with her. Then I'd dash home with the goodies; a loaf of challah bread and three hot cherry cheese Danish. I can remember to this day, the mouth watering smells of that bakery.

As we drove I hoped that maybe something along the way would bring back an inkling of my being here years ago but everything seemed unfamiliar. If I was here, if I had ever traveled down this road before, it was a total blank now. It troubled me how this period in my life, when I was sixteen, was now completely absent from my memory. Was I in some type of accident or had some type sickness that caused this void? I seemed to be able to remember things before and after this summer but something or someone erased this period in my life and I didn't have the vaguest idea of how or why or when it happened and the more I pondered the question, the more frightened I became of learning the truth. Maybe, I thought, I should heed the age old advice, "let sleeping dogs lie."

Then, just above a rise, I slowed down to get my bearings to inspect a field on the left side of the road surrounded by an old rusted chain link fence. As we rolled over the crest of a hill, there in front of us, down at the base of the hill was a large blue green lake surrounded by little white cottages. Elated, I called out to the boys, "hey look, there's a lake," but they were too involved attacking their Gameboy villains to bother looking.

"I think that's Sackett Lake!" I said with some excitement.

"Are we there yet?" they questioned in unison.

"I think so," I said hesitantly.

"Let's go down to the lake and check," I said.

At the base of the hill, just across from a small boat

rental shop was an old General Store. Its porch was cluttered with what looked like, yard sale rejects and a large sign which proclaimed in bold letters, 'BAIT' and underneath it, 'Night Crawlers for Sale.'

I parked the Volvo in front of what looked like a hitching post and told the boys to wait in the car while I went in to check where we were. Since the place didn't look like it had anything to eat or amuse them, they were happy to continue their life and death struggles against their Gameboy foes.

The General Store was a combination grocery and hardware store. The big items on sale this week seemed to be, "flypaper and rat traps." In the middle of the room, next to a large black wood burning stove, were stacks of 50 lb bags of cracked corn and rabbit food. On one side of the room the shelves were filled with fishing equipment and the other side groceries. Bags of rice, dried fish, condensed milk, bread, yellow mustard and ketchup were stacked here and there. Behind the counter was a stocky, grey haired woman wearing western gear. She reminded me of a modern day 'Dale Evans' with her black cowboy shirt and string tie. Behind her, hanging on the wall were black and white photos, most likely her children and grandchildren; a framed two dollar bill with some kind of writing on it; and a man standing proudly next to a large cow.

"Is that Sackett Lake over there?" I said, pointing towards the lake with my thumb.

"Yep," she said without looking up from a magazine she was reading on the counter.

"I'm looking for ah, The Laurels Hotel," I said.

She gazed at me for a few seconds expressionlessly, then said, "It's gone, burned down years ago."

"Gone, burned down," I repeated discouragingly.

"Yep," she said nodding her head.

I was shocked and didn't know what to say so I thanked her and slowly walked out of the store. I stood there, on the porch, looking at my car and the lake. I took the postcard of The Laurels out of my pocket and tried to determine where the hotel complex once was. It must have been the field we passed on the way down the hill, I thought, the one with the chain link fence. I went back into the store and using the postcard as a visual aid, asked the woman if that area we passed was where the hotel once was.

She took the card from me and after adjusting her glasses, nodded her head saying, "Yep, it was up on the hill. Has a fence around it." She came out from behind the counter, still holding onto my postcard and went to the open door to point using the card to where the hotel once stood. At first I thought she wanted to keep my card but she surrendered it as I thanked her.

When I got back to the car, I told the boys of the bad news and they wanted to know if that meant that we'd be heading home. I told them that, since we'd come this far, we'd might as well visit the site anyway.

"You know," I said, "We'll go exploring." They agreed and I swung the car around to go back up the hill. I found an opening in the fence and parked on the shoulder as close to the fence as I could.

Kenny, who had at this point stopped playing with his Gameboy, asked in utter disbelief, "Is this what we came to see? There is nothing here, Dad."

"Well, let's walk around anyway," I said in a quiet voice showing my disappointment for the first time.

We squeezed through the fence and walked up a path until we found a vantage point where we could look around the site. As I stood there, I couldn't believe what I saw. The site was flat, without any sign that it once housed one of the most popular resorts in the Catskills. As we wandered around the grounds the boys spied a light blue, Olympic sized swimming pool with puddles of green brown algae in its deep end. The twisted metal frame of a lifeguard's chair was still there facing the pool as well as a couple of pool ladders that were still attached to the inside walls of the pool. From where we were, we could see Sackett Lake just 100 yards down the hill.

Between patches of concrete, grass and weeds had grown to about two feet high around the pool and what looked like the black asphalt outline of a basketball court was now a garden of tall weeds. I wanted to tell the kids that they could imagine what once stood here by examining the aerial view of the hotel on the postcard but they had already started walking down towards the lake.

As I walked around in circles, I tried to imagine what the place looked like back then but couldn't. I also realized that it was impossible to describe the place to the kids from the postcard since every vestige of that celebrated resort had been carted away. Even the outlines of the crude foundations, where three or four story buildings once stood were merely lines in the dirt. Unlike foundations today, the makeshift construction practices of that era probably called for buildings to be merely stacked on top of cinder blocks or concrete slabs.

After finding nothing to occupy their attention at the lakefront, the boys rejoined me. I told them that we'd probably be heading out in a few minutes and that I was sorry to take them on such a wild goose chase and that I'd make it up to them. It was about then that Randy found an old spoon in the grass and rather than show it to Kenny, threw it with all his might over his head. Whereupon both boys raced, high stepping through the knee high grass, to find the spoon. Kids don't need toys, I thought, anything will keep them busy. When I caught up with them, Kenny had found the spoon sticking out of the ground, and proudly showed it off to Randy. It was like finding a needle in a haystack I told them.

Then a strange thing happened. As we stood there, I had the eerie feeling that time had stopped. That everything around me had just stopped moving. The trees, the sky, the grass, all had stopped moving. It was perfectly still. When I turned to see what the boys were doing, they were standing there facing the forest, their arms at their sides, frozen, like mannequins in a department store. Then, I felt a chill come over me, down to my bones. And as I stood there, I could have sworn I heard someone call my name, "Max," and as I turned in the direction of the voice, I saw a flash of light from deep within the woods and then again, a voice called my name, "Max."

As I stood there, gripped with fear, I was shocked back to reality as Randy grabbed my arm to ask, "When are we going back, Dad?"

I tried to make a mental fix, as I would when I'd try to retrieve an errant golf ball in the woods, as to where the flash of light came from. And as I headed for the woods, I called for the boys to follow me. Kenny came running up alongside me to ask, "Where are you going, Dad?"

"Just follow me," I said briskly, concentrating on a spot in the woods I thought the light came from.

We walked for a while through a thick wooded area, stepping over and around fallen trees. The ground was damp with a blanket of leaves and pine needles and had a sweet smell of rotting vegetation. The deeper we went into the woods, the darker and more menacing it felt. Then we saw it, in a small clearing surrounded by a stand of dead trees, an old rusted car resting on its frame. It looked like, over the years, the car had settled into the ground. The hood had plunged through part of the windshield and the body was just a rusted shell. Inside the car, a literal forest had grown with weeds and wild flowers spouting from where windows once were. At the rear of the car, a large branch had fallen on the trunk and jutting out from the opened trunk, a small pine tree was sprouting. Inexplicably, the boys picked up sticks and began reciting some sort of mumbo jumbo while circling the car and banging on it like it was a drum.

As I leaned against a tree staring at the old heap, something began stirring within me. There was something about the car, something familiar, something ominous. I watched in amazement as the boys performed some type of primitive ritual, racing around pounding on the car with their sticks. It seemed that the faster the boys ran, the louder the pounding. They were moving so quickly and the pounding, the pounding, that my mind began spinning. The boys ran and ran around the car until they were merely a blur. They were merely a blur, as I sank to my knees and all I could feel was the pounding in my head. I was dizzy and nauseous and felt as if I was going to faint. I shut my eyes and clenched my fists to ward off falling face down onto the wet ground. Then, a chill came over me like a wet blanket and my nose started running.

I felt cold, very cold. I snapped out of it to the sound of Kenny hitting the car with a rock and a loud ... BANG!

"Guys, guys," I cried out stumbling to my feet.

Both boys stopped their jousting around and looked at me with puzzled expressions.

It was at that instant, as the boys stared at me, that I realized I knew something about that rusted old car. For some inexplicable reason, I knew everything about that car, the year, make and model, but I didn't know why.

"You know boys, this is an old Hudson," I said.

"What do you mean? Did you have a car like this?" Randy asked.

"No," I said. "These were before my time. They were popular after the war."

"Then how do you know it's a Hudson?" inquired Kenny.

"You see that insignia on the side? That's a Hornet. It's a Hudson Hornet," I said matter-of-factly.

"Maybe they left something in the car, you know under the grass." Randy said, pulling at the weeds growing out of the windows. Kenny taking his cue from Randy went around the back of the car and grasped a small seedling growing out of the trunk; pulling it out with one big yank. Then he froze in horror upon seeing, entangled in the roots of the seedling, the brown skeletal remains of a hand and part of an arm. In utter panic and shaking from limb to limb, Kenny dropped the plant on the ground and rushed to his brother's side screaming, "It's dead, look it's dead."

"What's dead?" I asked rushing to Kenny's side.

"Look at the tree," Kenny said pointing to the seedling lying on the ground next to the car.

"What's dead?" asked Randy backing away from the car.

I looked over at the seedling and saw the unmistakable outline of a human hand caught up in its roots. Then I gingerly lifted it off the ground and held it up to get a better look. I hoped that it might have been an animal but it clearly was the unmistakable skeleton of a human hand.

While I placed the seedling back in the trunk, I tried to reassure the boys that, "Dad's going to call the police and tell them what we've found."

As they both looked at each other in bewilderment, I backed away from the trunk and said, "Just put your sticks down and let's ... a, let's not touch anything, O.K.?"

"Do you know who it is Dad?" asked Randy.

"What?" I said still staring at the contents of the trunk.

"Are we in trouble?" asked Kenny hesitantly.

I looked at the two boys each with fear in their eyes.

"Listen daddy doesn't know who this person is or was. We have nothing to fear for finding it," I said.

"Leave every thing alone," I said, grabbing Kenny by the arm and motioning to Randy to follow. We made our way back to the field without saying anything. Once we got to the fence near the car, Randy asked what we should tell the police. Whereupon Kenny voiced his doubts about getting involved and that maybe we should just forget that we had found a skeleton. I looked back into the woods we'd had just come out of and knew that unless the police were told, the question of what had happened there in the woods would haunt each one of us forever.

As I sat in the car with the boys safely buckled up in the back seat, I fumbled with the car phone wondering who I should call. Whose jurisdiction was it? The best thing I decided was to call the New York State Police. The boys, now over the shock of what they'd just seen, bantered away in the back seat over the various scenarios that brought the victim to their eventual demise and ultimate burial in the trunk of the car. To them, it was just like a TV program, allowing for commercials, it would be solved in thirty minutes.

# FOUR

About twenty minutes later, from over the crest of the hill, bearing down on us came a blue and white New York State Police cruiser. The trooper glanced briefly at me as he passed our car, and then made a sharp U-turn pulling in behind us. Before I got out to speak with the trooper, I admonished the boys to act nice. Excited over the arrival of the State Police cruiser, they were all wide eyes and nods.

As I walked over to the cruiser, I noticed that it probably had just come out of a car wash. Water was dripping from the bumpers and along the sides of the car. The trooper made a brief call on his car radio then slowly got out of his car with a clipboard in his hand. He looked as if he was in this mid-twenties, with a short crew cut, spit-polished black boots, and wearing a tightly starched navy blue uniform.

"Are you Mr. Rosen?" the trooper asked looking at me from over the top of his dark sunglasses.

"Yah," I murmured.

"You called in the finding of human remains?" he asked.

"Yes, I think it's someone's hand. Ah, skeleton I mean," I blurted out. I must have sounded like an idiot, I thought. I couldn't put two words together.

"I can show you where … it is," I volunteered while thinking if I should have used the plural, 'they are,' instead of the singular, 'it is.'

"Let's start with some details before we go to the site," he said in a very official sounding manner.

"OK." I replied nervously, while the boys came up on either side of me.

"It would help if I could have your license and registration," he said, extending a hand towards me.

I fished around with the button in my back pocket and finally getting it open, removed my wallet. My driver's license was tucked behind my Mobil gas credit card and after fumbling around in my glove compartment, came out with the car's registration. I handed them to the officer who stuck them under the clip of the board.

While copying down the information, the officer would every so often glance coolly at me. That's when I started worrying that maybe Kenny was right and we should have just forgotten about getting involved.

"OK, I've got what I need here," he said returning my license and registration back to me. "Why don't you lead me to the site? You told the dispatcher that you found a skeleton on the grounds of the old Laurels Hotel?" he said, referring to some notes he had on his clipboard.

"Yes, it's in the woods over there," I said pointing in the general direction from which we had just come, while stifling the thought that I once again used the wrong noun. "I'll show you," I said.

With that, the boys took it as a cue to bound through the field in the direction of the woods to find the old wreck. As I walked alongside of the trooper, I studied the woods trying to find that reflection, that flash of light again. I wanted to point it out to him, but everything now seemed dark and foreboding. When we got to the wreck, the boys were waiting just a few yards from the car. As if to say, 'we found it.' Upon closer inspection I noticed that the car's hood had been separated from its hinges and was pushed back into the windshield and that several small trees were growing alongside the car.

As the officer approached the car, the boys pointed to the small tree whose roots encircled the skeletal remains in the trunk. We all stood there while the trooper examined the contents of the trunk with his flashlight.

"You just lifted this up?" he asked, as he carefully lifted the sapling with a gloved hand to examine it further with his light. Seeing the hand, he then slowly put it back and returned his flashlight to its holder on his belt. He made some notes on his pad, then looking around, made a sketch of the site. When he was through, he motioned to the boys and me to come back with him to his cruiser. I walked ahead with the boys who were babbling to each other their impressions of the trooper.

"Did you see how big his gun was?" asked Kenny.

"It's like an old time six-shooter," replied Randy.

"He must think he's a cowboy," giggled Kenny.

"Shush, boys. You said you'd be nice," I said in a whisper.

As we made our way back to the cars, I noticed that the boys' jeans were covered with that stuff that clings to your pants when you walk through a field of weeds. I also noticed when I looked down at my own pants that in addition to two large wet spots on my knees, my pants were also covered with the stuff too. I'll have to change my pants, I thought, when we get back to the motel.

Once back at the cars, the trooper called his dispatcher to confirm, as he put it, "…the vehicle might contain human remains."

"Where are you staying?" he asked.

"Pine Lodge," answered Randy, proud that he could beat out his brother with the answer.

"On Route 17?" he asked writing it down.

"When did you check in and how long do you plan to stay?" he continued quickly.

"We only got here last night and … ah, plan on leaving this afternoon," I said.

"A very short stay," he remarked with a frown.

"Dad wanted to show us The Laurels," blurted out Kenny looking at his brother with pride.

"Then it was no accident your finding the remains," he stated.

I started to say something about finding it by accident but he interrupted me with, "wait here," while he went over to his car to speak to his dispatcher.

I had the feeling that his tone and his body language had changed all of a sudden and that he suspected I knew more about the skeleton than I was telling him.

I overheard him asking the dispatcher to send a forensic team to the site. He told them where and how to find the field and then began questioning me again on why we had come here.

I explained that I wanted to show my sons where I once worked 44 years ago, and that I didn't know that the hotel had been demolished and that, as he could see, only a vacant lot was left. That during our exploring the area I had seen a reflection in the woods and decided to investigate, whereupon we found the car.

"Well…. and you discovered the skeletal remains. How did that exactly happen?" asked the trooper.

I could see he was asking me the same questions trying to catch me in some inconsistencies. "One of the boys, Randy, pulled a little tree growing in the trunk out and entwined in the roots was the hand," I said.

"Why did he do that?" looking towards the boys leaning against the Volvo.

"I don't know, you know kids," I replied.

"And then you called us, right?" he said writing something down.

"Listen, I gotta get something for the boys to eat, when can we leave?" I asked.

"They shouldn't be long. We have to wait for them.

Then you can get something for the kids," He said looking back at the woods.

"Do you still need me?" I asked.

"Stick around, until the detectives get here," He said looking up from the clipboard.

I could tell from his demeanor that his comment wasn't a request, it was an order.

# FIVE

About an hour later, what seemed like a small entourage, descended upon us from out of nowhere. A couple of unmarked State Police cruisers and a black van that said, 'New York State Crime Lab,' came rumbling to an abrupt stop alongside the fence. Two of what I presumed were plainclothes detectives, moseyed over to me and the kids. One was wearing a light brown suit and cowboy boots, the other, a dark blue blazer with wrinkled gray slacks and scuffed black penny loafers.

The one in cowboy boots introduced himself as Detective Russell, and motioned with a nod of his head to his partner saying, "that's Marty." Cleaning his teeth with his pinky, as if he'd just finished eating, Russell gestured to me and the trooper to show him what we'd found. I stood there as Russell and the trooper started walking towards the woods followed by several members of the crime team who piled out of the van.

"Can't the trooper show you the way?" I protested.

"Look, don't you want to get this thing over with?" said Russell cocking his head to one side.

"Yes, but I've told him everything that I know," I said as I noticed Marty beginning to question Randy and Kenny.

"Oh, they'll be OK," Said Russell noticing my concern. "Now you just come along with us and we'll make this as quick as possible," he said.

Reluctantly, I took a deep nervous breath and began walking with them towards the woods. The day had suddenly become cloudy and it started feeling cold. I glanced at the woods hoping that I'd see something, anything that I could point to and say, 'look, look, do you see that light?'...but everything now looked very dark. My mind was racing and I felt a little light-headed. What had I told the trooper? Did I mention hearing someone call my name? I don't remember mentioning that. They'd think I was crazy if I told them now, I thought. Just stay calm ... calm down and everything's going to be O.K., I told myself.

"So you used to work here. How long ago was that?" asked Russell as we made our way through the high grass.

"Ah, I think it was '55 . . . 1955," I said, glancing back at the boys. Kenny was now sitting in the back seat of the detective's car and Randy was leaning on the car speaking to Marty.

I stopped, feeling a rush of fear grip my body and said, "What's going on with my boys?"

"Nothing to worry about. He's just chewing the fat with them," he said with a smile. "Come on," he said with a wave of his hand. "Fifty-five, that was a long, long time ago. How old were you then?" he asked as we entered the tree line.

"I am not sure, 16 or 17." I said.

What did you do at the hotel . . . what was it called, The Laurels?" he asked stepping over a downed tree truck.

"I . . . I was a busboy during the summer," I said in a quiet voice.

"And, and why did you come up here again?" queried Russell.

"I wanted to show the boys where I worked years ago," I said as we reached the old car.

A few moments later, two men and a woman surrounded the car each seemingly responsible for a different task. One of them was a photographer who took photographs of the car and its contents from all angles while the others waited patiently for him to finish. Then the woman, who had donned a thick green plastic apron and white surgical gloves, began carefully collecting the skeletal remains from the trunk. She placed the entire sapling encasing the hand and arm into a black plastic bag. The third member of the team wore what resembled a white plastic biohazard suit that covered the upper and lower parts of his body. He also wore white surgical gloves and used a small shovel to collect the entire contents of the trunk, placing the contents into two large black garbage bags. After collecting and labeling everything from the trunk for analysis back at the Crime Lab, one of the techs walked around the scene dictating into a small, hand held tape recorder.

"Bud, come over here will you?" asked Russell gesturing to the photographer.

The photographer looked up from what he was doing and came over to us. Russell put his arm around him and turning him around, walked him a little ways away from me to whisper something in his ear. Bud shook his head, affirmatively and then went back to lining up his next shot.

"Now, from what I read here, you found the car while walking in the woods. Is that correct?" asked Russell reading from the trooper's report.

"No, not exactly," I said, and just at that moment, while looking at that old car, I suddenly thought of my friend Larry, Larry Kahn. We were friends back in Brooklyn 50 years ago. We lived in the same tenement house on 97th Street. He was a gifted musician. He played the piano and I think a couple of other instruments. Why the hell was I thinking about him, I thought as the flash from the photographer's camera momentarily blinded me.

"Hey, I think, this has gone on long enough," I said with irritation upon being unceremoniously photographed without my permission.

"Must have been an accident," replied Russell with a smirk on his face.

"Now, you be careful of what you shoot," said

Russell to the photographer, who now had his back to us.

"OK, boss," replied the photographer moving around for another shot of the crime scene.

"I've gotta get back to the boys," I said in frustration.

"All in good time," said Russell reassuringly.

"Now, why would someone go walking in these woods anyway? You didn't work in the woods did you?" asked Russell sarcastically.

"I told the trooper that while we were walking around out there, pointing over toward the clearing, that ... that I thought I saw a flash of light come from in the woods. And we ah, walked in the direction of the ..."

"Yeah, yeah, you told us that," interrupted Russell

Then he paused, folding his hands across his chest, to compose his next question. "Now why would you go toward the light, unless ... unless, you knew what was here in the first place? Especially with your kids. You don't know what dangers there might be in the woods. What if the light was the reflection from a hunter's scope? He could have shot you for a deer or bear," said Russell walking around the car. Then, peering over the hood of the car at me, Russell looked me in the eyes and said, "Is this your car?"

"What do you mean?" I said.

"Just that," he said and when I didn't immediately reply, he repeated the question again. This time, pronouncing each word slowly, like he was talking to a deaf person, "Is ... this ... your ... car?"

"Of course not," I said beginning to back away.

"What's your hurry, Max?" he asked.

"I've … I've gotta get back to the kids…that's what." I said with a bit of a stutter.

"Well, just before we get back, come over here," ordered Russell, now standing by the empty trunk.

I slowly walked over to Russell who was peering into the empty trunk.

"What model car do you make this out to be? Olds? Chevy? Ya know, I don't see any marking. Guess I'll have to get a car buff down here to identify it. You know, Max, you could really help us out if you could tell us something about this car and who the victim was," said Russell twisting his head and moving closer to me.

"I don't know what kind of car this is and I don't know who was in the trunk," I said.

"O.K.," said Russell, throwing the stick into the trunk. "Let's get back and see how the boys are doin'."

# SIX

"Where's my kids?" I demanded as we entered the clearing.

"You said they were hungry. I guess Marty took them to McDonald's," replied Russell.

"What the hell's going on?" I stammered angrily.

"Don't get yourself into a thither," said Russell sympathetically. "It's O.K … it's O.K., we'll meet them over at the barracks and finish up our interview over there," he said reassuringly.

"What barracks?" I asked in frustration.

"Just have to type up the transcript … let you look at it, you know . . . make sure it's accurate. Then we'll file it and you'll be on your way," he said opening the door of my Volvo.

"Just follow me," he said as I reluctantly got into my car.

On the way to the State Police barracks, I was so distracted with thoughts about the kids that a couple of times I almost hit the back of Russell's car. I noticed that he would occasionally check on me through his rear view mirror to see if I was still behind him. The only thing I could think of was how stupid I was to get the kids involved and that this whole trip was a terrible mistake. What did I think I was going to accomplish? Whatever memories I sought, burned down years ago. Now I have to pretend I know something about a time that's a complete blank.

As we drove past the same old dilapidated bungalow colonies, fast food restaurants, and gas stations that we passed on the way to Sackett Lake, my mind began to wonder as to what I could tell my wife, Vicky. I know she'll be upset. Actually, upset isn't the right word, ballistic might be closer to her reaction. She was suspicious as to why I was going to begin with and now, I was in deep shit. Funny, sometimes at the strangest moments, my mind flashes back to images of my youth. I remembered when I was a kid and did something wrong, I would tell myself, 'that it just didn't happen.' Yep, there's nothing to worry about because, whatever I did, 'just didn't happen.' It didn't always work but it did temporarily help me get over the panic of being beaten with my father's belt, which in honesty, he threatened but never used.

I followed Russell's car around the back of a plain looking two story red brick building. And after he gathered up his paperwork, he led me through a back door, up a flight of stairs, into one of the empty rooms.

"Would you like a cup of coffee or something?" asked Russell.

"No, let's just get this thing over with. Where are my kids?" I started.

"I'll check ... Ah, let me just get myself a clean cup," he said peering into a coffee cup he took off the table.

He left me alone in, what I presumed, was an interrogation room. In the center of the room was a solid looking, 4 x 6 wooden table, which was fastened with metal brackets to the floor. The chairs were those heavy, unbreakable wooden variety that you find in family restaurants. A water bubbler stood in the corner with some paper cups stacked on top. There was only one window in the room, and it had bars on the outside. The floor was a faded gray linoleum tile with scuff marks under the chairs.

When Russell returned, he was carrying a cup of coffee in one hand and a small portable tape recorder in the other. He set them both on the table and just before he eased himself into a chair, he retrieved a notepad from his back pocket.

"My kids?..." I started to ask, when he put up a hand saying, "Oh, Marty's gone to see if we have any cokes. They're right big boys you have there," he said.

"I want to see them," I said, walking over to him.

"Sure, have a seat. Let's just get this over with and you'll be on your way home," he said pointing to a chair while fumbling with the record switch.

When he finally got it going, he said, "Why don't you just say your name, address, telephone number, social security number, date of birth, OK?" He rattled off pushing the recorder closer to me.

"I'm Max Rosen, live at 15 Wilder Street, Hull, Mass, telephone number is 617-590-1239. My date of birth is: 11-9-39. Is that what you want?" I said.

"Social Security Number," he said.

"612-58-2532," I said.

"OK," he said, sitting back. "Why don't you tell me what brought you to our fine part of the country?" He said smiling.

"I came to show my boys, where, Daddy . . . I mean, where I worked when I was 16 or 17. The Laurels on Sackett Lake," I said.

"You worked there when?"

"I think, to the best of my recollection, " '55 or '56 . . . 1955," I said nodding my head.

"And you were a waiter?" he said.

"Busboy" I said.

"Right, Oh yes, you're married? Your wife's name is ah?" He asked.

"Yes, married, Vicky," I stammered. "I mean, my wife's name is Vicky," I said slowly looking down at the table and thinking that I may not be married when she hears what happened.

"OK, continue," he said looking to see if the tape recorder was working.

"We came to Monticello yesterday," I said.

"That was Friday, June 12th," he recited for the record.

"Yes, and we drove to where The Laurels used to

be. But it had been demolished. Burned down and then I guess demolished," I said.

Get a hold of yourself . . . you're sounding like an idiot, I told myself. "There wasn't anything there except the swimming pool." I said.

"When you got there, were you walking all together, you and the boys?" he asked.

"Yes and no. We started to and then they went to the lake to look around. They came back while I was by the pool. I said to them that I saw a light, a flash of something coming from the woods. And we went to see what it was," I said.

"Did the boys see the flash?" he asked.

"I don't think so, no they didn't. It was just an instant flash," I said.

"Like a flashlight?" he asked.

"Brighter, like light reflecting off a mirror," I said.

"Then what happened?" he asked.

"We found the old car and...," I stated.

"Did you know a car was there?" he said inching his chair closer to me.

"Nope, we just happened upon it," I said sitting back in my chair.

"It was pretty deep in the woods?" he asked.

"I guess so," I said.

"Maybe 200 feet in the woods?" he asked.

"I can't say how far," I said.

"That would be quite a reflection, that far through thick woods," he said.

"I don't know, I just saw a flash," I said.

"Then what happened?" he asked.

"Randy . . . he pulled out a little tree that was growing in the trunk and . . . ," I said when Russell interrupted to ask, "Did you?" Then reconsidered and said, "Never mind go ahead."

"The hand was caught in the roots. I mean, he got scared and dropped it. That's it. I think you know the rest. I want to get my kids and leave," I said rising to my feet.

"Sure, sure, let me just have this tape transcribed so that you can sign a copy," he said looking at the tape recorder.

"Just a couple of questions then we'll be through. Sit, just a second more," he said.

I decided to stand, waiting for his next question, leaning on my chair. He put the recorder back on the table and thumbed through his notepad, when his partner, Marty came in.

"Almost through," Russell said to Marty.

Marty nodded to Russell and they huddled together speaking to each other just out of my earshot.

"Good question," Russell said to Marty as he came over to me shaking his head.

"About the car, did you tell the boys?" he paused, "What did you say to your boys about the car?" he asked.

"I don't remember what I said."

"Did you ask them if they could find the model of the car?"

"I might have, you know, is it a Chevy or Buick, or something like that. I really don't remember," I said.

"Why did you want to know the model?" he asked.

"If I asked … it was just curiosity," I said.

At that, Russell looked over at Marty with a smile. "Have you ever been in any trouble, Mr. Rosen?" asked Marty.

"No, never," I said.

"Ever been arrested?" asked Russell.

"No," I said.

"That's good," said Russell picking up the recorder.

"And that's it?" I said.

"That's it," said Russell. "I'm going to have this transcribed and after you sign it, you'll be on your way."

"Can I see my kids now?" I asked.

"Sure, they'll be right in." he said.

"Oh, yes, before I go. Anything you'd like to add to your statement?" he asked.

"No, I think you've got it all," I said feeling a sense of relief that the interrogation was over.

Just as I thought that he'd be going, he came back and sat on the edge of the table. He looked at Marty, then me and said, "I gotta be honest with you, Max, this story; it's not exactly the same as the boys told us. Seems that they were under the impression that you were, well, familiar with the car. Are you sure? We can save a lot of time and aggravation, if you'd tell us the truth about the car," he said.

"They were mistaken, they were under pressure, seeing the skeleton," I said.

"You could make it easy on everyone," he said,

looking at Marty "If you just level with us. Come on Max, you came back to find that car, didn't you?"

"No, it was like I said, an accident," I replied angrily.

"You mean you killed them by accident?" he asked.

"No, finding the car was an . . . ," I blurted out in frustration.

"Yes, yes," he interrupted me.

"You followed a ray of light to the skeletal remains," he said sarcastically.

I just stood there looking at Russell as he adjusted himself on the table. His hands were curled over the lip of the table as he began slowly moving his legs up and down like he was on a swing. He did it for a few moments then, like a cat, sprung to his feet and walked to within a few inches of my face.

"Tell me who the skeleton is?" He shouted spraying my face with spittle.

As I turned and wiped my face, he said, "You know we'll eventually find out."

"I have no idea, who ..." I cried out.

Russell raised his hand as if to stop me, "OK Max, have it your way. We'll find out about the car, and who was in it, and then, it might get rough on you and your family. Do you understand me?" he screamed.

"I want to go. I want to go now," I said.

# SEVEN

I found the boys in a conference room on the first floor thumbing through wanted posters.

"Hi Dad," said Randy seeing me.

"Doesn't this guy look like Uncle Charlie?" he asked holding up a wanted poster for me to see.

"Let's put that back where you found it," I said dryly.

"Can't I keep this one to show Mom?" Randy pleaded.

"No, it doesn't belong to us. Just leave it on the table," I told him shaking my head to emphasize the point.

After successfully herding the boys out of the building and into the backseat of our car, Kenny announced that he had to go to the bathroom.

"Please wait until we get to the motel," I pleaded, desperately not wanting to set foot in that building again.

"But Dad ..." Kenny began saying.

"We'll be there in a moment, I promise you." I said hoping to reassure him.

"Do they know whose bones they are?" asked Randy.

"No, and let's talk about it later," I said, not looking forward to the long ride home speculating as to who the remains were and how they got there. Luckily, we got back to the motel just in time for Randy to grab a comic book from his rucksack and make a mad dash to the bathroom. Whatever the cops fed him did not sit well with his delicate constitution. Kenny on the other hand could eat anything without encountering any digestive problems.

After gathering our belongings from our room, we checked out of the motel and headed home. It had been a long, stressful day and I wanted to badly put it behind us. I tried to make small talk with the boys about pit stops and food but when I glimpsed into the rear view mirror to see what the boys were up to, I could see that Kenny and Randy were bent over with their heads unusually close to each other, speaking in muffled voices. It made me feel very uncomfortable because this was not the typical way they communicated with each other. Most of their conversations are at arm's length, at best.

"What are you whispering about?" I asked.

"Nothing," replied Randy. When I looked up into the rearview mirror, I saw an anguished look on his face.

"Come on, what's going on?" I asked.

"We're afraid that something will happen to you," said Kenny speaking for his brother.

"Why? We didn't have anything to do with the

bones," I said avoiding the temptation to call it a crime or murder scene.

"I mean what if the car was your old car, wouldn't that mean, you know … wouldn't it cast suspicion on you?" asked Kenny, using terms I didn't think he knew.

I adjusted the rearview mirror so I could see both boys, and wondered how they made the leap from babes to adults so quickly, in only a few short years. How they possessed such probing minds amazed me. It must be television or the movies, I thought.

"Look," I said, "The best thing we can do is put this horrible episode behind us and … ," I started to say.

"No, we can't," interrupted Randy, "Only after the body is identified and the year of their death, or disappearance is known can we be sure."

"Isn't there some kind of test they can do on the bones that would tell when they died?" questioned Kenny.

"I don't know, maybe there is a way of dating bones or maybe there's a missing persons file they can check … but I am not sure," I said.

During the long ride home, the boys mostly kept to themselves and uncharacteristically, didn't fight once. We stopped several times to call home and tell Vicky that we were on our way, but there was no answer. It actually wasn't until we reached our house and saw her car parked out front, that they asked. "What are we going to tell Mom?" almost simultaneously.

"Let me handle it" I said bravely.

I'd been rehearsing what I'd say to her during the long ride home and thought that I'd basically tell her the same story I'd told the police. That if they questioned her, and I didn't think that it would ever go that far, at least our stories would be consistent. The real trouble I had was the impression I'd left on my boys. My fear was that they might suspect me of being involved in a crime. More than anything, that thought had me really worried. I didn't want to shatter the illusion of their Daddy, that he could be guilty of some heinous crime. I had tried so hard to be a model father and not make the mistakes I perceived my parents had made with me; to be there for them, to watch them play soccer or a class play or a birthday party or all the other important events in a child's life. They were a gift in my later years and I wanted to enjoy what moments we could share as father and sons.

# EIGHT

"**W**hat do you mean you didn't tell them?" asked Vicky furiously.

I turned away from my wife's glare and said, "Honey, I wasn't sure it was the car."

She walked over briskly to close the French doors which led to our bedroom, then turned saying, "Now you're a suspect. By not telling them, then and there about the car, you're the only one they'll investigate."

"Look anyone could have placed that body in the trunk," I explained.

"Yes, but you're the one who went looking for the car...after forty years . . . in the woods . . . with your own children." Vicky blurted out in exasperation.

"I mean, how could you have taken the children?" she said.

Vicky then went to the window which overlooked the backyard and said with her back to me, "What were you thinking? Have you completely lost your mind?"

"I didn't go looking to find a body ... I mean, skeleton. I thought I was just reminiscing, you know," I went on.

"I don't understand why." she began but was interrupted by Randy's knock on the door.

"Honey, Mom and Dad will be right out," said Vicky.

But Randy opened the door anyway and asked, "Can we talk to you?"

"About what?" I asked.

"You know, the police," replied Randy as Kenny came along side him carrying a serious look on his face.

"I know you both have many questions about . . . about what happened at Sackett Lake ... but," I said walking over and sitting on the edge of the bed.

"O.K., this has been a very emotional time for all of us," said Vicky as she ushered the boys out of the room. Just before closing the door, she said to them, "We'll be right down, let me speak to Dad for a few moments, O.K.?"

With that, Randy and Kenny retreated with troubled looks on their faces. After closing the door, Vicky came over and sat next to me on the bed. She grasped my hand in hers and asked, "What are you going to do?"

"I don't know, maybe try to find Sam," I said, looking at her for help.

"Who's Sam?" she asked.

"You know, I mean, the picture I found in the box with The Laurels postcard," I said.

"Don't you think the police are better suited for that type of work?" she asked.

"Why get Sam involved if he had nothing to do with it. I mean . . . it's been over forty years, he might even be dead," I said looking at her for approval.

"What are you going to tell the boys?" she said getting up.

"Let's tell them, Daddy's going to play detective, they'll love the drama," I said feigning a smile.

"Be serious, I don't want them getting involved," she said with great urgency.

I grabbed Vicky by the wrist and looking her in the eyes said, "I want you to believe me. I had, I mean, I don't know anything about . . . about what happened up there. Let me see what I can find out and then I'll call the police and tell them all about our suspicions. I promise, I won't get you or the kids involved."

As I tried to get up, Vicky said, "Wait, I want to talk to you about something."

"What?" I asked.

"Look, I spoke with Dr. Holland..." she began.

As she said that, I felt a flush come over me. The last time I saw Dr. Holland, I brushed him off when he suggested I see a neurologist for tests. I remember him sitting there in that tiny exam room at our HMO with a sheepish look on his face and telling me that memory loss is a common occurrence in men my age. That there were tests and drugs I could take to slow down ... I can't even say the word ... dementia.

"What'd he say?" I asked.

"He's concerned about," . . . as she hesitated

searching for the right word, "he wants you to see a specialist," she said softly.

"I know and I promise that I'll call him for a referral," I said nodding my head indicating that I would follow through with her suggestion.

"Are we O.K.?" I asked. "If so, I want to look through some papers in my office," I said.

Grudgingly, she moved away without acknowledging me to the window, folding her arms across her chest, and just stood there staring out at the woods behind our house. I took a deep breath and I left Vicky standing there and as I went down to the kitchen. I passed the boys, who had helped themselves to snacks and were now engrossed in a cartoon on TV. They looked up with questioning eyes as I stopped to tell them that I was going to work in my office for a while and then would take them out for Chinese food. They merely nodded without taking their eyes off the action on the screen as I went down the stairs to my office.

The room I called, 'my office,' was once a bedroom before the boys were born. Since then, we've added and added and added. Today, the onetime tiny ranch, was now was a sprawling three level, six bedroom home. On the wall facing my desk was twenty or so photos of our family taken at locations all over the globe. The boys at the Parthenon in Athens, on a cable car in San Francisco, at the Eifel Tower in Paris, in Covent Gardens in London, and the Lincoln Memorial in Washington, D.C. were some of my favorite pictures.

What times, what memories I thought. Will they also be erased? I was even afraid to think about it.

I took out a pad of paper and I turned on my calculator. I punched in 1939, the year I was born, then added 16 years to that, hit the plus sign, and presto, 1955. That's about the time I worked at The Laurels I surmised. I opened the box and put the postcard of The Laurels County Club I'd been carrying into it and took out the photograph of the handsome young man wearing a Temple University Athletics Department T-Shirt. On the back of the photograph was written, Sam Bergman. I had also remembered seeing the name, 'Sam', on one of the waterlogged pages in the Journal I found with the pictures.

I tried to open the Journal using an Exacto knife and a pair of tweezers but the pages seemed to have been glued together into a solid block. However, there was this one break in the Journal and I was able to decipher a few words here and there.

Halfway down the page, I was able to make out, 'don't stare at the short order cooks in the morning'. And then later, 'Sam says he will watch my back'. I was also able to make out, 'never whistle in the kitchen'.

I was really feeling drained and decided to tackle the Journal in the morning. In any event, we had a date with Beijing Gardens for their boneless spare ribs, General Tsao's chicken, pork fried rice, and shrimp chop suey. The finale would consist of the boys harpooning chunks of pineapple with umbrella toothpicks while smashing their fortune cookies with the palms of their hands on the table. This behavior often brought looks of disgust from other dining patrons but with all they'd been through, it was a small price to pay for a little happiness.

I recalled the lines from an old poem, the author of which is unknown, some of the lines were:

*Youth is full of pleasance*
*Age is full of care.*
*Youth like summer morn,*
*Age like winter weather;*
*Youth like summer brave,*
*Age like winter bare.*
*Youth is full of sport,*
*Age's breath is short;*
*Youth is nimble,*
*Age is lame;*
*Youth is hot and bold,*
*Age is weak and cold;*
*Youth is wild,*
*and Age is tame.*

# NINE

Oh…, I've overslept, I thought to myself as I noticed the alarm clock next to the bed said, 9:57 AM. Wearily, I hung my feet over the edge of the bed in search of my LL Bean fleece slippers. When I looked down, they weren't there. Probably hiding under the bed, I thought getting down on all fours and blindly sweeping an arm under the bed frame. Ah, I got one, I said to myself reaching under to grab it. After determining it was my left slipper, I resorted to a full-body press, lying on my stomach to get a better look of what was under the bed. Socks, a ballpoint pen, a nickel, and a TV guide from seven weeks ago . . . but no slipper. Oh well, it'll turn up I thought as I put on my bathrobe, slipper and hobbled into the bathroom. I've found that as my prostate grew, so did my appreciation of the pleasures of just relieving oneself. Wherever I went nowadays, the first place I sought out was a friendly bathroom.

In the kitchen, I put on a pot of coffee and clicked on the TV to see what the weather was likely to be today. A cold front moving in from Canada, chance of rain, high's in the 80's, low's in the 60's. Same old, same old, I thought. Weathermen were like politicians, they hardly ever got it right but who kept score?

With a steaming cup of Joe, I limped into my office. I put on the desk lamp and shuffled some papers looking for a coaster to rest my coffee on. Unable to find one, I rested the cup on, what I hoped was, a blank CD. I took some scrap paper from a drawer and my favorite, Uni-ball GEL IMPACT pen. With all that had transpired in the last couple of days, I knew that I had to organize my thoughts and the best way I had found of doing it, was to write it down: the who, what, when, where, and why scenarios.

Let's see, the boys are in school until 3:30 PM and Vicky's at the hospital until, maybe 5 PM or 6 PM today. That will give me six hours to figure out what I should do about my situation. I was thinking that if I could decipher some of the Journal, it might give me a leg up on what happened at The Laurels that summer long, long ago.

I took out the Journal and using a kitchen knife, stuck the point into the middle of the book. Then I gingerly wiggled the knife back and forth trying to part it where the blade was to no avail. So, I retrieved a hammer and chisel from my toolbox and standing the book on its end, I gave the chisel a good rap splitting some of the pages from the book. Eureka! I shouted under my breath.

I could see some of the writing. It was only a short paragraph but it told me a lot about Sam:

> Lucky to have Sam ... told me to roll up my clothes and follow him ... ran barefoot through the rain in our underwear ... to a small guest cottage where the guests shared a bathroom. It was great... took turns showering and getting dressed ... even though clothes were wet ... Sam said stuff newspapers in them at night and never leave anything on the floor.

Interesting, I didn't need a degree in linguistics to figure that one out. Being an only child, I probably looked upon Sam as an older brother, someone to teach me the ways of the world, so to speak. I lifted the black and white photo of Sam and examined it with a magnifying lens. He was wearing shorts and a Temple University Athletics Department T-Shirt. He was a strong, handsome looking boy with curly dark hair and a big smile. He gave the appearance that he was confident and intelligent. If he was a freshman or sophomore in college, he'd be around 20 or 21 years old compared to my 16 or 17 years old. I could see how I could be taken under his spell, in that he was much older and worldlier than I was.

I decided that the first thing to do was track down Sam Bergman so I called Temple University in Philadelphia and asked to speak with someone in the Alumni Office.

"I'm looking for an alumnus, Sam Bergman, he might have graduated in 1957, '58 or '59. I'm not exactly sure," I said. "Do you have a current address for him?"

"That's a long time ago, mused the woman on the line. Let me pull up the graduation records. Was it an undergraduate or graduate degree?" she asked.

"I think he did his undergraduate work there," I said.

As I held on waiting for the information, she advised me that Temple had numerous schools: Nursing, Law, Medicine, and others. Then after a few moments she said, "Yes there was a Sam Bergman who received his BA in 1957 and his MA in 1958. Do you think that's the one?"

Relieved, I said, "Yes, I think so. Do you have his current address?"

"There is no current listing for Mr. Bergman and frankly even if there was, we're not at liberty to disclose it," she stated for the record.

"OK, I understand," I said hanging up.

Well that was something; he graduated from Temple University with his Masters in 1958. I figured that they probably wouldn't give out his home address even if they had it. They'd want to protect their alumni's privacy. I realized that the only way I might secure more information on Sam Bergman was to visit the Temple University Alumni Association in Philadelphia. Maybe a well placed $50 or $100 bill could pry his address out of someone there I thought.

Invigorated, I kicked off my slipper and jogged

upstairs to pack. I found an old rucksack in the closet that passed the sniff test, meaning the cats hadn't peed in it and threw some underwear, a couple of shirts, socks, and my toiletry kit in it. I have a habit of over-packing I told myself; this time I took enough for a couple of days.

I looked in my wallet and realized I had only eleven dollars in cash. Why did I pay for the Chinese food last night in cash? Who uses cash nowadays? I've got to stop at a bank machine before I get on the road, I thought. A hundred should be enough. If I needed more, I had Mobil and Shell gas credit cards, a VISA Card, and a AAA Card for emergencies. No, I wasn't thinking. What if I had to pay for the information? A hundred wasn't enough. Two hundred is more like it. No, tolls, fast food, miscellaneous this and that, two-fifty is more realistic. Yap, two-fifty is it.

I tried several times to compose a note to Vicky telling her of my plans, but each time I crumpled them into a ball and threw them into the trash. I'll call her from the road I decided. After all, she didn't want me to go, her idea was to cooperate with the New York State Police and tell them that I recognized the car. Yeah, that's all I had to do, trust them. Well, she hadn't met Detective Russell. If there was anything on their minds, it was to connect me to the hand in the trunk. That's how they rise in the ranks, by closing cases, especially cold cases. The trouble is, I did remember something about the car. It was a Hudson, a Hudson Hornet. I decided that there was enough time before running down to Temple University to do an Internet search of the Hudson Hornet. The picture that popped on the screen was a 1953 Hudson Hornet. It was a sleek, two door model with those large white wall tires. Even by today's standards, it was a beautiful looking car. The article said that it was also one of the most popular stock cars of its time with a six-cylinder 308 cubic inch engine and won 27 of the 34 NASCAR Grand National races. It was hard to imagine that the pile of rust I saw in the woods was once a luxury race car back in the '50's. But then again, the more things change, the more they remain the same.

# TEN

I stopped off at the drive-up ATM at my bank and got $260 dollars in crisp twenty-dollar bills. I had forgotten that the ATM's only dispensed cash in twenty-dollar increments. Oh well, I'll probably need the extra ten-dollars, I thought as I headed to the Massachusetts Turnpike and the start of my six hour jaunt to the City of Brotherly Love. I had driven on several occasions to Philadelphia in the past and I knew that the tricky part was how to get from Connecticut to New Jersey without the madness of having to travel through New York City. Because traveling, either over the bridges or through the tunnels bisecting Manhattan was a test of ones faith. For on any given day, for no apparent reason, the traffic could backup for hours. I've heard that it's gotten so bad, that some motorists have been known to abandon their cars and walk aimlessly around the city looking for other means of transportation.

Several hours later, while racing south on the Henry Hudson Parkway, the moment of decision was at hand as I approached a large green sign with white lettering directing me to either; the always treacherous, Triboro Bridge or the infamous top deck of the George Washington Bridge. Where to go? It was time to set my sail into the wind and hope that I made the right choice. Bravely, I headed for the top deck of the George Washington Bridge. If I could weave into an inside lane, I might avoid the vertigo of being suspended 1,000 feet above the Hudson River without a parachute. Just keep your eyes straight ahead I told myself. However, almost by instinct, I did glance once in a while to my left and right only to see my fellow motorists drive by with the fear of death in their eyes. It's comforting to know I'm not the only chicken in town.

After arriving in Philadelphia 5½ hours later following the directions from MapQuest and a few students, I finally found Temple University's Alumni Offices. They were housed in, what looked like, a restored colonial mansion a few blocks north of the main campus.

I had a few ideas as to how to pry the information I needed from them but decided that I'd have to sort of, 'play-it-by-ear' at first. My thought was that at best, I didn't want to box myself in with a request for information that was so patently transparent that they would become suspicious of my real intentions and thereby block any further maneuvers I might attempt.

Once inside, I was welcomed by an attractive coed who was seated behind a large antique oak desk, efficiently typing away on a laptop computer. I told her that I was doing research and had to locate an old alumnus who had information I needed for my book. She showed me to an ante room just off the entrance saying, "please wait here, someone will be right with you."

It was a spacious room with high ceilings and a large decorative stone fireplace. The furniture looked like antiques from the colonial period and the paintings on the walls depicted naval revolutionary battles. Men-of-War with cannons blasting and others showing the effects of the destructive power of a thirty pound ball filled with gunpowder. The paintings were of such exquisite detail that you could make out the sailors on the ships.

While waiting, I perused through some of the literature on a coffee table. One brochure dealt with, 'Tax Deferred Bequeaths'. It always amazed me how many tax loopholes there were for the wealthy. And it also struck me that whomever I was about to deal with in the Alumni Department understood the importance of confidentiality for fear of upsetting a donor. Depending upon who walked through that door, the appropriateness of offering a gratuity, a bribe, would have to be based on chemistry. A subtle suggestion that, "I don't expect it for nothing," or "I'd like to give you something for your trouble," or "I'm willing to pay someone to research it," had to be weighed by my perception of that individual. Because I knew that the wrong word, the wrong attitude, the wrong body language would ruin my chances.

"Can I help you?" he said walking into the room

carrying a large yellow legal pad. I guessed he was in his mid-twenties, sporting a pair of snappy Nautica dress chinos, Cole Haan loafers, and a light blue button-down Ralph Lauren shirt with the familiar little polo pony and coordinated Dior silk tie. "I'm Seth," he said with firm handshake and a wide smile displaying his perfect teeth.

"Hi," I said thinking to myself that he could be the, 'yuppie poster boy of the year'. "My name is Max Rosen from New York. I'm writing a book … I'm actually at the part that … ," Relax, I said to myself, you're speaking too quickly … "some background information that one of your old alumnus may have … and, and I need to contact him," I said.

"Are you one of our alumni?" he inquired, still smiling.

"No, actually, I attended NYU." I said.

"O.K." he said pointing to a chair. "Why don't we sit and you can tell me exactly what you need from us," he said.

We sat facing each other on these two wing backed chairs separated by a small cocktail table and 35 years while I concocted a story about my research for a book about life at a summer camp during the summer of 1955. That the person I needed to contact, Sam Bergman, was my co-counselor and that the only thing I remembered about him was that he was attending Temple University. I also told him that in checking, I'd discovered that Sam graduated in 1957 with a BA and a MA in 1958.

"Ah, ha," he said nodding his head while scribbling something on his pad.

"And you need," he said looking up at me.

"A current address," I replied.

"The customary procedure in that event is to send us a note, with the request for it to be forwarded to the alumnus and we in turn sent it to them. In that way, we maintain the alumnus' privacy and their avoidance of unsolicited materials," he advised me.

"Seth, I can understand your reticence to opening the files to those wishing to market their wares to unwary alumnus but I'm in the midst doing research and time is of the essence," I explained trying to sound academic.

To this, Seth merely sat back and tapped his gold Mont Blanc pen against his lower lip.

"You know, he might for that matter be deceased. It's been over 40 years," I said.

"Good point," he said rising. "If you can kindly give me a few moments, let me see what I can find in our database," he said.

"Thanks," I replied also rising, "I'd appreciate any information you can find."

When he left I thought to myself that the story about why I wanted to locate Sam was plausible but that the part about, 'time is of the essence,' wasn't. If you were conducting research for a book, what would a week or two matter? That excuse just didn't hold water. I also decided that Seth wasn't a starving student who might be tempted by a bribe ... but you never could tell.

Ten minutes later, Seth returned with the news that

the Sam Bergman in question, wasn't on the active alumni database. However, he did say that there might be a chance that Sam attended an alumni reunion or he had a subscription to one of the University's Journals and that he would be happy to make some inquires. He asked me how he could get in touch with me and I told him that I planned on spending the night in Philadelphia. He gave me his card and told me to call him later.

# ELEVEN

I found a Quality Inn just a few blocks from Temple University. The room was of the standard bill of fare: a full size lumpy bed, dresser with an old 24" RCA TV on it and a small bathroom whose toilet seat was dressed with a white paper ribbon boasting it was, 'sanitized for my protection'. A card on top of the set advertised X-Rated Movies for only $6.95. I turned on the TV for background noise, adjusted the two slim pillows against the make believe headboard and eased myself onto the bed. This was the first rest I'd had since leaving home.

I thought of a dozen ways I could have or should have conducted the interview better with Seth in the Alumni Office. Like Sam was some long lost relative I had to find for Aunt Nell who's dying or he's inherited some money. But then again, what if he'd asked for credentials or the telephone number of the insurance company? No, I thought, as I drifted off to sleep, I played it close to the truth.

At around a quarter to five, I awoke with a start. Groggily, I took out the card with Seth's telephone and extension on it and after deciphering how to make a local call, I dialed the number.

"Seth, this is Max Rosen, I was in earlier looking for information on Sam Bergman," I said.

"Yes, Mr. Rosen, I've made some calls and it turns out Mr. Bergman doesn't seem to have attended any of the reunions and is not a subscriber to any of the schools publications," he said.

"Oh, I see" I said as I felt the blood drain out of my limbs.

"The only thing I could find was at the Registrar's Office. They said that in 1958 they forwarded an official transcript of Mr. Bergman's grades and degrees to a, Mount Lawrence in Rutland, Vermont," he said.

"Mount Lawrence, in Rutland, Vermont" I repeated.

"Yes, it's a school. That's all I could find. Sorry we couldn't be of more assistance," he said.

"Seth, I want to thank you for all your help. Is there anything ...," I started to say when he cut me off, only wishing me good luck on my book.

As I sat back, I looked at the notes I'd written on my pad. Not much, I thought. The school sent someone in Vermont a transcript forty years ago. I still had no idea of where Sam used to live, if he had any living relatives, friends, anyone ... I had a big fat zero.

I opened the Philadelphia White Pages to see how many Sam Bergman's or S. Bergman's there were and only found fourteen. Oh well, a shot in the dark, I thought and just as I was going to call the first name, I realized that I hadn't spoken to Vicky yet to tell her where I was.

"Hello," said Vicky on the first ring.

"Honey, it's me," I said.

"Where are you? I was worried about you. Did the police get hold of you?" She asked.

"I'm OK, what about the police?" I asked.

"They called looking for you. They left a message on the tape for you to call them," she said.

"What time did they call?" I asked

"The caller ID said 2:30 PM. But where are you calling from?" she asked.

"I'm at the Quality Inn in Philadelphia," I blurted out.

"WHY!!" She replied.

"Yeah, I got a lead from the registrar on Sam," I explained.

"Do you want the telephone number for the police?" she asked.

"No, if they call, tell them I am out of town and haven't called in yet, OK?" I said.

"Why the suspense?" she asked.

"I'll tell you later. How're the boys?" I said trying to change the subject.

"Tell me now," she demanded.

"There's nothing to tell, he ... Sam, graduated in 1958 with a master's degree and the only thing in his file that I could get is that they sent some school in Vermont his transcript," I said.

"When are you coming home?" she asked.

"I'll call them in the morning to see if they have any idea where Sam is," I said.

"I don't feel good about lying to the police. Get a pencil and I'll give you their number," she stated.

"OK, give it to me and I'll call and find out what they want," I said.

"What's the telephone number there? When are you coming home?" she asked.

"It's 216-555-2376 Room ... ah, 545," I said fumbling with my reading glasses to make out the numbers on the phone.

"I'll be at work until 5 AM., call me there," she said.

"I will, kiss the kids for me. You take care of yourself and don't worry. I love you," I said.

"I love you too, but just come home," she said sounding exasperated.

"I will. Goodnight sweetheart," I said.

I decided to call all the Sam and "S" Bergman's in the Philadelphia White Pages on the chance that he might still be living in Philadelphia or possibly someone might know where he is. It was a long shot but I had to start somewhere I thought. I got out my pad and favorite pen and scribbled down a few lines of dialog I'd use to question the recipients of my phone calls. I felt that I had to come up with something right off the bat to alleviate their innate apprehension to speak with a stranger, especially one who calls at night. If it were me, I would probably just hang up on them. So, "Hi is Sam Bergman there?" was out. I put the pen down and lay back on the pillows. I closed my eyes and tried to come up with a good opening line. Should I be an old friend? No, that was too obvious a ploy. How about an old business associate? No, that was too lame. Then I got it. "Hello, this is Marshall Tucker of Temple University Alumni Association," that should work. That one line should rule out anyone not associated with Temple University. That statement should necessitate a response and from there, I'd have to play it by ear. After all, if someone there was an alumnus or knew someone who was, they might make reference to it. In any event, they were less likely to just hang up on me.

I also decided that I'd need some sustenance to help me through the stress of making unsolicited telephone calls. I needed food, any kind of food. I slipped on my shoes and with one arm in my coat was out the door in search of some old fashioned home cooking. As I hit the street, the wind had picked up and it started to rain so hard it ripped leaves off their trees. It was quite a sight as debris whisked past the old fashioned street lamps like flocks of blackbirds. Pedestrians leaned into the wind in an effort to cross the street. Others with umbrellas ran with the wind like sailboats with billowing spinnakers. As I pressed myself against a wide oak tree and tried to decide which course to take, it stopped, stopped dead. The rain stopped. The wind was gone. It was eerily calm. I imagined it was like passing into the eye of a hurricane. The wind, the fury, the destruction, then the calm. Was this an omen of things to come I wondered?

Around the corner and a half block from the motel was Wendy's, good old Wendy's. Chicken, hamburgers, fries, and Cokes, what more did a hungry pilgrim need? At first glance I thought the place must have been part of Temple University's meal plan since it was packed with boisterous students but then, they let me in without an ID. Go figure? As I waited in line, I noticed that all the girls were wearing blue jeans. There were basically two types of jeans; tight and torn. The tight ones probably required some type of magical ability to shrink one's body long enough to get into the jeans then return to one's normal proportions. Or for that matter, maybe they greased their legs to squeeze into the jeans. It was a puzzlement. The others, were a collection of jeans torn in every conceivable place; the more tears the merrier. As the queue moved closer to the register, I decided that the only way to enjoy my meal was to take it back to the room. I shouted my order to the girl at the register who was carrying on a conversation with a boy making fries who was talking to a customer about a video game who was talking to . . . I just had to get out of there before my head got unscrewed from the pinball machine like chatter.

As I got to the old elevator in the lobby of the motel, I fished around my pockets looking for my room keycard. I couldn't remember what floor I was on and didn't want to get into the elevator until I knew what button to push. I put the Wendy's takeout bag on top of a waste barrel and found the plastic keycard in my wallet with my credit cards. "Oh shit", I said to myself as I realized the card merely said, "Quality Inn". No one gave out room keys anymore I murmured to myself in disgust. I picked up my goodies and went over to the front desk with card in hand to ask the clerk what room I was in. Unfortunately, a new clerk was on duty. "I've forgotten what room I'm in," I began. The clerk was a tall thin man with greased black hair combed straight back in an old fashioned style. All he needed was a part in the middle of his hair and he could have been a member of the, "Our Gang," of silent movies fame. As he looked down his nose at me, he nodded to the keycard in my hand saying, "were did you find that?"

"I didn't find it," I said feeling somewhat tired.

"You're a guest?" he asked inquisitively.

"Yes, I'm a guest. What room does this open up . . . I mean what room am I in?" I said getting a little frustrated.

"No need to get uppity," he replied. "I'll just have to see some identification. You could have found that on the street and ... ," he started saying when I realized that I could be here all night explaining to this guy.

"I'm Max Rosen." I said handing him my driver's license.

He took it and perused some registration cards in a file behind the front desk. Satisfied that I was a guest, he handed me back my driver's license and said, "You're in room 545."

I nodded to him and retreated to the elevator

repeating to myself, 545, 545, 545. Boy, from now on, I'm going to have to write things down, I thought.

Once in the room, I arranged the banquet of burger, fries, and packets of mustard and ketchup on a towel at the edge of the bed. I then pulled the chair up to the bed and after depositing my Coke on the night table began eating my lukewarm dinner while circling the Bergman's in the telephone directory to be called.

I spent the next hour munching on my dinner while calling the Sam Bergman's and S. Bergman's in the phone book. None of the one's I contacted attended Temple University nor knew anyone who was an alumnus. One of the numbers was disconnected and one was not home. I decided to call it a night and try contacting the one I didn't get a hold of later. All in all, it was probably a waste of time coming all this way to Philadelphia when I could have gone to my library and found a Philadelphia phone book. But then, there was that lead, albeit 40 years old, of Sam requesting official transcripts for a school in Vermont. As I closed my eyes I tried to figure out what I should do tomorrow.

# TWELVE

When I went to check out of the motel in the morning, there was an old coffee urn with small Styrofoam cups waiting at the front desk. While sipping a cup of strong black coffee, I briefly reviewed my bill and the ridiculous charges for phone calls from the night before. I had decided that since my phone calls had drawn a blank, my only option was to follow up the Mount Lawrence School lead in Rutland, Vermont. But where the hell was Rutland, Vermont? When I got down to my car, I rummaged through my glove box for a roadmap of Vermont but could only find torn copies of Massachusetts and Connecticut, so I bought a couple of roadmaps at a Mobil gas station and mentally plotted a route to Rutland. I figured that since it was all highways, it should take about 6 hours to get there. And just in case this was all a wild-goose chase, I planned to call the school administration offices half way there to check if Sam once worked

there. The way I saw it, it was then either 3 hours to
Rutland or 3 hours to get back home.

Around 10 AM and just west of the New York City,
I pulled into a rest stop to call the school in Vermont.
I got the Personnel Department on the phone and
after a short wait, was elated to discover that a Sam
Bergman had been an instructor at the school from
1958-1962. That he had taught English literature and
as the woman on the line put it, "other than that, we
are not at liberty to release confidential information
on a prior employee." I said that I understood and
asked her for directions to the school. After I told her
that I was coming up Route 7, she said the school was
off Route 7, on Woodstock Ave.

It was something. Sam was an English teacher
and for the first time, I was able to feel like I had
accomplished something, albeit small. I was definitely
on his trail and with a little luck; I might find another
lead in Rutland to where he went next. But before I let it
get to my head, I remembered promising Vicky that I'd
call the police in New York. I took out the scrap of paper
from my pocket which had the telephone number that
Vicky had given me the night before. As I looked down
at the number, my heart began pounding and I stood
there, with my hand on the phone for several minutes
working out what I was going to say. Finally in what
seemed like an eternity, I decided that my best course
of action was to just duck his questions until I knew
where I stood in the investigation. Then, with great
trepidation I dialed the number and asked to speak to

Detective Russell. Luckily, he was out. Relieved that I had ducked the bullet, I left word with the operator to tell him that I had returned his call. Breathing a sigh of relief, I pealed out of the rest stop, brought the car up to 75 mph, set the cruise control and sat back to enjoy listening to my tape of the 'Platters'.

Oh, this was wonderful I thought, I'll have three hours to do nothing more than drive, listen to music, and contemplate how to find Sam. After all, how difficult could it be? I'm only looking for someone I know nothing about, who worked at a school I've never heard of, in a town that I've never been in and to make matters worse, it was only 40 years ago. Piece of cake. Even better, no one wants to talk to me. If only, if only, I could have gotten into the student files at Temple University I thought. At least I could have discovered where Sam called home and who was listed to call in case of an emergency; all that good stuff that's in a student's file.

As the sun peeked out from between the clouds, I began laughing to myself as one of my favorite tunes began to play:

> *Oh– Oh, yes, I'm the great pretender;*
> *Pretending that I'm doing well.*
> *My need is such I pretend too much*
> *I'm lonely but no one can tell.*

I arrived, just as I had predicted, three hours to the minute at the gates of the Mount Lawrence

School. After getting directions to the school library from a young coed carrying a stack of schoolbooks, I parked in a lot behind the building. Once inside, the Reference Librarian directed me to the second floor Alumni Room, where the school's yearbooks were kept. I assumed that the reason the library was virtually empty was because of the hour. On a bottom shelf, I found a row of yearbooks, dating back to 1937. I grabbed the 1958-1962 books and brought them over to the nearest table. The books were bound in black leather bindings with gold lettering on the spine. The paper was the smooth, glossy variety with black and white photos of students and faculty. I flipped through the 1958 yearbook realizing for the first time, Mount Lawrence was an all-girl's prep school dating back to 1937. As I began to look through the yearbook I froze. The first few pages were devoted to faculty and staff and there, staring up at me was a picture of Sam Bergman, English instructor, BA, MA, Temple University. At first the shock of seeing Sam, his picture, took my breath away. I fumbled through my case and found the picture of the boy wearing a Temple University T-shirt and compared photos; it was him, it was Sam.

The 1959 and 1960 yearbook's carried the same photo and information on Sam. Taking one of the yearbooks to the copy machine, I made 4 copies each 50% larger than the previous one. Well, where do I go from here, I thought as I made my way down the stairs to my car clutching the copies in my hand, what's next?

Food always helps me put things into perspective so I found a restaurant nearby called the Campus House of Pizza. I took with me a pen and a pad of paper to make notes on. The restaurant had that nice smell of bread baking with tomato sauce, oregano and cheese. Most of the customers were a mix of book bag toting co-eds and office workers. I ordered a couple of slices of pizza and a coke and took it over to a counter and sat on a stool next to two young women engrossed in a conversation about the inequities of secretarial salaries in Rutland as opposed to Burlington. When I noticed that one of the women's elbows was resting on a copy of the Mount Lawrence Student Newspaper, I tapped her on the shoulder and I asked if I could read it. Without missing a beat nor a backwards glance, the woman shoved the paper with her elbow backwards so that it landed on my lap. Amused by her actions, I could only smile and thank the back of her head. The newspaper was a slick monthly rag put out by the students highlighting their social activities, sports, theatre, calendar, news, and op-ed. Actually, it was quite attractive. The photos were mostly of students in tennis or golf tournaments, or at a horse show, or TV production but a smattering involved some of the faculty. Last month one of the teachers gave a slide show of his climbing Mt McKinley in Alaska. Another was cultivating orchids in the conservatory attached to the library.

Why didn't I think of that? I thought, as I finished my pizza and headed back to the library.

# THIRTEEN

I drove back to the Mount Lawrence School Library and parked in the same spot as before, however, before entering the building, I walked over to a small Victorian conservatory which was attached to the building. It was an ornate structure reminiscent of the great conservatories at Kew Gardens in London. Inside, just as the article in the school newspaper reported were rows of lovely, delicate orchids. I wondered if they allowed the public into the conservatory to view the orchids up close.

Luckily, the staff that ran the library over the years had been a succession of pack rats, they saved everything. After I explained what I wanted to a pair of upturned eyes, I was escorted to the basement of the library where copies of the Mount Lawrence Student News were stored. After pulling out several dusty boxes from a shelf I seated myself on a step stool and began perusing back issues of the paper from 1958 to 1962.

Considering their age they were in remarkably good condition. The librarian instructed me, before she left, to handle the materials with care. Thankfully, the editions were monthly and composed of the usual school banter; sports, schedules, academic honors, trips, snow storms, etc. I made myself comfortable and began skimming the papers for any news of Sam Bergman. Then in one the last issues, which was devoted to memorial services for a student who tragically died, I found a group photo of the Drama Club who put on Hetta Gobbler and in the notes there was a reference to Sam Bergman, Drama Coach. I made a photocopy of the article and carefully replaced the back issues of the student newspapers into their respective boxes. Before leaving I asked the librarian if the conservatory was open to the public. She advised me that it was, "By Appointment Only" and that I should call the science department to make arrangements. I thanked her and just as I was about to leave, my cell phone rang. I made my apologies to the librarian and went outside to answer the call.

"Hello," I said.

"Hello, is this Max Rosen?" The voice asked.

"Yes," I said. "Who is this?"

"Mr. Rosen this is Detective Russell of the New York State Police," he said. I thought I had recognized the voice and it momentarily took my breath away. I stood there, searching my mind for what to say when he said, "Mr. Rosen we have a few things we'd like to go over with you. It's important we get together? And by the way, where are you?" he asked.

"What do you mean?" I asked.

"Well, your wife says that you're in Philadelphia. Is this right?"

I was afraid to answer the question so I ducked it with my own question. "What do you want to go over with me?" I replied.

"Look Max, we just need a few more details, that's all," he said.

I knew he was playing me, wanting to get on my good side but I couldn't act as if I was guilty. I just had to play along with him. I needed more time. "Max, are you there?" he asked.

"Yah, I'm here." I said. "Let me get back to you," I said.

"Whatta you mean?" he said exasperatedly.

With that, I ended the call and turned off my phone. If he wanted me, he could leave me a voice message.

When I got back to the car I was shaking so much I had to use both hands just to unlock the car door. I sat there for a good five minutes just staring out the window and trying to calm down. My head was pounding away and I was sure my blood pressure was through the roof. I took a prescription bottle out of the glove compartment and inspected the label. They were my blood pressure pills. What if I took a couple of them now I wondered? Will I die? Since it didn't say anything about imminent death, I took a couple of them with a swig from a tepid bottle of water I found under my seat.

Where do I go from here? I asked myself. At that moment, I felt like I was a character in a Laurel &

Hardy film, when Hardy looks over at Laurel and says. "Well, what kind of predicament have you gotten us into now?"

In hindsight I should have pursued other avenues for information. I should have concocted some kind of story or found some way of squeezing the information from the people at Temple University. After all, why was I playing games? The police probably think I had something to do with the crime at Sackett Lake. Maybe I should have called all the Bergmans in the phone book within a 30-mile radius of Philadelphia. There were a lot of things I should have done, but didn't. Most likely with my luck, the Bergman I was searching for would probably live 31 miles from Philadelphia.

Without a clue as to where to turn next, I drove over to a phone booth to check the Yellow Page listings for local newspapers. Besides some listings for out-of-town newspapers, there was one for a Rutland Free Press. When I called them to ask how I could review back issues of their newspaper from 1958-1962, I was told that I'd have to call back at 6 PM and speak to Nate, the janitor. I wasn't certain I heard her correctly so I asked her to repeat it. "Yes, Nate the janitor," she said with a thick Vermont twang, "Nate knows where they're kept. They're not at this locale, understand?"

I decided I had time to kill so I checked into a motel that I had passed on my way into town, The Green Mountain Inn, which advertised on a neon sign, Color TV, Movies, $49 singles.

At 6:10 PM I called the paper and after an eternity

was connected to Nate. I explained what I wanted to a hesitant Nate, and after hinting that I'd make it worth his while, got directions to a warehouse on the outskirts of town where copies of the old newspapers were kept. Nate gave me some instructions as how to find the building, and told me to be there at 7:30 PM. He also made it quite clear that I could stay until 9 PM.

The warehouse was housed in an old building that probably was once a textile mill back around the turn of the century when the State was dotted with mills putting out cloth for the garment factories in New York City. At 7:35 PM an old battered green pick-up truck pulled up at the loading ramp and a man in his 50's wearing a blue work shirt and pants hopped out and limped over to open the door. Putting on the light, I could see large rolls of newsprint paper stacked 15 foot high on palates from floor to ceiling. The rooms smelled with an acid like aroma, probably from something that they treated the paper with. The smell was reminiscent of the printing plant that my father worked for in Brooklyn, so many years earlier. He led me to a back room where rows of cardboard boxes were stacked on metal shelves. The boxes were marked with the month and year of publication.

"That's 'em," remarked Nate, as he pulled over a large wooden dowel. "Everything stays in this room, OK? I'll be back at 9 PM to close up." With that he turned and limped away.

Fifty-eight, nine, sixty, O.K., sixty-one, I stepped on the bottom rung of shelving and reached behind some boxes, finally pulling out a cardboard box labeled 1958

Part I. In it I found an accordion like file, with 26 issues of the Rutland Free Press, January 1958 through June, 1958. Another box along side was labeled 1958 Part II. Pulling both boxes out and lowering them to the floor, I put on my reading glasses and began to thumb through the issues, not exactly certain what I was looking for. I looked for anything on Sam that I could find; new instructor at the school, drama coach, benefit diner, awards, buying a house, anything. I soon decided that an hour wasn't going to give me enough time to scan all of the papers. I had to ask Nate for another day or two to complete my work. I thought that maybe giving him $20 for his time was enough but on second thought I decided to up the ante to get in there again.

As expected, Nate came limping in at 9 PM. After he gave me a hand lifting the boxes back onto the shelf, he asked. "Did ya find what ya wanted?"

"Nate, I appreciate your taking time out to help me. Here take this," as I placed two folded twenty dollar bills in his hand.

"I'll give ya the same amount if I can come back tomorrow night and finish my research," I said.

Nate took the money and stuffed it in his shirt pocket, then looking at me with his head cocked to one side asked, "What ya lookin' for Mister?" "I'm trying to find an old friend who taught at the Mount Lawrence School back in the late '50's."

"Wasn't here then," said Nate, closing the light and locking the door. "See ya 7:30 tomorrow," he said with a nod.

When I got back to my room, I called home to speak to Vicky and the boys but only Randy was home.

"How are you, Dad?" he said excitedly.

"I'm fine I said softly. I miss you son, I'll be home tomorrow, OK?"

"What time are you coming home? We have a dance at the 'Y' tomorrow night," he said.

"I'll be home late honey, you'll be sleeping," I said with regret.

"Are you in any trouble Dad," he whispered. "Mom said . . . ."

"No, I'm OK, I mean . . . I'm not in any trouble. Tell Mom I called and I'll call back later. OK?"

"What?" he asked.

"Remember I love you." I said.

"Right, I love you too Daddy," he said.

The next night, the forty dollars had done its job; Nate was waiting for me at the ramp. He opened the door, switched the lights on, and over his shoulder he said, "Be back at 9:00." Then he got into his pickup and drove off. The previous night I had scanned 1958 through 1960 and had only 1961 and 1962 to review. So far there wasn't a single reference to a Sam Bergman. There was lots of news about schools, graduation, local politics, snowstorms, sales, TV listings, assorted petty crimes but nothing that had Sam's name or picture. By that time I had pretty much given up. That was until I read the July 10, 1962 headline; 'Girl's Body Found in Trunk'. There on the front page was a picture of a 1958 Ford Fairlane being examined by two Vermont

State policemen. The article said that the body of a 15-year-old girl, Mary Ellen Mullen, a student at Mount Lawrence, was found in the trunk of her car and that the cause of death was under investigation. I got out my pad and pen and made some notes as to the names and dates in the article. I found additional coverage of the murder in subsequent issues of the newspaper that detailed the funeral services and the memorial held by her classmates.

As I sat there staring at the stacks of newspapers piled around my feet, I couldn't help think that there might be a connection between the crime in Rutland and the one in Sackett Lake. That if the skeleton in Sackett Lake was a girl … no. That would be ridiculous. But, there was something bothering me about it that I just couldn't put my finger on. Something didn't feel right. Something I was overlooking maybe. Then it hit me. Those little gray cells had recorded something … "the connection." I'd seen that name before, yesterday at the school library while going through the old student newspapers. She was the one they had the memorial services for. I took out the photocopy from the school newspaper of the Drama Club and there she was, Mary Ellen Mullen, the same Mary Ellen Mullen whose body was found in the trunk of her car and the same Mary Ellen Mullen that Sam Bergman coached.

# FOURTEEN

Is Sam a serial killer who leaves his victims in the trunks of cars or is it more likely that these were merely random acts of violence? It's pervasive today, I don't think anyplace is immune anymore. And the abandoned car in Sackett Lake, was it Sam's old car? Or was it, the scene of a mob execution. For all I knew, it could have been Jimmy Hoffa in the trunk. Anyway, I decided that I had to find out what the police had learned about the identity of the skeletal remains we found at Sackett Lake. Was it a male or female? How old was the person? How long have the remains been in the trunk of the car?

As I sat there, waiting for Nate to return, I felt very alone, isolated. I had always prided myself on being an individual, an independent thinker; an iconoclast, a spectator to life's events, avoiding the need other's felt to join clubs or churches. What would they do for me now anyway? I thought. What I needed, were facts. And what

I had going for me was, no experience and no resources to call upon. In other words, 'I was up a creek without a paddle.' Just then I heard the sounds of the warehouse door open and knew it was Nate by the sounds of his leg dragging along the concrete floor coming towards me. I had to think of some way of convincing him to allow me to copy some of the articles about the 1964 murder.

"Hi Nate," I said taking off my glasses and rising as he entered.

"Ya finished?" He inquired noticing the newspapers I was holding under my arm.

"I ah, found a few that I'd like to make copies of," I said, which didn't go over well with him.

"Ain't no copy machine here and … ya can't borrow anything," he said pointing to the papers under my arm.

"Look, Nate, they must have a copy machine back at the newspaper. Why don't we just run back and I'll make the copies there?" I said handing him three twenties.

He glanced at the money in his hand and said, "I'll hold on to them," taking the papers from me. I followed a couple of paces behind Nate as we exited the warehouse and got into his pickup truck for the ride to the newspaper building. The cab of the truck reeked of a combination of stale tobacco and cow manure. I assumed that Nate's second job was at one of the dairy farms that surrounded Rutland.

The offices of The Rutland Free Press were housed in a two story brick building which probably dated back to turn of the century. When we pulled up in front, the lights were on and the place looked empty.

Nate had keys to the offices and as we entered he pointed to a large Xerox machine against the wall.

"Ya know how to use one of them?" He asked handing me the newspapers.

"Sure, they're all the same," I replied hoping I could figure it out.

Luckily, they had left it on. No telling how long it would have taken to warm up I thought. I stared at the directions on top for a few seconds to get my bearings. It was one of those new copiers that does almost everything . . . and you need a Ph.D. to run it. I decided that I'd have to fold the paper in order to fit the standard 8 1/2 X 11 format. This wasn't the time to experiment with reductions or larger formats. I folded the paper to expose the date and headline first, then held it in place with one hand while I fumbled under the paper to find the copy button. The flash momentarily blinded me as a copy of the front page slid out. And as I stood there squinting, out of nowhere a young Asian looking girl had taken the copy from the machine and was reading it.

"I didn't know you were a reporter, Nate," she said smiling.

Nate, who had been resting against a desk, stood up displaying a guilty look on his face. "I thought I heard you leave a half hour ago," she said studying the photocopy in her hand. With that, I felt a pang of responsibility for getting Nate in trouble and tried to makeup some story to cover him.

"I'm sorry if I disturbed you . . . Um, I'm doing some

research ... research for a book and ... and just need some copies, ya know. Be out of here in a minute," I said looking from Nate to the girl.

"Kind of late to be doing research isn't it?" she said looking up at the clock on the wall above the copier.

"Look, I just have a few more items to copy," I said.

"I'd best get the papers back to the warehouse," Nate said coming towards me.

"No, let him finish," she said to Nate still holding on to my photocopy of the front page.

"Thanks, I'll make it fast," I said adjusting the newspaper on the Xerox to make another copy.

"Are you researching a murder?" She asked.

"Yes." I said trying to quickly copy the remaining papers.

"Oh my, this is a long time ago. I wasn't even born yet," she said noticing the date above the headline.

"What have you written?" she asked. "Maybe I've read one of your books," she continued.

"Oh, mostly ... really, just ... short stories that kind of stuff," I said fidgeting with the papers.

"Ya'll through now?" pressed Nate.

"Yap," I said gathering up the copies and feeling around for the off switch.

"You can leave it on," she said handing me the photocopy of the front page she'd been holding.

"Thanks" I said with a silly little bow.

That was stupid I thought. She wasn't a Japanese dignitary. She's a young, attractive Chinese woman. I probably offended her with that bow, I thought.

"Good luck with your book," she said as we wound our way around desks en route to the front door.

"Oh yes," she said.

"What was your name?" she asked coming up besides us.

"I'm Max Rosen," I blurted out; realizing I probably should have used an alias. With that, we got into Nate's pickup for the ride back to the warehouse. I could see that Nate was disturbed by the encounter at the newspaper and I figured it was best not to pry.

I got out of the pickup as Nate stopped by my car and I simply nodded to him. He put the truck into reverse and burning rubber, backed out into the street. That move on his part spoke volumes of what he was thinking. I had gotten him into trouble for a few lousy dollars. I wanted to offer to return the newspapers to the correct boxes but he didn't give me a chance. I wouldn't blame him if he just threw them in the trash.

# FIFTEEN

As I turned the overhead light on in my car to organize the photocopies, a car with its headlights on high beams entered the alleyway and came to an abrupt stop alongside my car. When the driver's window came down, I saw it was the girl from the newspaper. However, this time, she wasn't wearing a smile.

"Mr. Rosen," she said "I've never seen Nate so scared. How much did you pay him?" she asked.

"Nate was good enough ..." I started to say when she cut me off with, "Please don't hand me that bullshit Mr. Rosen. Nate's an old Yankee and wouldn't give you the time of day for free," she said.

I quickly saw that she didn't buy the research story but I couldn't come up with any fresh material to feed her at a moments notice. I found it hard to ad lib when I was tired. And I was very tired ... both emotionally and physically.

"Now why don't you tell me what you're really doing at our papers archives at ten o'clock at night or better yet," she stopped to think for a few seconds then said, "Why don't you follow me? I know a diner where we can speak."

I nodded my head as she put her car into reverse and backed out of the alley. When I got onto the street, I found her waiting for me. She was driving a new red BMW M3. I followed her back to Main Street in Rutland, which looked like they rolled the sidewalks up at night it was so dead. I figured that she was a little leery of me and picked a place she'd feel safe. Near the end of town was an all night diner/truck stop. We parked out front and found a booth in the back. After ordering coffee from a sweet looking old lady, she began by introducing herself. She told me that her name was, Phyllis Cho and that she was a staff reporter for The Rutland Free Press. She also told me that she didn't believe my story about writing a book and that if I was involved in some crime, I wouldn't get out of town. She said that she could make one call and in a matter of minutes I'd be in custody ... and that they'd find out who I really was.

As I sat there, cradling the hot coffee between my fingers, looking at this sweet young thing, I knew she had me by the balls. I could either tell her another tale or worse, the truth.

I decided on the latter and spent the next twenty minutes recounting my story to her without leaving anything out. Throughout my ordeal, she sat motionless, looking directly into my eyes, without saying a word. When I was through, she asked me where I was staying.

"I'm at the Green Mountain Motel," I said wearily.

She told me she'd call me at the motel in the morning to arrange another meeting. Then she said, "Give me your driver's license."

"Why?" I said. "Everything I've told you is the truth."

"Max, just give it to me," she said reaching across the table.

I reluctantly took my license out of my wallet and slid it across the table to her. She glanced at it for a moment and stuffed it in her bag saying, "I'll give it back to you tomorrow."

She can be one mean son-of-a-bitch, I thought as she put a couple of bucks on the table and left.

When I got back to the motel I debated whether it was too late to call home or not but decided that it would be probably worse if I didn't. I knew that Vicky was probably worried to death about me and wouldn't go to sleep until she heard from me.

"I thought you were coming home today. What's up?" she asked groggily.

"I'm at the Green Mountain Motel in Rutland," I said.

"But you told the boys you'd be home today and that Detective Russell's been calling. He doesn't sound nice. He said you can be in a lot of trouble," she said.

"What did you tell him?" I asked.

"I told him that you would be home, that's what you said you'd do," she said.

"Honey ... ," I started to say when she interrupted me.

"Max, I don't want to deal with him. I don't want to get involved with something I don't know anything about. Do you understand?" she said.

"Honey, just listen, I found something unusual here in Rutland and I need to look into it further. There are some similarities between Sackett Lake and a murder that occurred here while Sam was a teacher in Rutland. A fifteen year old ... ," I started to say.

"Max, what are you getting yourself into? You're not a policeman, call this Russell guy and tell him your story ... then, come home," she said sounding frustrated.

"Honey, I will, I promise you ... just that I've told someone that I'd meet them tomorrow. Right after that ... ," I tried to say.

"Who do you have to meet?" she asked.

"Miss Cho, she's a reporter with the Rutland Free Press," I said.

"Why did you go to the newspapers?" she asked.

"I didn't exactly go out of my way to involve her. She came across me copying some articles in her newspaper on the murder in Rutland back in 1962," I said.

"And now she's involved?" she said with a sarcastic laugh.

"She knows people at the school where Sam worked and might be able to get access to stuff I can't. Where he was from, his home, next of kin, I mean confidential stuff in his personnel file," I said.

"Max, I can't discuss this anymore. I want you to call the police and come home," she said.

"I will, I will . . . tomorrow, I promise," I said.

"Tomorrow" she said.

"Tomorrow, I promise ... I love you," I said as she hung up.

The next morning at 10:30 AM my phone rang and it was Phyllis in a bright and excited voice she said, "While you've been sleeping I've made some calls and I might have some more information on your friend Sam," she said.

"He's not exactly a friend, only someone I worked with ...," I started to say.

"Yes, I've heard that story. I want you to meet me at my office in one hour, 11:30 and I'll show you what I've got," she said.

I showered, dressed and ran over to an IHOP restaurant across from the motel. There I wolfed down bacon, eggs, pancakes and coffee while reading a copy of the Rutland Free Press. I tried to find some articles written by Phyllis Cho, but couldn't find any. I wondered what information she might have gleaned during the morning hours.

The Rutland Free Press was only a short drive from the restaurant, but parking close to the building was difficult and I had to settle for a spot, some 3 blocks away. While walking to the newspaper, I pondered what Vicky had said about the police. I decided that as soon as I had left the newspaper, I would call Detective Russell and tell him everything I knew. Then, non-stop to home and family, I really missed them all. It was one thing I didn't want to lose because of some nightmarish situation that I was getting myself deeper and deeper into. It must have been a coincidence that girl being killed while Sam was teaching at the school. And the skeleton in the car at Sackett Lake, that could have been 15 or 20 years ago, not even remotely near the time that Sam and I worked at The Laurels. I felt better after rationalizing the circumstances and approached the meeting with Phyllis on a positive note. After all what could she have discovered in a few hours anyway, I thought.

"Sit down," said Phyllis closing the door to her office. She was dressed in a red dress with a wide white belt and white high heel shoes. Her hair was brushed back and looked still wet from her morning shower. She exhibited a perkiness and scurried behind her desk, clutching a folder.

"He was Sam Bergman, an English teacher, freshman literature, married, wife's name was Joanne, graduated from Temple in 1957 with a BA and 1958 with an MA prior address was; 49 Rutledge Road, North Philadelphia, born 1935, Scranton, Pennsylvania," she said with a smile.

"Does that fit your," she almost said friend but quickly remembered and said, "...man?"

"Sam Bergman, yes, the Scranton part, I'm not sure," I said, nodding my head. "Does it say where he went after leaving Mount Lawrence?" I asked.

"It doesn't say, but there is a letter in his file, a request for a reference from a Spaulding Library Company in 1962."

"Spaulding, where is their office?" I asked.

"Spaulding's office was at 2440 Broadway in New York, but there is no listing in the NYC directory for them. They may have gone out of business or been sold to another company. It's been over 40 years," she said.

I stared at the folder on Phyllis' desk, then sat back and asked her, "Where . . . how did you get this information?"

Phyllis smiled and closing the folder said, "A little bird gave me it."

"OK, I've gotta get home," I said rising, "My family hasn't seen me for . . . ," I started to say.

"Where are you going?" said Phyllis, "We've just started. We've got leads. Spaulding may be gone, but someone's got their records. Sam's possibly got relatives in Scranton, and even better, I've got his social security number. Do you know what I can do with a social security number?" she said with a smile on her face as she tossed my driver's license to me.

As I sat there looking at her, I realized that she pulled the same shit on me. She had my social security number too, and if she was running a profile on Sam, she was probably doing the same on me. I told her that I was tired and wanted just to get back into my station wagon and head home. I had had enough, I thought.

"In a few hours I'll have a report on everything he's done this year. Where he currently lives, eats, drinks, travels, shops, banks ... you name it," she said tapping on the folder.

"You leave now, and that asshole in NY will try to pin everything on you. They don't give a hoot about Sam, it's you they have. For all that matters, Sam could be long dead ... you're CNN, FOX News and Greta Van Susteren. Nothing helps a career more than solving an old murder, especially when you can hang it on an old man. No offense, you're not that old," she said.

"What if I just leveled with them about Sam and the car and the murder here in Rutland?" I said.

"They'll grab you for the NY State murder ... Rutland's not their problem, someone else's turf. They don't have jurisdiction here, and the last thing they want to do is hint at an interstate crime and lose it all to the FBI. What's another few hours anyway? I'm thinking of calling libraries to find out about Spaulding; do you want to help?" she asked.

"My wife is going to kill me," I said.

# SIXTEEN

Phyllis told me that she had some errands to attend to and that we should meet back at the newspaper in a couple of hours. I decided to run over to the Rutland Public Library and use their computer to check on this Spaulding Library Company. But after spending a half hour of fruitless searching on the Internet, I could not find a single reference to them. However, I did print out a list of companies that serviced the library market for follow-up. I even asked the Reference Librarian if she had heard of the Spaulding Company but she too had never heard of them. She did suggest contacting the National Library Association in Washington, DC saying: "They have records back to the Civil War." I thanked her and wondered if I gave her the impression that I was old enough to serve in that conflict.

I drove back to the newspaper to see what, if anything, Miss Cho had found. Stopping at the reception desk I was advised that Miss Cho was out and would be back in a little while. I decided to wait in the lobby since I noticed a pay phone and thought it a good opportunity to check-in with Vicky.

"This is your wandering husband," I said as Vicky answered the phone on the first ring.

"There were two men from the Massachusetts State Police here this morning looking for you," she said hesitantly in a low voice.

"What do the State Police want with me?" I asked.

"What do you think? They were here at the request of the New York State Police to confirm you lived here. They think you're a skip, fleeing from justice. I told you, I begged you to call them, why ... just tell me why?" She pleaded.

"I'm sorry honey. I had no idea that it would be blown out of proportions," I said.

"What do you mean blown out of proportions, they think you murdered someone and that you're trying to hide," she shouted.

"I'm not hiding and I'm not running, I'm still here in Rutland and ... ," I said in a low nervous voice.

"That's what I told them," she said.

"You told them what?" I asked.

"I told them everything. About Sam, about the murder in Rutland, about the girl," she said beginning to sob.

"Honey, don't cry, you did the right thing. I don't know why I didn't just call them. I'm sorry, I'll take care of it," I said as Phyllis entered the lobby.

"Look, I've gotta go, I'll call you later," I said hanging up and hearing a faint, "but," from Vicky.

"Have you been here long," inquired Phyllis as she picked up her message slips from a carousel on the receptionist's desk. Phyllis rifled through the pink slips until she got to one and said "Hmmm, a Detective Russell from the New York State Police called, very interesting. How did he get my number?" she said angrily.

"Um, I'll tell you, can we talk somewhere," I said, as I touched her elbow.

"I thought we agreed to keep them out until we found Sam," she said.

"I know, but it's gone too far. The police were at my home in Massachusetts this morning and they suspect me of a crime," I said to Phyllis in a low, hesitant, shaky voice careful not to be overheard by the receptionist.

"Well, I've got news for you. We're real close to tracking Sam down. I've put feelers out through credit agencies, Trans Union and Equifax, and should have a preliminary report at any time," she said.

"That's nice, but I'm still in deep shit," I said, "and my wife, Vicky told the police everything."

"I figured," said Phyllis waving a pink message slip at me.

"That means that they'll be looking for me too in a little while," she said.

Phyllis took my arm and told me to follow her as we walked out of the building onto the sidewalk, where she asked, "Where are you parked?"

"Across the street, over there," I said pointing.

"Go to the warehouse where we met the other night and wait for me. I've got to get some things from my office and ... ," she started to say.

"What are we doing?" I asked removing Phyllis's hand from my arm.

"We're going to get you out of trouble ... trust me," she said in her most sincere manner.

"That's what I'm afraid of," I replied.

"And don't do anything stupid like calling the police. They'll only grab you up and by the time they're through with you, your face will be all over the Six O'Clock News. Even if you are exonerated, the image of you being led into a police station in handcuffs will haunt you forever," she said.

"OK, OK, the warehouse,... but when...?" I asked

"I won't be long," she said as she turned on her heel and marched back into the building.

I got into my car, put the key into the ignition and just as I did, my cell phone rang. The caller ID said 'Blocked Call'. I just sat there, holding the ringing cell phone in my hand, until it stopped. 'Blocked Call', I thought, most likely the police. Why didn't I just answer it I thought, are they really after me?

# SEVENTEEN

After I left Phyllis, I returned to the motel to pick up my belongings and check out. I ran around the room throwing my stuff into my rucksack, then checked the bathroom, closet and finally, under the bed before dashing down the stairs to my car and tossing everything into the back seat. With my room key in one hand, I drove around the parking lot to the office to drop off the key and pickup a receipt for the room when I saw a Vermont State Police car parked in front of the office. Gripped with fear, I quickly negotiated a U-turn and deftly exited the motel parking lot hoping they didn't see me. I made my way, looking all the while through my rearview mirror, to the warehouse to wait for Phyllis.

As I sat there, slouched low in my car alongside the warehouse, my whole miserable life flashed before my eyes. Why can't I act, instead of always reacting? I asked myself. Because you're a counter-puncher, I said to myself in defense. Let the other guy flail around and get tired and in the doing, one good punch is all I need. Bob and weave, keep out of his reach. He'll get tired and when he does ... just as I was about to raise my fist in mock recognition of winning an imaginary hard fought battle, Phyllis's red BMW came abruptly to a stop alongside my car. It took me a few seconds to adjust to the shock of seeing her.

Opening her window she smiled at me; then, still looking at me, took a folder from the seat alongside her. "I've found a teacher who worked with Sam and she has agreed to speak with us. She still lives in Rutland. Come on quickly, get in my car," she ordered.

"Wait," I said. "The Vermont State Police were at my motel," I said.

"I assume they didn't see you since you're here," she said frowning.

"O.K., O.K. let me think," she said biting her lower lip in thought.

A few seconds later she looked over at me and said, "O.K., follow me."

"Wait, where are we going?" I asked.

"Just follow me. We have to ditch your car," she said.

I was about to protest but she turned to look out her back window as she shifted the BMW into reverse and deftly weaved her way backwards out of the alley. I took a deep breath, started my engine, and began down the alley after her. I followed her down several side streets until we reached a road leading out of town. I guessed that she was avoiding the main roads in case the State Police were looking for a dirty old Volvo wagon with Massachusetts license plates. I found myself following her down a two lane country road. Once out of downtown Rutland, the land was spotted with dairy farms. These farms probably supply the dairy products used to produce Vermont cheese I mused. After about four or five miles, she took a right turn at a mailbox that just had the number 147 on it. The road meandered through a stand of trees to a small farmhouse hidden from the road.

"Just leave it here," she said taking things off the passenger seat and stuffing them into the trunk of her car.

"Won't they object?" I asked.

"They're away visiting their daughter in California. They'll be gone for another week," she said.

I was about to question her but decided to just go along, since I really didn't have any better ideas. I adjusted my seat back and fumbled with the seatbelt thinking how nice the interior of a BMW is. The first thing I noticed was that it was clean. There weren't any candy and food wrappers stuck under the seat and it smelled nice too or maybe it was the fragrance Phyllis wore.

"Tell me about this teacher?" I inquired.

"My source at the school said that she taught math and science while your Sam was a teacher there. As I remember, she said the teacher, Mrs. Swanson, taught there for over thirty years," she said.

"Is it far from here?" I asked.

"No, but it is back in the heart of Rutland, so keep your head down," she said.

We once again took a surreptitious route through the back streets of Rutland until we found our destination, 767 Parker Street. The house was a large turn of the century White Victorian with a spacious wraparound porch. The woman that came to the door was dressed in a soft green cardigan and a long brown skirt which swept the door as she walked. She led us into a large country kitchen that smelled of fresh herbs and bread baking in the oven.

"Would you care for some coffee or tea?" she asked as she filled a kettle at the sink.

"Tea would be nice," replied Phyllis.

"That would be very nice of you" I blurted out loud realizing that she probably wasn't deaf.

She adjusted the flame on the range and placed the kettle on it asking, "Would you like some fresh baked scones?"

"Please don't bother" replied Phyllis. Only to be told that they were already in the oven and should be done in a minute.

She motioned us over to a very unusual looking rectangular wooden table surrounded by four matching chairs. As I pulled out one of the chairs, I realized that they were exquisitely handmade like the table and as I moved my hand over the surface of the table, I was amazed at how lovely and soft the grain of the wood was. Seeing my appreciation of the set, Mrs. Swanson advised us that the table and chairs were called a Classic Diamond Mission design which was very popular with Amish furniture makers.

"You said something on the phone about investigating the murder of Mary Ellen Mullen?" she asked.

"Yes, yes," Phyllis said as she took out a steno pad to take notes.

"And you're a reporter for the Rutland Free Press?" Mrs. Swanson continued.

"That's right," said Phyllis as she took out her ID to show Mrs. Swanson.

Satisfied, she turned her attention to me asking, "Are you a newspaperman too?"

"No," I said "I'm doing research for a book," wondering if she believed me. It was hard to tell looking at her but then, as a school teacher for thirty or so years, she's probably heard every cock-in-bull story ever told. I decided then that it might be better to get to the point of our visit as soon as possible, before this clever old lady caught us in a web of deceit.

"We believe that a teacher who worked at the school may be implicated in her murder" I said, upon which Phyllis shot me an angry look. However, Phyllis quickly recovered and asked Mrs. Swanson to describe Mary Ellen.

"Well," she started to say as the tea kettle began whistling, "She was a very lovely girl. She was from around here, Vermont I think. Such a pity," she said with a sigh.

"They never solved the case, did they?" Phyllis interjected.

"No, I don't think so. It was a long time ago. As a matter of fact, I think it was my first or maybe my second year teaching at Mount Lawrence," she said pouring three cups of tea. I got up to help her with the tea cups while she checked the scones in the oven.

"Just warming them up," she said as she removed a tray of cinnamon raison scones. "Do you take them with butter or clotted cream?" she asked.

"Whatever's convenient," I said catching a whiff of their delicious fragrance.

"I like them with clotted cream and a dollop of strawberry preserve on top," Mrs. Swanson said with a smile.

Phyllis, who was all business, declined the scones and went ahead with her questions leaving me thinking if it was polite to eat both my scone and hers. I decided to wait, in case Phyllis changed her mind or Mrs. Swanson insisted I eat another one. I guess that being on the run gives one an excellent appetite. You know, is this the last meal I'll have as a free man?

"Who is this person of interest?" asked Mrs. Swanson as she stirred honey into her tea.

"How well did you know Sam Bergman?" Phyllis asked.

Her reaction was very subtle. She gently put down her spoon and sat back folding her hands in front of her and began tapping her two index fingers together. Her mouth was open as if she was speaking but no words came out. As I looked over at her I got a glimpse of her profile. She was a lovely looking woman and I could only imagine what type of beauty she was forty years ago.

"What can you tell us about Sam Bergman?" Phyllis said repeating her question.

Mrs. Swanson collected herself and replied, "Sam Bergman was a very handsome and charming man. He was very well liked and respected at the school and in addition, his command of Russian literature and poetry was very impressive."

"I saw in the school yearbook that Sam Bergman was the Drama Coach and that Mary Ellen Mullen acted in one of his plays," I stated. I could see that the mention of Sam's name had an effect on Mrs. Swanson and decided to change the focus and learn more about the victim, Mary Ellen Mullen.

"We've read all the newspaper clipping of the crime; do you remember anyone the police suspected of the murder?" I asked trying to get her out of her brown study.

"Try to remember," said Phyllis.

"Yes, there were rumors about an ex-boyfriend," she said almost in a whisper.

"Do you remember his name?" Phyllis asked.

Mrs. Swanson sat back again closing her eyes and began tapping her index fingers together. She slowly shook her head up and down; then she opened her eyes and said, "Billy ... Billy Archer."

"Was he arrested?" I asked.

"I don't think so," she replied "But then again, it's been a long time," she continued.

Shifting the conversation back to Sam, I asked "Tell us more about Sam Bergman please. Was he married or single, do you remember?"

"He was married but I don't recall his wife's name. Why you think Sam was involved in the girl's death?" she asked.

Both Phyllis and I picked up a slight sense of familiarity in Mrs. Swanson referring to Sam Bergman as, 'Sam'. Was she one of his conquests too? In that case, she might become defensive about her relationship with Sam. Thankfully, Phyllis came up with a real zinger. "We understand that Sam Bergman was interested in young girls and was seen driving them around Rutland at night."

"Really?" commented Mrs. Swanson.

"There are also reports of him at The Stage Bar & Grill in the company of young girls," Phyllis said.

"Well, I never heard anything of the kind," Mrs. Swanson stated as she picked up her cup and brought it over to the sink. I could tell we had touched a sensitive spot and that the interview, for all intents and purposes, was over. Mrs. Swanson made some lame excuses about errands and a meeting as she began walking us to the door, when the telephone rang. Since the closest phone was in the living room, we followed Mrs. Swanson as she went to answer the phone. The living room was also furnished in the Amish motif with a large sofa in the shape of a sleigh and what I later learned were designer Prairie Round Chairs. Against the far wall was brick fireplace which had been painted white. On the mantle was a framed photograph of a man and woman in formal attire. On either side of the photo were 4"X 6" religious tablets. The tablets reminded me of the ones you might see in a museum. One was of a man in royal garb and the other was of a woman tending her sheep. I assumed that they were reproductions since real ones were probably priceless relics. Finally, the party on the line got the message and Mrs. Swanson continued to show us to the door.

Once inside the car, I leaned over and grabbed Phyllis's arm. "What was that all about?" I demanded.

"Hey," she said angrily removing my hand.

"Why didn't you tell me that Sam was seen around town with young girls in his car? And what was that thing about the Stage Bar?" I said.

"Cause I wanted to see her reaction," she said as she started the car.

"What do you mean, 'reaction'?" I said in frustration.

"Just that; . . . let's get out of here and we'll talk," she said.

After we drove a couple of blocks from Mrs. Swanson's house, Phyllis pulled over to the side of the road and said, "Did you see her reaction when we told her we suspected Sam Bergman? After all these years, she's still in love with him."

"What do you mean?" I asked.

"Don't be naive, didn't you see how upset she got after hearing about his alleged liaisons with high school girls?" she said.

"But why didn't you tell me about this before?" I pleaded.

"Because I made it all up," she remarked proudly.

"What, are you crazy? How could you ... ," I blurted out.

"Trust me, she had something with Sam Bergman, a woman can tell," she said.

"So that whole thing about sightings with high school girls ... was all, bullshit?" I said.

"Sort of, but she did give us ... ," she started to say; then stopped.

"I've got to get back to the paper," she said with a sense of urgency as she pulled away from the curb.

"What about me?" I asked.

"I'm going to drop you at the library," she said.

"Like an overdue book?" I joked.

"Stay out of trouble until I pick you up," she said.

Just before she dropped me off I asked her if there was anything I could do while I was in the library. Any research involving the case. She just looked over at me as I was exiting the car and said. "Yeah, you might check if New York State still uses the electric chair," then drove off.

I didn't think it was very funny but the stop at the library would give me an opportunity to use the Internet. Those tablets stuck out like a sore thumb. I had a funny feeling about them.

# EIGHTEEN

P hyllis arrived at the library to collect me just before it closed. It was a good thing, since the librarian had passed my desk several times and was starting to give my computer screen the fisheye.

"Hungry?" she asked.

"I could eat a horse," I replied tightening my seatbelt.

"Good, I know a nice takeout," she said.

Phyllis probably stopped at her place since she was now wearing a short tight black skirt which she hiked up to negotiate the floor pedals. She did have some nice looking gams for a kid, I thought. After a few minutes we turned into a Burger King and got into the takeout queue.

"I was only kidding about the horse, I didn't think you'd take me serious," I said. When it was our turn, we gave the order to an invisible microphone and pulled up to the takeout window. I fumbled with my seatbelt in order to get at my wallet but Phyllis already had some cash in her hand.

"Thanks," I said.

"That's O.K., you can get the next one," she replied handing me the bags.

"Where can we eat?" I said feeling a slight growl in my stomach.

"We're going to the farm," she said.

"All the way out there?" I said.

"It's safe," she replied.

I tucked the bags between my legs as Phyllis deftly negotiated her way out of the Burger King parking lot.

"Do you remember those tablets on the fireplace mantel?" I asked while fishing for a French fry.

"The Russian icons?" she replied.

"Why didn't you tell me they were Russian icons?" I said exasperatedly. "You could have saved me time searching the Internet for those damned things," I said.

"I thought you knew," she said.

"Well, they were Russian icons; one was of Jacob, and the other was of Rachel," I replied.

"O.K., she's religious," she said matter-of-factly reaching over between my legs to close the Burger King bag.

"Yes, but their story might be significant, especially if they were a token of love between Sam and Swanson," I said. "And by the way, what is Mrs. Swanson's first name?" I asked.

"That's a bit of a stretch," she said. "And her first name is, Rachel."

"I thought so," I said excitedly. "Listen, here's a story of a guy, Jacob, who falls in love with beautiful girl named guess who ...Rachel, only to be forced into a marriage with someone else. Despondent, he prays to God for help ... and guess what? His prayers are answered and he eventually ends up with the one he loves, Rachel," I said.

"A Hollywood ending but without the credits," she replied.

"What do you mean?" I asked.

"You have no proof Sam gave them to her," she replied.

"But you're the one who said she still loves him," I said.

"Yes, but Russian icons?" she replied looking over at me in disbelief.

"Remember the part about Sam being a Russian scholar, well why should she treasure two biblical icons from the Book of Genesis? ... Especially, one of the Hebrew patriarch, Jacob?" I said. When she didn't reply, I thought that I might have convinced her of my theory or at least, the plausibility that the icons were connected to Sam. That was, until she threw me a zinger.

"Spoke with Detective Russell," she said.

"Why'd you call him?" I asked facing her in disbelief.

"Because he called me," she said shifting into third gear.

"What did he say?" I asked.

"He wanted to know where you were," she said

pushing down on the clutch and shifting into fourth gear.

"Did you tell him?" I asked.

"Of course not," she said with a smile.

"You know, you drive like Mario Andretti," I said.

"Who?" she asked.

"Mario Andretti, you've never heard of him?" I said.

"Is he that little Nintendo character?" she asked.

"No he was a famous race car driver," I said.

"Don't worry, Max, I'm a good driver," she said proudly holding one hand on the wheel and the other on the stick.

"Yeah, I remember Mario said the same thing as they wheeled him into intensive care," I said.

"Do you want to know about Detective Russell, or not?" she asked looking over at me a bit too long for my tastes.

"If we live long enough, sure. Keep your eyes on the road," I said as she shifted into fifth gear.

"From what I got out of him and by the way, I think he takes things much too personally, he wants your ass," she said checking her rearview mirror.

"Is there anybody following us?" I asked.

"Nope," she said.

"Exactly, what did he say?" I asked.

"At first he was 'Mr. Nice Guy', you know, we're both on the same side, seeking truth and justice. Then, 'Not Mr. Nice Guy', you don't want to obstruct a criminal investigation, do you?"

At that point, she shifted down into 3rd gear as we entered the driveway leading to the farmhouse. She stopped behind my car and grabbed the Burger King bags from between my legs saying, "Take your things, you can stay here tonight."

"But I was thinking of going home tonight, I promised my wife," I protested.

"Didn't you hear what I said? This Russell guy has a screw loose. He'll show up at your home with a Swat Team and drag you back to New York in chains. He wants you dead or alive hombre."

As I collected my things from the Volvo, I felt a little woozy from the ride. Phyllis disappeared around the house and next thing I saw were the lights inside the house going on. She opened the front door and led me into the kitchen. With the lights on, the house had a warm and comfortable feeling to it. The furniture was Early American with braided rugs here and there and, from my untrained eye, what looked like original oil paintings of pastoral country settings on the walls. The kitchen was lit by recessed lights in the ceiling and indirect lighting under the walnut cabinets. Phyllis walked over to a rectangular dining room table with four chairs around it and divided the contents of the bags into, hers and mine. I mentioned to Phyllis that the room had a bit of a stuffy smell to it and she went around opening some of the windows. In front of the windows were festively painted flower pots with geraniums, hostras, and azaleas growing in them.

Since they were quite large, I assumed that they put them out in their garden in the summer.

"How long have they been gone?" I asked as I spread ketchup on my fries.

"It's been two weeks ... and I should have stopped by sooner to water the plants," she said gingerly picking the onions out of her Whopper. A small puddle of condensation had formed around my Coke and I asked her if there was any ice. She went over to the refrigerator still holding onto her burger and extracted an ice cube tray. She then began to fumble with the tray, eventually putting her burger in her mouth as she wiggled and twisted the tray to no avail. I went over and took the tray from her saying, "there's a trick to it." I ran it under the water and twisted the plastic tray until two cubes popped out and landed on the floor. I picked them up quickly as I counted to five out loud and dropped them into my drink. Perplexed, Phyllis said, "What was that all about?" I told her that it was a game I played with my boys. If they dropped food on the floor, it was O.K. to eat it if they picked it up before they counted to five.

"You miss them?" she asked.

"They're my life," I said.

After we finished, she put the wrappers, tomato ketchup packets, and cups into the bag. Then she moistened a paper towel at the sink and began to wash down the table, deftly sweeping the crumbs also into the bag. Then she sat down and started looking through her handbag until she found what she was looking for, a brass business card holder. She extracted one of the cards and tapping it on the table in front of her said, "there's a guest bedroom in the rear," pointing to a hallway off the kitchen, "and a bathroom through that door," motioning with a nod of her head to a door adjacent to the refrigerator.

"Oh yes, one other thing, please don't make any long distance phone calls from their phone," she said.

"No problem," I said.

I felt that there was something bothering her, since she continued to absently tap the business card on the table so I asked her, "What's on your mind?"

"Max, I'm a little confused by something that Detective Russell said on the phone. He says you're feigning amnesia. Are you?" she asked looking me directly in the eyes.

"No, I've told you that I can't remember working at The Laurels Hotel," I said.

"Max, that's hard to believe, this selective amnesia story. Did you have some type of accident, injury, or drug thing that you're not telling me about ... what?" she asked.

"No, no it's just a blank. Look . . . ," I started to say.

"No, you look ... this story of yours is a farce, you know it and I know it," she said disgustedly.

All I could do was sit back and shake my head.

"Max your brain isn't a loose-leaf binder where you can selectively remove pages you don't like," she said.

"Believe me, I've tried to remember the past but ... ," I blurted out before she cut me off.

"You know, you're either the world's greatest bullshit artist or a case study for a psychiatric journal," she said.

"What do you want me to do?" I pleaded.

"Just be honest with me," she said.

"I swear to God, I am being honest with you!" I said.

"What if you're an atheist?" Well, I am but that's besides the point I thought. No need to add fuel to the inferno.

"O.K., I'll give you the benefit of the doubt. But if you're lying, I'll hand deliver your head to Russell on a silver platter," she said.

"Oh, tomorrow were seeing Mr. Archer," she said.

"You found him?" I exclaimed.

"Yes and it's Billy's father we're seeing. I neglected to tell you, he's in a nursing home in Gatesville."

"Is that far from here?" I asked.

"About 20 miles," she said fishing for her shoe under the table.

"How'd you locate him?" I asked.

"Advanced research . . . he was in the phonebook," she said with a smile.

"When he didn't answer his phone I went over to his house, a small cottage on Green Street, and a neighbor said he had broken his hip and was recuperating at the Franklin Nursing Home in Gatesville."

She slid her business card over to me and told me to call her on her cell if I needed her. I walked her out to her car and just before she left she did what every woman does, gives you last minute instructions, "I'll be back in the morning around ten, don't make a mess, and water the plants."

"Right," I said obediently.

# NINETEEN

I watched her speed down the driveway until the little red taillights disappeared into the trees. It was getting cold, so I hurried back inside and locked the door. I decided that I should checkout the farmhouse to make sure, 'Freddy Krueger' from 'A Nightmare on Elm Street,' wasn't hiding somewhere in the dark recesses of the house, so I decided to take a look-see of the second floor. I flipped on the light switch at the foot of the stairs and made my way up to the second floor hallway.

The second floor had two bedrooms and one full bath. One of the bedrooms was converted into an office/study. I poked my head in and noticed a large walnut desk with a fluorescent lamp on it and a black executive desk chair in the corner. I walked over and sat down at the desk and switched on the desk lamp. On top of the desk was a white pushbutton telephone, a calendar from the State Farm Insurance

Company, a couple of envelopes containing bills, a Miller Light beer coaster, and what I presumed was a family photograph of the residents and their two teenage daughters. I realized that I didn't even know the names of these nice people who were allowing me to rummage through their things and spend the night in their home, so I picked up one of the bills from New England Electric Company and read who it was addressed to, an Abraham Pike. 'Well, Mr. Pike, I'd really like to thank you for letting me stay here,' I said to no one in particular as I rifled through his desk. Finding nothing of interest, I walked over to a four drawer filing cabinet and perused the folders. They were mostly the usual personal papers people hold onto for no other reason than they're either afraid or unwilling to throw them away.

Gripped with fear investigators from the IRS will swoop down and demand to see that receipt for a contribution you claimed for some what-cha-ma-call-it charity.

"What, no receipt?  BOOK HIM, DANO."

Satisfied that Freddy was not lurking under the desk, I closed the light and went into the other bedroom. I found a light switch on the wall by the door and switched on the overhead light. In the center of the room, was a four poster Early American Queen sized bed. On either side of the bed were night stands each with a brass lamp and white shade. Across from the bed on the opposite wall, was a matching four drawer dresser with a Sony television sitting on top of a VCR player. I could immediately see that one of them was, 'the boss,' since all of the remote control clickers were on one of the night stands. I shut the light and went across to the bathroom. Since I was the new 'Lord of the Manor' in residence, I decided to mark my turf before any further exploration of the farmhouse. Relieved, I went down stairs and grabbed my rucksack and carried it into the back guest bedroom. The room was small with two twin sized beds on either side. A large color photograph of the girls on horseback was hung above a dresser in the corner. The room had two windows with light blue country curtains held open on each side with a matching sash pinned to the wall. A small digital clock sat on a night stand flashing 12:00 next to one of the beds. I sat on the bed and reluctantly reset the clock to 8:05 PM. I hate it when the power goes out at home. We must have a dozen digital clocks and appliances that have to be reset each time the power goes out.

I crossed through the kitchen and turned on one of the floor lamps in the living room. It too was furnished in Early American with two recliners, a moss green velour couch with a colorful American Indian blanket thrown over the back, a large hutch, and a brown and red 8′ X 12′ braided rug on a wide pine floor. In one corner of the room was a Vermont Castings wood burning stove sitting on a raised brick hearth. Next to it was a green plastic recycling container filled with firewood. Under different conditions, I would have loved to start a fire in the stove but feared that I might burn the house down by accident.

On the hutch, was a Sony stereo/CD/record player with speakers on each side. Underneath, I found a treasure trove of old long playing records from the 1940's, 50's, and 60's. There was Frank Sinatra, Perry Como, Nat King Cole, Ella Fitzgerald, Mel Torne and Tony Bennett. I turned on the stereo and stacked a bunch of LP's on the turntable. The first record was a 'Sinatra's Golden Oldies,' circa 1967. While Frankie sang, I went into the kitchen to find where my hosts kept their spirits. After a bit of crawling around on all fours, I found their stash in a base cabinet under a silverware drawer. There were a couple of opened bottles of gin and vodka and one unopened bottle of Johnny Walker Scotch. With the thought that they might be saving the Johnny for a special occasion, I decided that I might fill the bill. I opened the bottle and poured two fingers, then another finger into a glass. Then I added a splash of water from the sink and an ice cube from the freezer as Frankie began singing:

*"I've got you under my skin."*

I took a long sip and murmured:

*"I've got you deep in the heart of me."*

I eased myself into one of the recliners and pulled the lever to raise my feet. Oh, this was heaven, I thought. To be able for the first time in days to relax with a drink while listening to the, 'Chairman of the

Board' sing melodies from my past; music that my parents would sit and listen to in the evening. As I closed my eyes, I could see the old neighborhood so vividly, the long line of row houses on East 97th Street, Brooklyn. I remembered the exultation of racing up three dizzying flights of stairs to the brown painted metal door with the tiny peephole. Our apartment had a small bathroom with a cast iron tub, a galley kitchen with a window opening to a fire escape, a living room with a couch I called my bed for fifteen years, and my parent's tiny bedroom. The apartment was so small, it could literally fit in our master bedroom at home. I took another sip of the Scotch and I could hear the noises of the neighborhood, the horns, sirens, and screams of the children playing in the alley below. The intoxicating smells of cabbage and chicken and breads baking in ovens, and the girl upstairs endlessly practicing scales on the piano. The jingle, jingle, jingle announcing the arrival of the fruit man and his horse drawn cart overflowing with fruit and vegetables or the call from the knife sharpener in his broken English, 'bring ah-me your knives, bring ah-me your scissors.' It was like something out of a Fellini movie. Here was this young handsome Italian man, shirt open exposing his massive chest, pants held up with a rope and women pouring out of their homes helter-skelter with knives in their hands, racing to his little cart. But my favorite, hands down, was the musical tune that signified, 'The Good Humor Man' had arrived with ices and popsicles.

On warm nights, people would gather in front of their buildings and sit on wooden folding chairs to watch the world pass by while smoking Camel's cigarettes and drinking warm glasses of beer. Every so often, a one of the kids ran around the corner with an empty pitcher for a refill at the local saloon. They swapped stories about their kids or their jobs or about the lack of hot water in the morning. Sometimes, usually after several rounds of beer, they'd talk about the war. Many had served in the armed services or merchant marine. Some fought their way across North Africa, others disembarked from landing craft in waters up to their necks while Japanese snipers picked them off, and some stood watch on frozen decks of cargo ships as they slowly zigzagged their way across the North Atlantic. I took another sip of Scotch as the old crooner, with that perfect pitch, sang a song my father would sing to my mother.

*'I'll be seeing you*
*In all the old familiar places*
*That this heart of mine embraces*
*All day through'*

As I sat there with my eyes tearing up I had one of the earliest memories of my past I'd ever had. I was walking with my uncle Joe down Church Ave in Brooklyn; it was a hot sunny day and he was dressed in his green paratrooper's uniform. There were lots of medals and ribbons on his chest. His boots were big and brown and very shiny. He wore a cap with a parachute insignia on it. As we walked, people came over to him, complete strangers, to shake his hand; others smiled and nodded their heads. I was very proud of my uncle Joe. He had survived the Normandy invasion and 'The Battle of the Bulge.' The next day, he put his uniform away and never wore it again. I was four years old. I opened my eyes just in time to accompany Frankie with:

> *'I'll find you in the morning sun*
> *And when the night is new*
> *I'll be looking at the moon*
> *But I'll be seeing . . . you.'*

After that, I dried my eyes, wiped my nose and went to bed.

# TWENTY

I spent a restless night pondering the possibility that a combination of alcohol and music, specifically the music of the 1950's, might unlock that period in my life that I had no memory of.

After making my third trip to the bathroom, I decided that I desperately needed some sustenance. Unfortunately, the Pike's left little or nothing in the refrigerator. A jar of orange marmalade, a half jar of green olives, a can of Dole pineapple chunks, a bottle of concentrated lemon juice, a stick of unsalted butter, and an opened box of Baking Soda. As I stood there in one of my famous 'refrigerator poses,' arm propped on top of an opened refrigerator door, body leaning forward with head bent into the refrigerator, eyes staring at the food, I broke from my trance and grabbed the can of Dole pineapple. I brought it over to the counter and opened it with a can opener I found in the silverware drawer. I poured the contents into a bowl and after further exploration, came up with a box of Social Tea cookies, which I crumbled into small pieces and sprinkled on the pineapple. I then took a spoon and my concoction up the stairs to the Pike's bedroom and switched on the television.

Perched on their bed, I ate my breakfast while watching 'The Valley News,' on Channel 26. A young girl with a permanent smile was reading the news; 'war, more war, and war' . . . then she turned to her colleague and said, 'and now for the Valley Weather Report.' Happy that nothing had changed while I was on the lam, I turned the television off and decided I needed a hot shower to clear my mind and get the kinks out of my body. I got the shower real hot to steam up the bathroom, and then I turned down the temperature so that wouldn't scald my body. As the warm spray engulfed my body I moaned with delight and thought out loud . . . 'what a luxury, mankind's greatest invention, indoor plumbing'. I dried myself with one of the Pike's pink Turkish towels and with it wrapped around my torso, made my way down stairs to find fresh clothing. Picking up my clothes from yesterday, I held them to my nose to see if they passed the 'sniff test.' Wow, did they stink. I had no idea that they smelled like burnt rubber tires. I guessed that was why Phyllis used the deodorizer in the car. Oh, I felt so ashamed that I didn't even realize I had such an offensive odor. I assumed that it must have been caused by all the tension I've been under. In any event, I had a couple of clean shirts and underwear in my bag which did pass the 'sniff test.'

At around 9:45 AM Phyllis arrived with hot coffee and fresh blueberry muffins from Dunkin' Donuts.

"You haven't made a mess, have you?" she asked while glancing around the kitchen.

"Nope, I've been real good," I replied.

She placed a couple of napkins on the table then gingerly deposited a blueberry muffin on each napkin. Then she cut each muffin in half with a plastic knife and placed a pad of butter in-between the halves. I slid one of the muffins over towards me while I removed the plastic lid from my coffee and poured two of the mini-creamers into it. Then I licked the crumbs off the knife and stirred my coffee with it.

Phyllis looked up at me disapproving and said, "That's gross!"

I shook my head in agreement while I sipped the hot coffee. Anxious to tell her of my theory of how I might recall the blank spot in my past, I tried an analogy. "You know, the brain is like a computer in many respects," I said.

She looked at me with a confused expression on her face. "What?" she said.

"Let me tell you of my theory," I said.

She had this blank look on her face as if she were thinking, "Is he for real?"

"Bear with me," I said. "A computer is merely a device, a machine, which requires an operating system to run software applications like, 'Microsoft Word'. O.K. so far?" I said. She nodded her head while sipping her coffee.

"OK, you enter data . . . reports, correspondence, articles, what-have-you into the computer's memory, its' hard drive, just like a person does in life but in our case, the information is stored in the brain," I said as she got up to empty her coffee into the sink.

"Keep talking, I need some water," she said as she rinsed out her cup and filled it with cold water.

"All right," I said "I'll keep it short." As she walked back to the table and stood behind her chair.

"What I'm getting at is that when I was in the business, the computer business, we wrote code for companies to run their applications. Invariably, these were sensitive materials and we installed, 'firewalls,' to protect their data from hackers," I said.

"Look, Max we should be getting along. I want to be at the nursing home before they have lunch," she said shifting from one leg to another like a kid that had to pee.

"O.K., here's the best part," I said "Some of the time, especially in the early going, there were glitches in the software . . . and we needed to install a, 'patch', a 'fix,' and we had to get into their systems by bypassing their firewalls. We did this by secretly building a, 'backdoor' to get into their systems. Are you still with me?" I asked.

"Yes, what's your point, I'm familiar with all that, my father is an engineer at IBM," she said.

"Oh, really," I said. "Then you should understand my theory. What if there's a 'backdoor' to the brain?" I could see she was beginning to get restless, so I cut to the chase.

"What if, everything that happened that summer was locked in my brain, and protected by my, 'firewall'. What if, we could bypass my defenses and get at the memories through sort of a, 'backdoor'," I said.

"And how do we do this, brain surgery?" she said with exasperation.

"No music," I blurted out.

"Max, let's discuss this theory of yours in the car," she said ending my presentation as she gathered up the cups and papers into a bag.

"OK," I said as I retreated to the guest bedroom to collect my rucksack. Meanwhile, Phyllis busied herself checking out the house making sure I hadn't made off with the silverware.

"You got water all over the bathroom floor," I heard her scream.

"Sorry," I shouted up to her.

When she came down the stairs she was holding a wet towel and said, "What did you do, swim laps in the bathtub this morning?"

While I put my bags into the Volvo, Phyllis locked the doors and replaced the, 'hide-a-key' on the back porch. She used the wet towel to wipe her headlights and then threw it into her trunk.

"You don't have to use so much air freshener," I advised her.

She looked over at me with that, 'pardon me,' look on her face.

"I've showered and put on clean clothes," I confessed.

"Thanks," she said as she threw the clutch into first gear without warning.

"Would you like to hear more about my theory?" I asked.

"Why don't you save it for later?" She said looking both ways before popping the clutch into 2nd gear and heading north on Route 31 to Gatesville.

That's when her cell phone rang. She glanced at the caller ID then flipped it open and said into the phones microphone, "Kathy, what's up?" She switched ears so that I couldn't hear what the caller said. "Yes I'm on my mobile today . . . and only if it's important, understand?" With that she closed the phone ending the conversation.

"Everything O.K.?" I asked.

"Usual office horseshit," she replied as she drove with wild abandon.

"Careful, you're going to get nabbed for speeding," I cautioned her realizing that kids usually did exactly the opposite of what you tell them to do. In retrospect, I should have said, 'go get yourself killed, see if I care'.

"I'm sorry Max, I was distracted. What did you say?" She said.

"Oh, it was nothing, just a prayer before dying," I said tightening my seatbelt.

Phyllis had a printout of directions to the Franklin Nursing Home which she passed to me saying, "When we get off exit # 7, tell me where to go."

I glanced at the MapQuest directions and nodded my head.

# TWENTY ONE

The MapQuest directions were dead on and we pulled into the Franklin Nursing Homes parking lot at 10:45 AM. The nursing home resembled a sprawling ranch house with the offices in the center and patient rooms on either side. The building looked like it had just been repainted and sported white cedar shingles in contrast with its black shutters and a new black asphalt tile roof.

"Let me do the talking." Phyllis instructed me as she reached behind and took a paper bag off the backseat of her car.

"Do you want me to follow you three paces to the rear?" I jested.

"Not funny," she snapped back.

Realizing I made a cultural faux pas, I followed her as she made her way up a long wooden ramp into the nursing home. When we entered, there were several patients sitting on either side of the entrance. One of the women nodded to us and said hello. The others just sat in a catatonic state staring at the floor or sleeping. The receptionist was a sweet looking woman in her 70's with light blue hair who looked up and smiled at us asking, "Who are you here to see?"

"I called earlier." Phyllis said "We are here to see Mr. Archer."

"Oh, O.K., go right at the end of the hall and he's in room #12 . . . . and Oh, please sign the Visitors Log," she said.

Phyllis signed the log for both of us and after collecting her bag from the floor started down the hallway with me on her heels.

"That was easy," I said.

She nodded her head as she walked along the narrow hallway looking for room # 12. Some of the patients were in their beds and others sat on upright chairs in their room. The unmistakable odor of urine permeated the air and I wondered how long I could hold my breath. Not long enough I decided, we had to make this short. Phyllis stopped at one of the rooms and said, "Are you Mr. Archer?"

When I caught up, Phyllis was walking over to a man in a wheelchair. He was thin, probably in his eighties, with a few grey hairs pulled back behind his ears and hairy stubble on his chalky face. He wore light blue pajamas and a thin food stained matching bathrobe. His expression was one of bewilderment. The room was small with two twin beds with safety rails, a couple of small night stands each with lamps and cubby holes built into the wall for their belongings. Archer's roommate, if he had one was not there. Bending down, Phyllis took a box of assorted chocolates from her bag and placed it on Archer's lap saying, "Nice to meet you Mr. Archer. You are Mr. Archer, aren't you?"

"Do I know you?" He asked looking up and squinting at us.

"How are you today?" inquired Phyllis trying to break the ice.

"The other guy, what's his name, isn't here ... um," stuttered Archer.

"No, no, we are here to see you," Phyllis said with her warmest smile.

"Who are you?" asked Archer.

"Mr. Archer, we want to have a talk with you about Billy," Phyllis said.

Archer looked at us with a blank expression then lowered his head taking a deep breath. He sat motionless in that position for a few moments. Getting concerned, I asked Phyllis if he was all right? Whereby, Phyllis moved closer to Archer and placing her hand on his shoulder and asked, "Are you all right Mr. Archer?"

Then, Archer's head rose in anger as he suddenly turned his wheelchair around and moved away from us saying over his shoulder, "I don't talk about Billy."

"Stay here." Phyllis ordered me as she followed Archer to the other side of his room. She came up behind him and leaned over to whisper something in his ear. Then I saw Archer shake his head and say something to Phyllis. She tapped him on the shoulder and coming back my way, motioned to me to follow her outside the room.

"Get him some cigarettes," she said.

"What?" I asked.

"Two packs of Marlboro's, a butane lighter, and two packs of Wrigley's Spearmint chewing gum," she said with a smirk on her face.

"Where?" I replied.

She walked over to Archer and once again began talking to him in a whisper. Then, shaking her head in agreement, she came back to me and gave me directions; turn right after leaving the nursing home and walk one block to the stop sign, turn right and a QuickMart was one block down diagonally across the street. I was just about to ask her if I could borrow her car, when she gave me one of her, 'Don't even ask me for my Beemer,' looks.

Happy to get some fresh air, I smiled at the receptionist as I left and briskly walked the two blocks to the QuickMart. I found the spearmint and a Bic lighter at the checkout counter. "Two packs of Marlboro's," I said to the cashier, a girl of about 16 or 17 sporting a Red Sox baseball cap and a ponytail sticking out the back of the hat.

"Got ID?" she asked, cocking her head to one side.

"Don't I look over 21?" I replied, giving her one of my famous smiles.

She pointed to a sign above the cigarettes which read:

## 'You Must Be Over 21—And Prove It
## No Exceptions—No Excuses'

"Oh." I said, "I didn't notice the sign."

I handed her my Massachusetts driver's license and I could see the wheels turning in her head as she crossed off the 2 and made it a 1 and carried the 1 and made it 11 then subtracted the 9 . . . . then handing me back my license saying, "It's probably O.K." and got me two packs of Marlboro's.

"Would you like a bag?" she asked.

"Do I need an ID?" I teased.

She just stood there dumbfounded, then getting the joke, said in a common youthful colloquialism, "Whatever."

When I returned to the nursing home, Phyllis was sitting on Archer's bed talking to him. "Got everything?" she asked.

"Yep," I replied.

"O.K." she said. "This is the plan; he can't smoke in the building . . . . there's a side exit just down the hall that leads to an outside patio. I'll have them shut the alarm so we can open the door. Push him down to the door and wait for me," she said.

I did as instructed and a few moments later, Phyllis rushed back and told me to open the door. I did so while she maneuvered Archer's chair through the door and down a small ramp onto the patio. The patio was rectangular with a cement floor that was surrounded by a five foot chain link fence. Scattered around were aluminum chairs in various forms of disrepair, a couple of red painted picnic tables and a rusted barbeque grill.

No sooner had the front wheels of the wheelchairs hit the cement; Archer turned to me and asked, "Got the smokes?" I took out the cigarettes, lighter and gum and handed it to him. Like an addict eager for a fix, Archer dislodged a cigarette from the pack and was lighting up in a matter of seconds. He took a long drag and threw his head back inhaling every bit of smoke he could into his lungs . . . then sighed, "God I needed that," he said as he brought the cigarette up to his lips again for another hit. "Now, what do you want to know about Billy?"

# TWENTY TWO

I pulled over a couple of aluminum folding chairs and after wiping off the pine needles, placed one on either side of the wheelchair. The wind had picked up and the smoke from Archer's cigarette swirled around his head like a turban. He was now in the other world of cigarette induced nirvana.

Hoping to capitalize on his trancelike state, Phyllis opened with, "Mr. Archer, tell us a little about your son Billy?" she asked taking out her notepad. Unfortunately, the sight of Phyllis's notepad brought Archer down from his temporary trance. I could see the anxious look on his face and tried to reassure him that . . . "No, it's O.K. Mr. Archer, she's always taking notes. You know, to get it accurate," I said.

Archer was still a little ruffled and fearful he was getting into something that he might one day regret, remarked, "This is just between you and me, right?"

At which point, Phyllis and I both nodded our heads

in agreement. Satisfied, Archer shifted his position in his wheelchair and lit up another cigarette. He began, "Billy was the boy every father dreams about. He was a nice boy, nice to everyone. Finished the Voc Tech and started working for me at the garage the day he graduated. No job was too big or small for him. Held his own with the other men, men who had ten, fifteen years experience. Got to work at seven and didn't come home until the job was done . . . sometimes after closing."

"That sounds wonderful Mr. Archer," I said seeing that just the thought of Billy was upsetting to him. He took a deep breath and was just about to say something when Phyllis asked, "How did he meet his girlfriend, Mary Ellen?" With that, Archer snapped his head up and gave Phyllis a terrible stare that cut right through her. They both sat there staring at each other for a moment seeing who would blink first. Finally, Archer swallowed and wiped the sides of his lips with the back of his sleeve before speaking and when he did, it was low and deliberate. "I don't know when he met 'Miss Pretty' but he fell for her in a big way. Spent all his time and money trying to impress her; bought her a watch, and a ring, clothes and what-have-yah . . . then, she just dumped him like he was garbage," he said shaking his head.

We sat there for a few moments giving the cigarette and opportunity to calm him down before continuing our interview. Seeing that the nicotine had once again relaxed him, I asked, "Did you ever meet her, Mary Ellen?" Archer looked over at me and smiled saying, "Yah, I met her."

Where upon Phyllis followed up with, "How would you describe her?"

Archer now intoxicated by the tobacco merely mumbled, "God gave me a son and took him away. They said it was the cancer but I know it was because of her."

Phyllis looked down at her notes then said, "I know her death must have had a profound effect upon Billy, but wasn't he a suspect?" To this, Archer merely rocked back and forth in his wheelchair without speaking. "And he was exonerated as well," she said as Archer continued to rock back and forth every so often taking long drags from his cigarette.

Sensing that I might be able to bring him back, I told him about my boys. "I've got twins . . . boys, almost thirteen." I said with a smile. "So I know how you must feel, I can't imagine life without them." He looked at me and for that brief instant, I felt we connected.

"I heard from people who knew her that Mary Ellen was a good girl, popular and very pretty. No matter what happened between Billy and her, she didn't deserve to die . . . she was just a kid," I said.

"But she broke his heart . . . and he was never the same," he said choking up with tears. "That whole trip, the hunting trip I sent him on was to cheer him up, to forget about her, get him out of town, clear his head. Some good it did, came back and found she was dead," he said.

"Why do you think they broke up?" asked Phyllis.

"It wasn't because of anything he did . . . she was screwing someone else," he said with disgust.

"What do you mean?" I said.

"Are you deaf? She had another guy all the time," he said "Screwing him behind Billy's back."

I could sense Archer was getting very uncomfortable discussing the past and knew we'd have to wrap it up soon before he blew us off. Phyllis sat there satisfied to let me continue the interview maybe sensing that Archer favored speaking to me, man-to-man, as apposed to a woman who might think favorably about Mary Ellen.

"This other guy," I started, "Do you know who it was?"

"I don't know, maybe Billy knew but never said," Archer said looking up at the trees swaying in the wind. The wind had picked up and leaves started falling from the trees landing all around us. Then, all of a sudden, it came out. "Someone said she was screwing this older guy . . . a married guy to boot," he said.

With this revelation Phyllis and I both perked up and Phyllis beat me to the all important follow-up question. "Who told you that?"

"I don't remember. It might have been a cop. One of them who came to ask Billy some questions," he said shaking his head and taking another long drag.

"Is this guy still on the force?" I asked which brought a laugh from Archer.

"He's probably been dead a long time now," he

replied. Then completely out of the blue, Archer says, "They even wanted him to take a blood test."

"What kind of blood test?" I asked moving my chair closer to Archer. Then, just as the words came out of his mouth, the blast of a passing fire engine's siren muffled his reply. However, I thought I was able to read his lips. Did he say she was pregnant? So I repeated it, "Did you say Mary Ellen was pregnant?"

"They told him he had to go with them to a clinic and have his blood taken. Would you fuckin' believe that?" he said spitting out the words.

"What are you talking about? Mary Ellen was pregnant?" asked Phyllis as she scribbled like mad in her notebook.

"From what they said, she was pregnant," he said looking at his cigarette.

"But there were no reports in the newspapers about her being pregnant," I said to Phyllis.

"Sometimes these facts are kept out of the papers to protect the family," she said.

"Well, did Billy take the test?" I asked.

"No, he didn't. He swore that they never had sex and I believe him," Archer said proudly. "Anyway, he was nowhere near Rutland when she was found in her trunk wearing a garbage bag on her head . . . . he was up north in the White Mountains hunting," he said with a smirk on his face then, putting his hand on my arm, he leaned over and whispered, "I'm getting a little thirsty, can you get me a bottle of Jack Daniels'?"

"Sure I can," I said with a reassuring smile.

"Mr. Archer, do you know anyone that can shed some light on this case that we can speak to?" Phyllis asked.

"Speak to, no they're all dead, all gone by now," he said.

"Did you ever hear the name, Sam Bergman?" I asked.

He thought for a few moments, searching his mind and finally said, "No, I don't think so."

I took out the photo's I had been carrying and showed the picture of Sam Bergman to him. He took in it his hand and putting his cigarette in his mouth, he used his other hand to remove a pair of reading glasses from his bathrobe pocket. With the glasses perched on the bridge of his nose, he studied the photo for a few moments before returning it to me saying, "Never saw this guy."

"He taught English at Mary Ellen's school," I said.

"Let me see it again," he said studying it.

"How about her?" I said handing him the picture with the inscription on the back that said, "My Daisy Mae."

He took it and holding it up a few inches from his eyes, began nodding his head. "That's her all right . . . Miss Pretty," he said.

Confused, I repeated his remark, "That's Mary Ellen Mullen?"

"Yap." he said, returning the photo's back to me.

I looked over at Phyllis for support but she merely sat there with a smile on her face. He might have known Sam Bergman but it was impossible . . . I mean, that wasn't Mary Ellen Mullen.

With that, the door to the nursing home sprung open and a nurse's aide dressed in blue scrubs strolled over to us announcing that it was time for Mr. Archer's lunch. Noticing the cigarette butts surrounding the wheelchair she smiled at Archer and remarked, "You know guests aren't allowed to smoke on the property."

Stomping on the cigarette butts she kicked them through the chain link fence and began to wheel Mr. Archer to the door. "Would your friends like to stay for lunch?" she asked Archer.

But before he could reply, Phyllis said that we had to get going and that we appreciated the offer.

As we made our way past Archer towards the door, he reminded me to, "Stop back with Mr. Daniels real soon."

Phyllis signed the Visitor's Log on the way out and once out of ear-shot in the safety of the car I could not control myself. "He thought the photo was of Mary Ellen, what do you make of that?" I exclaimed.

"We'll talk about it later," she said as she started the engine.

"Wait." I said touching her arm, "What did you say to him when we first got there and he said he didn't want to talk about Billy?"

"I told him that if he didn't talk to us, I'd take back the chocolates." With that, she threw the car into reverse and backed out into the street without looking.

# TWENTY THREE

Phyllis had a great sense of direction; she found her way back to the highway without any help from me or the directions I was holding on my lap. As I looked over at her, I could see she was deep in thought, probably trying to process the information we had just gleaned from Archer at the nursing home.

"Do you think Mary Ellen's pregnancy was the reason for her murder?" I asked.

"Maybe." she replied staring out at the open road.

"What'd you think of Archer?" I asked.

"I don't know about him. I have a funny feeling that he didn't tell us everything he knew," she said.

"What do you mean?" I asked.

"I can't put my finger on it but he just seems to be a conniving old man," she said.

"I know what you mean. I had the same feeling of him." I said.

"That still leaves Sam as the prime suspect in my mind," I said.

When she didn't say anything, I continued with my theory of the crime. "Look, Sam was married, probably having affairs all around town with the young and old and wham . . .this kid, Mary Ellen, gets pregnant, threatens him and he kills her," I said.

She was about to say something when her cell phone rang. Retrieving it from her bag, she glimpsed at the caller ID and frowned before flipping it open and saying, "Yes, Martha, what's up?" She listened for a few moments, then told Martha in no uncertain terms to; "Tell Harrison that I'm working on it . . . that I need more time and I can't turn in those god dammed time sheets." At which point, she was told to wait while Martha got Mr. Harrison on the line. "Yes, I'm here Mr. Harrison," she said, moving the phone to her other ear so that I couldn't hear what Harrison was saying. "Yes, I understand. . . but, I can't speak now . . . Right, Oh, one hour . . . Yes, thank you," she said quietly closing her phone.

"Are you O.K.? Who's Harrison?" I asked.

"The fuckin' publisher," she replied.

"It's because of me isn't it?" I asked.

When she didn't answer, I sat back and sighed, content to watch the countryside go by, while Phyllis calmed down enough to talk to. The weather was changing and the sky got that, 'I'm going to rain like crazy,' look to it.

"I'm heading home," I said.

Surprisingly, she merely nodded her head in agreement. I had expected a lecture from her comparing my plight to the characters in Les Miserable's, where Detective Russell was Inspector Javert who obsessed over capturing Jean Valjean, aka Max Rosen. Yeah, that would be a nice idea I thought, they could write a play about my misadventures. Nah, no one would believe it. No, the whole thing didn't make sense. The possible similarities between finding the skeleton of a hand in the trunk of a car on the grounds of the now extinct Laurel's Hotel and a girl's murder in Rutland, Vermont just didn't add up. Yet, there must be a way of conclusively proving that Sam was a murderer . . . by finding him. Otherwise, I was just a modern day Jean Valjean, forced to run and hide.

"We've got to get more information on the Mary Ellen Mullen murder," I blurted out.

To which Phyllis nodded and as if speaking to herself said, "I've got to get The Murder Book."

"What?" I asked.

"That's what they call the case file, the documents, the investigators notes and comments, the autopsy, witness statements, all the details pertaining to the investigation," she said checking her rearview mirror for visitors.

"Can you get a copy of The Murder Book?" I asked.

"I can't just walk into the police station and get The Murder Book. First of all, I'm not even sure it's in Rutland or if they transferred it to some offsite warehouse. In any event, I'll have to make a formal request to the Police Chief in Rutland or to the District Attorney's office in Montpelier asking them to release portions of the 'Book!.'" She said.

"How long do you think it might take?" I asked.

"You realize that anything they give me will be heavily redacted." she continued.

"What do you mean, 'redacted'?"

"The original pages will be photocopied, then they'll use a black marker over the portions they don't want us to read and then, they'll photocopy the redacted pages and after being checked again, they'll release some." she said.

"Why would they do that?" I said "It could take forever."

"Sometimes it's to protect their sources but most of the time it's to cover up their incompetence," she said.

"Do you know anyone in the Attorney General's office?" I asked.

"No, I don't but I think my editor might know someone who knows someone who was involved in the Governor's election campaign," she said.

"Do we have a chance of reopening the case?" I mused.

"From what we've gathered to date, no," she said "Most of the time, it's just plain politics which cases they reopen."

As we approached the farmhouse, Phyllis pulled in front of my car and asked me to check if everything was still there. I got out of her car and using my key, opened the driver's side door and popped the trunk opening latch on the door. Then, I went back and lifted the trunk to see if my gear was still there. Seeing that everything was O.K., I shut the trunk and returned to start the car. It started right up on the first try.

While the car idled, I asked Phyllis if I could use the bathroom. While she ran around the house to open the door with the hide-a-key, I waited for her at the front door. She opened the front door, and then admonished me, for the tenth time, not to make a mess. When I returned a few moments later, I surprised Phyllis as she was putting something in the trunk of her car. As she slammed the trunk closed she looked up at me with that, 'little girl look,' they get when they're guilty of something. Then she went around to lockup the house.

"Follow me," she said "I'll get you to Route 4 East towards Boston."

"Thanks, you'll let me know about The Murder Book?" I said.

"Let me have your home address and phone number," she said handing me a pad and her gold Mont Blanc pen.

"I want to get to the bottom of this. . ." I said while scribbling down the information she requested.

As I handed back her pad and pen, she slipped into her car and said, "Just follow me until you see the cut-off to Route 4 East." Then she put it into gear and began driving off without even a goodbye. It felt good to be behind the wheel again. Vicky always told me that I was a bad 'backseat driver'. I followed her BMW for about 4 miles until I saw her motioning to me that the

Route 4 cut-off was just ahead. I flashed my headlights to tell her I understood and then, just like in Star Trek, she shifted into warp speed and blasted away.

After adjusting the seat controls for the long ride home, I opened the glove box and took out a fistful of audiocassettes. Then I randomly picked one and slid it into the cars cassette player and began to sing along to an old melody:

*"Earth Angel, Earth Angel, please say you're mine*
*My darling dear, love you all the time*
*I'm just a fool, a fool in love with you."*

It started raining in earnest after I had gone only about 25 miles from Rutland. The wipers did all they could to provide a modicum of visibility as I sped down the highway at 70 mph. But even at that speed and those conditions, people were passing me as if I were standing still. Don't they know that even the best tires hydroplane, making it difficult or impossible to control under these conditions? I guess we all get lured into a false sense of security once we get behind the wheel and close off the world around us.

Time to get back to reality, I thought as I patted my pants and jacket for my cell phone. Finding it in my jacket, I opened it up to see that the battery was too low to make a call. Remembering I had an auto cell phone charger tucked into the passenger side door pocket, I switched the car into cruise control then released my seatbelt all the while trying to keep the car between the white lines as I reached across the seat in search of the charger. Naturally, most people would first check their rearview mirrors before performing this type of dangerous maneuver but I didn't, as a truck flew by at 85 miles per hour and sucked me into its vortex. Not a good move, when it practically threw me into the passenger's seat. Fortunately, I was able to recover both control of the car and the cell phone charger telling myself I would never try that again.

I plugged one end of the cell phone charger into the cigarette lighter receptacle and the other end into my phone to see that I had 11 messages. I hate messages, especially old ones. People expect you to call them right back, even if you're on the backside of the moon. Why didn't you call me? I've left you three messages; and so on, and so on, and so on. You could be undergoing brain surgery when a doctor puts the phone to your ear and someone on the line says, "Cat got your tongue?"

Now, who called? I asked myself staring at the phone. After all these years, I still can't figure out how to work this freakin' thing. Why do my kids have no problem receiving messages and sending text messages when I can't even figure out how to check my messages. My phone must have a perpetual envelope on its screen signifying that I haven't retrieved my messages. It's annoying too. It means you're not technically competent enough to communicate effectively in today's society and that you should be relegated to the trash bin.

After several failed attempts to dial into my message center, I called information for the telephone number of Edward Webb, my attorney and thankfully, they dialed it for me.

"Ed, Max Rosen," I said.

"Max, how are you?" he replied.

"I've got a problem . . . and I need to speak with you," I said.

"What's wrong . . . are you in any kind of trouble?" he asked.

"I might be," I said.

"O.K." he said and then there was a pause before he spoke.

"Where are you now?" he asked.

"I'm in Vermont, on my way home. Do you have time now that I can tell you a little about it?" I replied.

"Om, right this moment isn't good," he said "I've got to go into a meeting, shouldn't be too long, maybe 30 to 40 minutes. Give me your number and I'll call you back," he said.

I gave Ed my cell phone number and decided to not to make another call until I had spoken with him. I had known Ed for over twenty years and I both liked and trusted him. In the beginning, I had sought his expertise in business ventures; Articles of Incorporation, contracts, stocks, liabilities issues, the run-of-the-mill business matters. Later, he helped me with more personal, family issues, when my mother was diagnosed with Alzheimer's disease and had to be moved from her home in Florida to my home in

Hull and later to an Alzheimer's nursing home near me. The time also gave me an opportunity to rehearse what and how I would tell him what's happened the last few days. I've found that like a doctor, a lawyer was ineffective unless you were prepared to be brutally honest with them. They can't help you if you make them guess what's wrong; and about 30 minutes later, Ed called me back.

"Max what's wrong, tell me?" he said.

Then as quickly and concisely as I could, I outlined what had happened starting from the time we found the skeleton of a hand in the trunk of an abandoned car near Sackett Lake to my investigation with Phyllis of the murder of a teenager in Rutland.

"Humm," he murmured in the phone, "And this Detective Russell is ah, he's been calling your home?" he asked.

"Yes, he's made several allegations and threats to Vicky," I said.

"O.K., Max, ah . . . I take it you want me to represent you?" he asked.

"Yes, I do . . . I do," I replied.

"O.K., let's get some of the details out of the way first. You know how it works; establish a retainer and set an hourly fee. This is a criminal case and they are usually hard to tell at the onset what it will eventually cost but 'cause I know you, let's say a $3,000 dollar retainer and I'll bill you a buck-in-a-half an hour, O.K.? That'll give you 20 hours. Is that O.K. with you?" he asked.

"Yes, that's O.K. with me. What do you plan to do?" I asked.

"To begin with, do you have a telephone number for Detective Russell?" he asked.

"Yes, I do," I said as I gave him the telephone number Detective Russell gave to Vicky. "Tell me, how does it look to you?" I asked.

"Well look, at this point in time, I really can't make any predictions. I'm going to have to speak with them and hear what they have to say," he said.

"O.K., I'll wait to hear from you," I said dejectedly.

"Look, Max it's too early in the investigation to be jumping to conclusions. Will they reach out for you in Massachusetts, I doubt it, they still have a lot of work to do," he said.

"All right," I said.

"Max, from now on, you and everyone in your household that means, Vicky and the kids, are not to speak with anyone about this case or anything remotely connected to it . . . do you hear me? If Detective Russell calls you or Vicky before I have any opportunity to contact him, tell him you're represented by counsel and tell him to call me," he said.

"What can I tell Vicky?" I asked.

"Tell her I'm representing you and her in this matter and that she must not speak with anyone about it and that I will be in touch as soon as I learn something, O.K.?" he said.

"In the interim, I don't want you to worry about this thing, we'll deal with it. From what you say, it's unidentified remains and you were forthright in bringing it to the attention of the authorities. You spoke with them, you answered their questions . . . and you have nothing more to add to the case. This loss of memory, well, this was over forty years ago . . . how the hell are you expected to remember what happened so long ago . . . right? And this murder in Rutland years ago . . . may or may not be connected, who knows?" he said.

"Thanks Ed, I feel a lot better after speaking with you," I said.

After we made our goodbyes, I called Vicky to tell her I was on my way home but there was no answer. I debated whether I should call her on her cell phone but decided to take the easy way out and I called the house again and left her a message that I had spoken with our lawyer, Ed Webb, and that she should refer all calls regarding the Sackett Lake matter to him and that I was on my way home. Satisfied that I had done as much as I could do at the moment, I turned the music on high and continued my Karaoke rendition of Oscar Hammerstein's, *"If I Loved You."*

# TWENTY FOUR

As I drove down the driveway to my house, it was like Christmas. All the outdoor lights, the floodlights, and all the indoor lights were ablaze. I slowed the car to a crawl as I pressed the clicker fastened to my visor and watched the garage door open. Then I slowly maneuvered the Volvo wagon into its tight quarters. As I turned the engine off I heard a rapping sound coming from the back of my car as my boys attempted to open the trunk to help me with my bags.

"Hi guys," I said as I opened my car door and pressed the trunk release for them.

"I got it first." Randy said as he wrestled my rucksack from the trunk.

"Did you get us anything?" Kenny asked.

Embarrassed, I told them that Daddy didn't have time to buy them anything, but that I'd make it up to them.

"When?" inquired Kenny, to which, I promised to take them to their favorite haunt, 'The Cyber Café', this weekend. It was a storefront in Cambridge that kids could play no end of video games to their hearts content.

"Where's Mom?" I asked as I followed the boys through the living room and up a short flight of stairs to the dining room.

"She's in the kitchen," Randy replied.

"Put the bags in the bedroom." I said as I headed for the kitchen. I found Vicky standing by the sink talking on a portable phone while rinsing off plates before depositing them in the dishwasher. She acknowledged my presence with a slight nod of her head and turned away from me as I approached saying goodbye to whoever was on the other end of the phone.

"Hi honey." I said as I wrapped my arms around her. When she didn't respond, I stood back and holding her at arm's length said, "Are you O.K.?" but she turned breaking my grasp to hang the phone up on the wall. "I know I should have called more frequently, but..." I started to say when she sat down at the kitchen table and moved a yellow legal pad closer to her.

"I've made a list of all the people you have to call back," she said turning the pad around to show me the names and some of the messages they left.

"I'll go over them later," I said "How have you been?" I asked.

"Honestly, Max, I'm tired. I've got to go to bed," she said as she rose and pushed her chair back from the table.

"What have you told the boys?" I asked as I reached out to embrace her again but she merely glared at me saying, "Oh, don't forget to call your girlfriend Phyllis. She's on the list," as she went up the stairs to the bedroom.

I took a deep breath and shook my head as I went down the hall looking for my boys. I found them sitting in front of the TV with their respective mouths wide open as the monster stuck a webbed claw through the porthole into the ship's cabin in search of its next victim. "Boys, Dad's tired from the long trip. I'm going upstairs to speak with Mommy," I said.

"O.K." said Randy frozen with fear.

"You're not going away are you?" asked Kenny.

"No, daddy's home," I said as I went over to each one and gave them a kiss on top of their heads.

When I got up stairs to the bedroom, Vicky was already in bed under the covers and as far as she could get on her side of the bed. What a homecoming, I thought as I sat on my side of the bed undressing. It was this thing with the reporter, Phyllis that was driving her crazy. I could steal from the poor, mug old ladies in the park, and terrorize the neighborhood and be forgiven; but fool around behind her back, and I was to be drawn and quartered. Even if nothing happened, it was the appearance of infidelity that aggravates women. I realized that she was probably no different than any other woman in her position.

The next morning I awoke around 9:30 AM to find that Vicky had left for work and the boys for school.

After a long hot shower, I put my bathrobe on and padded my way down the stairs in search of a nice hot cup of coffee. Being on the road had denied me the opportunity of grinding freshly roasted coffee beans for my morning ritual. I missed the intoxicating aroma the beans emitted as they were ground and hot water was poured over them.

As I waited until the coffee brewed, I perused the list of names on the yellow pad. On top of the list in bold letters was, Detective Russell, of the New York State Police, then Irv, my partner, followed by a reminder from my dentist that I had an appointment, then something from the boys' school, then the one that threw Vicky for loop . . . . Phyllis, with a comment about 'The Journal', had called several times looking for me. I decided to forget about Detective Russell for the time being and let my lawyer deflect his calls; however, I knew that I had to call Irv.

"Irving, its Max, how are you?" I asked.

"Well, when did you land?" he asked.

"Land?" I said.

"Yeah, you must have been in outer space, in a time warp, since you never called me back," he said half jokingly.

"No, I've been out-of-state," I said.

"Oh, was it the one that doesn't have telephones?" he asked.

"Yeah, that one," I said.

"Max, all bullshit aside, when are you coming in? We have to talk about CIC," he said.

CIC was our steak and potatoes account. We were one of a number of consultants they used to produce campaigns for their healthcare products and services. Our forte was designing multimedia productions. Both Irv and I had cut our teeth working at Madison Avenue advertising agencies and knew practically everyone in the business. In a pinch, we could put together a team of writers, actors, artists, still/motion and video production people, for any sized production anywhere in the world. However, it wasn't like the old days in 'The Big Apple', when advertising was, well . . . when it was fun. Today, corporations were led by "bean-counters" and advertising managers spewing psychobabble. They wanted us to . . . 'get in their heads' and 'scramble their brains.' Pitching our ideas to a room filled with these suits was like dipping your foot into a tank filled with piranha. Just that in deference to the piranha, they eat to live, whereas these guys do it because they love the taste of blood.

"Can we make it this afternoon?" I suggested.

"What time?" he asked.

"How about 2 PM," I said.

"Two's good," he replied, after which we made our mutual goodbyes.

I made a mental note to call the others on list later, deciding to call Phyllis and find out what she meant about the 'Journal' comment but before that, I had to have a my wakeup coffee. I put a dash of light cream into a cup and poured a generous amount of hot coffee into it. God, did it taste great.

"Phyllis, this is Max," I said getting her on her cell phone.

"Max, is that you?" she asked.

"Yes, I'm home," I said.

"I was just about to call you. I've found a person who might be able to reconstruct the pages in the Journal," she said.

"Great, where is he?" I asked.

"In Brooklyn," she said.

"Aren't there any companies in the Boston area?" I replied.

"Max, listen, there are only a handful of companies in the world who specialize in reconstructing old documents and they have more work than they can handle and in addition, they cost a fortune. Luckily, I've found a retired employee who has agreed to look at the Journal," she said.

"What would something like that cost?" I asked.

"He said that he would give us a price after inspecting the Journal," she said.

I wanted to tell her that I had spoken with my lawyer and that he felt that the police were a long way from indicting someone for the Sackett Lake crime since so much time had gone by but I realized that in the eyes of my family, especially my boys, the question of my involvement or lack of, was something I just could not live with. I had to know the truth, no matter how bad it was.

"I told him that I would see him tomorrow afternoon," she said.

"But I've just gotten home," I said realizing that she said, 'I would see him' . . . meaning her.

"Don't you want to find out what's in the Journal?" she said.

"Wait a second, did you take my Journal?" I asked.

"Oh, I've got it Max and it looks like . . . ," she started to say when I cut her off with a stern rebuke. "What do you mean you've got it? Who told you, you could take it?"

"Max, calm down, I thought we were collaborating on this case, sharing information, isn't that so?" she replied.

"Yes, but I didn't steal something from you and pretend you authorized me to take it," I said.

"O.K., I'm a bad person, so let's cut to the chase, are you coming to Brooklyn or not?" she asked

"You don't understand I'm having problems at home and . . . ," I started to say when she reminded me for the tenth time that this whole fiasco was my doing and that, with or without me, she was going to Brooklyn to see about reconstructing the contents of the Journal. Realizing that I had no other option, I agreed to meet her in front of the restorer's home in Brooklyn at 2 PM tomorrow. She also told me that there were some new developments in the Mary Ellen Mullen murder case. That somehow word had gotten out on the street that the case was going to be reopened. I wondered if Phyllis was the source of the rumor. I wouldn't put it past her.

"What about 'Murder Book'?" I asked.

"Nothing yet, but I was right, it's not in Rutland," she said.

"O.K.," I said as I made my goodbyes. I couldn't feel too bad about losing the Journal when in essence I was using her as much as she was using me. Just that in my case it was personal and in her case it was just blind ambition.

# TWENTY FIVE

I was unable to muster up the courage to tell my family that I once again had to hit the road in search of answers to the question of the murder at Sackett Lake . . . and yes, I've convinced myself that the hand in the truck was a victim of foul play and that in some way; I was involved. The next morning I left Vicky a brief note, packed a few things in my rucksack and headed south to New York City and my rendezvous with Phyllis.

On the previous day, I told my partner Irv that we should take a pass on a small project from CIC. It involved the postproduction of a video which was shot in India. It was a quasi-philanthropic fluff job sponsored by CIC through one of its Indian subsidiaries. They donate a few thousand dollars worth of used or defective medical products and write-off a few million dollars in taxes. They show the videos at stockholder meetings pretending they're saving the world. Everyone does it, it's a tax game but in this case, I told Irv that we may get shit from the unions. They take umbrage when corporations shoot abroad and do their postproduction here. I suggested we refer them to a company we've done business with in Bermuda.

En route, I decided to call my Aunt Norma in Great Neck to ask if I could spend the night at her house. Norma, my mother's sister, was the youngest of seven children, all of which were now deceased. Norma was a clinical psychologist. She began her career at the famous or by some accounts, infamous Bellevue Hospital in Manhattan. Bellevue had a reputation of having the craziest of the crazies. It was more a prison than a psychiatric hospital. I can only imagine the difficulty she had trying to help some of her patients. In any event, after eleven years at Bellevue, academia called and she joined the faculty of Rockefeller University where she taught a class in something she knew quite well, abnormal psychology. However, after many years of teaching she wanted to get back to seeing patients so she joined a group of doctors on Long Island and began treating adolescents. By all accounts, she enjoyed working as part of a group of mental health specialists but after her eyesight deteriorated and she could no longer drive to her office, she left and opened a practice in her home. She hired a secretary named Mrs. Anne McAuliffe, added an office with a separate entrance to her house and began to see patients. Norma was a wonderful counselor and she had no end of patients queuing up to see her. She was so busy at one point that it took six months to a year for a new patient to get an appointment. Finally, eight years ago at the age of seventy-five, Norma retired to write her memoirs . . . or that's what she told people. I think she still sees patients, but now on the QT.

"Norma, this is Max. How are you?" I asked.

"Max, is that you?" she replied.

"Yes, I'm on my way to New York. Do you have a spare bedroom for me?" I said.

"Tonight?" she asked.

"Yes, tonight," I said.

"What's tonight?" she asked.

"Tuesday," I said.

"Yes, of course. What time will you be here? I'll make some . . . ," she started to say when I interrupted her with, "Please don't bother, I'm not sure what time I can get there. I have to meet someone in Brooklyn at 2 PM and I have no idea how long I'll be there."

"O.K., Max, just come over. I'll see you then," she said.

"Wonderful Norma, I'll see you later," I said. I hated to turn down Norma's invitation to dinner, she was such a marvelous cook, but who knows how long I'd have to wait around while the Journal's pages are separated. The last thing I wanted to do was relinquish control of my Journal to Phyllis. I still couldn't get over the fact that she swiped the Journal from right under my nose.

I decided to give myself a good five hours to get

from my home to the address Phyllis gave me in Brooklyn; which turned out to be a good idea since the traffic in the morning heading into Boston was horrific. But once I was on the Massachusetts Turnpike, I was able to make good time keeping my speed five to ten miles per hour above the speed limits. Heading through Connecticut, I had a couple of options to Brooklyn. One was over the Whitestone Bridge into Queens and the other was over the Triboro Bridge which connected the boroughs of the Bronx, Queens and Manhattan. I took a peek at the directions I had to Montrose Avenue in Brooklyn and it looked like the most direct route was over the Triboro Bridge and down the Brooklyn-Queens Expressway or the BQE as New Yorker's refer to it.

Mistake, big mistake, the road was the narrowest, four lane, two on each side, dilapidated expressway, with a small 'e', I've ever been on. The road's surface was so uneven, it was like driving on a rollercoaster with sudden hairpin turns everywhere and to make matters worse, they drove like maniacs. I took the fist exit I could which would put me in the proximity of my destination, Montrose Street. Then I meandered my way to the address arriving at five minutes to two. As I passed 211 Montrose, I saw Phyllis's red BMW parked directly in front of the building with her sitting in it reading the newspaper. I wasn't sure if she noticed me since I couldn't slow down because I had another car on my tail. I found a spot large enough to park the wagon in and walked back to Phyllis' car.

Montrose Ave. was a two way street with a mix of old factory buildings on one side and rundown four story tenements on the other.

Between the tenements were vacant lots strewn with litter, rusted shopping carts, and construction debris. As I approached Phyllis' car, she put her paper down and looking over her shoulder to see if any cars were coming, opened her car door holding my Journal in her hand. She looked very chic dressed in tight designer blue jeans and a white jersey. She was a pretty kid, I thought to myself.

As we said hello to each other, I unceremoniously retrieved my Journal from her saying, "You could have asked."

Whereupon she said, "Would you have given it to me?"

"Probably not," I said.

With that, she turned and went up a few steps into the vestibule of the building. "He's in 1B," she said as I followed a few paces behind her. The hallway was dark and had the strong smell of detergents or ammonia; it seemed to burn your nose if you took a deep breath. Phyllis stopped at a door at the end of the hallway and began knocking.

"Fritz, it's Phyllis," she said. "Mr. Watt, it's Phyllis," speaking to the tiny peephole in the metal door. After a few moments, we could hear the locks clicking and the door opened a few inches until it was stopped by a sturdy chain. "It's Phyllis, I spoke to you yesterday. It's about the book we need reconstructed," she said.

The door closed and we could hear the chain being disengaged and opening to an equally dark apartment. "Go down, go down to the kitchen," he said motioning with a bony hand. While we made our way to the kitchen, he relocked the door and replaced the chain. The kitchen was surprisingly large with mustard colored walls and 1950's appliances. The countertops were sand colored Formica with a dull aluminum trim. Against one wall were a small white GE refrigerator and gas stove. The sink was an old porcelain relic with deep sides and a thick curved backsplash.

Under an old double hung window which looked out at an alley filled with trash, was a white Formica kitchen table with chrome legs and a pair of matching vinyl chairs.

Fritz Watt was short man, probably in his seventies, with dark eyes, bushy grey eyebrows and strands of grey hair on his bowed head. He wore a tattered pair of black suit pants, a frayed white shirt with its sleeves rolled up and black vest.

"Let me see, let me see," he said holding his hand out to me for the book. He brought the book into an adjoining room and put it down on a large drafting table whose top was slanted in a 30 degree angle. Attached to the table was a large circular fluorescent lamp with a magnifying lens mounted in the middle. He switched the lamp on and began examining the Journal with the use of the magnifying lens. After a few moments, he switched the lamp off and rejoined us in the kitchen.

"Can you separate the pages?" I asked.

"Do you know what type of writing instrument was used in the book?" he asked.

"Do you mean what type of pen?" I responded.

"Pen, pencil, what?" he asked with some annoyance.

"I don't know, I said.

"It would help if you knew. If it were written in ink, I would use one type of chemical vapor, if it were written in ballpoint, I would use another, and pencil, still another," he said.

"How will you know what to use?" Phyllis asked.

"I'll experiment," he said "We will sacrifice some to save others," he continued.

"But will we be able to read some of the pages?" I asked.

"Yes, if there is writing on these pages, he said motioning with the Journal; you will be able to read it. However, this book shows considerable water damage, mildew, and possible chemical deterioration," he said.

"O.K., I understand," I said.

"Where do you want me to begin?" he asked.

"What do you mean?" I replied.

"The beginning, the middle or the end?" he said quickly.

"Oh, I see what you mean," I said. "I'm especially interested in parts of the middle and as far back to the end of the book as possible," I continued.

"Good, yes," he said. "But also remember, this book may not have a beginning, middle and end. The middle may be the beginning or it might be the end, yes?" he said.

"O.K." I said.

"It will cost you fifty dollars an hour to reconstruct the pages. And you pay me today, three-hundred dollars in cash, on account," he said.

I looked over to Phyllis for her affirmation that this was the agreed upon price. However, when she said nothing, I reached into my wallet and took out two-hundred dollars in twenty's and handed it to Mr. Watt, assuring him that it was all the money I had on hand and that when I returned, I would have the balance in cash. He told me that if I wanted additional pages, I should bring enough cash to cover the cost of the additional pages.

"When can you have this done?" asked Phyllis taking the words out of my mouth.

"I will call you when they are ready, yes," he said.

"About when do you think they'll be ready?" I pressed.

"Sometime tomorrow, but I will call you first, yes," he said.

I wrote my name and cell phone number on a slip of paper and handed it to him. "Call me as soon as you have something to look at," I said.

With that, Mr. Watts showed us to the door. He made a slight bow as we left and we could hear him relocking the apartment door as we scurried out of the building.

# TWENTY SIX

It was good to get out of that apartment and onto the street. I was certain that Fritz was the cause of those terrible noxious odors and can only imagine what his neighbors are forced to go through living in that building. That's probably the reason why he has so many locks on his door I thought.

"Are you O.K.? You look a little green under the gills," Phyllis said.

"I just couldn't breathe in that place. There was something in the air that burned my nose, like an acid," I said.

As we walked over to Phyllis' car, she pressed her remote control to unlock the car doors; it also had the effect of simultaneously flashing her front and rear parking lights to the delight of two young girls who were gawking at the little red machine. "Man that's cool, some day I wanna get me a Beemer," she said to her companion who nodded her head in agreement.

But before moving on, they turned towards us and gave us big wide eyed grins. They looked like little movie stars.

"Where are you staying tonight?" she asked as she retrieved a newspaper from the front seat.

"I'm staying with my aunt in Great Neck," I said.

"Oh, that's convenient," she said.

"And you, where are you staying?" I asked.

"I'm crashing with a friend in Manhattan, a friend from college. She's in the publishing field with a loft in Soho. Ever been there?" she asked.

"A long time ago, I had an apartment on West 11th Street in The Village," I said nostalgically.

"I want to talk to my friend about a possible book deal," she said.

"What kind of a book deal?" I asked.

"Here's a copy of this morning's Rutland Free Press. I think you'll be interested in the article on the bottom of page 3," she said avoiding my question and handing me the newspaper.

"Remember you'll need more cash for Fritz," she said.

"I'll find a bank machine," I said as I opened the paper looking for the article.

On the bottom of page 3, the headline read:

**'Reporter Seeks Details in Unsolved Murder'**

Under the headline was a photograph of the victim. The copy said:

'Thirty-seven years ago, a young, bright, 16 year old student at Mount Lawrence School in Rutland was brutally murdered. Her name was Mary Ellen Mullen, daughter and only child of the late Bruce and Monica Mullen of Montpelier. An official request under 'The Freedom of Information Act,' has been made by this paper for details of this unsolved murder to the Criminal Achieves Division of the Vermont State Police. At this point in time, a number of promising leads are being followed up. Anyone with information regarding this unsolved murder are urged to call: Phyllis Cho, Staff Reporter (661-760-3000 Ext. 6)

"God, she looks like the girl in my photograph, my 'Daisy Mae' photo. It's uncanny," I said.

"She's a blonde. Don't you know, all blondes look alike to men?" she said.

"Do you think they'll reopen the case?" I asked.

"Based on some vague innuendoes about Sam Bergman? I don't think so," she said.

"Then why the exercise? Don't you have anything better to do than chase around with me?" I said.

"Don't flatter yourself, I have my own theory about this case and I want to loosen some tongues if I can," she said.

"O.K., I've got to get going. Call me on my cell if you hear from Fritz and I'll meet you," she said getting into her car.

"O.K." I said as she started her car and eased it out into traffic, a far cry from her cowgirl antics on the roads in Rutland.

I checked my roadmap for the best route to my aunt's house that would avoid taking the BQE. There was one that would take me through the heart of Brooklyn past my old neighborhood. It was a trip through memory lane and I felt it might jar something to help me recall some events of my past.

Once I found Flatbush Avenue it was easy. It was one of the longest and most popular streets in Brooklyn. As you went from one part of Flatbush to another, the shops changed from Latin, to Asian, to African, to Russian. It was like a 'Food Court of All Nations,' on both sides of the street. It was colorful, lively, vibrant and intoxicatingly alive. The smells, the music, the clothing, the people, the casualness, it was the Brooklyn of today and so much like the Brooklyn I remembered. I stopped along the way to grab a Gyro from a cart and peruse knockoff Gucci bags and Rolex watches being sold by street urchins. As I drove away I had the feeling that if so many people, from so many different places, with so many different customs, languages and religions could live together in peace as they do in Brooklyn, there may be hope for us all.

After an exhilarating jaunt around Brooklyn, I found the entrance to the Long Island Expressway, referred to as the LIE by the natives, and headed east towards Great Neck. The LIE is also known as Long Island's longest parking lot with good reason. At approximately 4 PM each day, there's a stampede of motorists leaving Manhattan via the midtown tunnel and all heading east on the LIE. And at approximately

4:30 PM it all comes to a screeching halt, with a long line of cars stretching from Manhattan to, what seems like the White Cliffs of Dover. However, after one hour of stop-and-go driving, I pulled up in front of my aunt's house in Great Neck. Her house was a modest four bedroom, red brick colonial on a quarter acre lot probably valued at $1.2 million dollars which was the low end of the scale considering waterfront property in Great Neck went for $10 to $25 million dollars. And don't ask about much it costs to join the exclusive Great Neck Country Club. Not to mention the troublesome one to two year wait for a new Bentley. Even the drycleaners in Great Neck are, 'By Appointment Only.'

I gathered up my things from the trunk and walked up the steps to my aunt's house. I rang the bell and when I didn't hear anything, I knocked on the door. After a few moments, I heard Norma say, "I'll be right there." She opened the door and upon seeing me, gave me a big smile inviting me into her home. As usual, Norma looked radiant for woman in her mid eighties. She wore a fashionable pair of beige woolen trousers, a light green blouse under a White Cashmere cardigan sweater. The furnishings were the same as they were for the past twenty years. Norma never saw fit to change anything after her husband Joe died. It was just the way they liked it, tasteful, comfortable, and unassuming.

"Would you like a cup of tea or a drink?" she asked.

"I've just got off the LIE." I told her, "A drink would be wonderful," I said.

"What would you like?" she asked.

"A good Scotch would do wonders," I told her. "With a little water," I said as she went to get a bottle from the pantry.

"Go into the conservatory," she said.

I left my bags by the door and made my way through the living room into the conservatory. Norma had decorated the room with a variety of flowering plants which all seemed to be in bloom.

"A good trip?" asked Norma as she entered the conservatory carrying a tray with a bottle of Chivas, a small sterling silver bucket of ice, a glass, and a small carafe of water. She placed the tray on a cocktail table in front of me and asked, "How are Vicky and the boys?"

"Good." I replied.

"Was your business in Brooklyn successful?" she asked as she eased herself into a leather armchair.

"I hope so," I said.

"What's wrong, Max? You look troubled," she said.

"Just a lot of things on my mind," I said. "How are you?" I asked trying to change the subject.

"Well, you know about the problem I've had with my eyes, the macular degeneration, well guess what? It's in remission," she said.

"That's wonderful" I said pouring two fingers of Chivas into my glass.

"Maybe those treatments really worked," she said as I put a couple of ice cubes into my glass and added a little water.

"To you, my darling aunt," I said as I took a drink

and felt the warmth of the Scotch as it made its way from my lips to my heart.

"And Brooklyn, was that a business trip?" she asked.

I looked at Norma and she looked at me and I knew, there was no way, no way of pulling the wool over her eyes. She was infinitely more intelligent than I could ever hope to be and second of all, deep down inside, I needed her help.

"Norma, you're not going to believe the story I'm about to tell you," I said.

Norma merely smiled and making herself comfortable in her armchair said, "Max, try me."

And I did.

# TWENTY SEVEN

"You mentioned some pictures; a postcard of The Laurels Country Club and two photographs, one of Sam Bergman and the other of a young girl referred to as, "My Daisy Mae'?" asked Norma after I had related the events of the past few days to her.

Norma was great that way, she was a great listener. She would just let you talk . . . and all the while analyzing and processing the information. In less than an hour, I had told her of our trip to Sackett Lake and finding the remains of someone in an old car in the forest, the interrogation at the State Police barracks, the search for Sam's records at Temple University which led to Rutland, my meeting Phyllis and our interviews with Mrs. Swanson and Mr. Archer and finally the conservator in Brooklyn.

"Yes," I said.

"Do you have them with you?" she asked

"Yes, I do," I said as I reached into my jacket to retrieve them and handed them to her. She put on a pair of thick reading glasses and began examining the pictures.

"The Laurels Country Club looks like it was once a very large complex," she said.

"Yes, my best guesstimate is that the buildings and grounds covered an area of approximately 200 acres," I said.

"And none of the buildings were still standing?" she asked.

"It was just a deserted field of weeds. The only clue that it was the site of The Laurels was the old swimming pool," I said.

"Tell me about this voice you heard . . . you were standing in the field looking at the forest when you heard someone call your name?" she asked.

"I'm not certain I was looking in the direction of the forest when I first heard my name." I said.

"Could it have been Randy or Kenny who called you?" she asked.

"No, no . . . ah, they call me Dad or Daddy, never Max and besides, I asked them if they had called me and they both said no." I said.

"And this coincided with a feeling that an icy breeze passed through your body, so-to-speak?" she said.

"Yes, the voice was so clear and the chill was so frightening that I still get the shakes just thinking about it," I said.

"The voice, was it a man's or woman's?" she asked.

"That's funny, I don't really know," I said.

"Then you saw a flash of light coming from the forest," she said.

"Yes, but . . . ah, another thing was the feeling that I was frozen in time. That time had stopped for just that moment. Out of the corner of my eye, I saw the boys standing motionless looking towards the forest, then the voice said my name and I saw the flash of light from the forest, I said.

"And you said the car, the old car, was familiar in what way?" she asked.

"It was a '49 Hudson Hornet," I said.

"Had you seen this car before?" she asked.

"I must have but I don't remember where I could have seen it . . . unless, I rode in it while working at The Laurels," I said.

"Have you been in contact with your lawyer, what's his name, Mr. Webb, about the investigation in upstate New York?" she asked.

"No, he said that he'd be in touch and that I should refrain from speaking with them without him being present," I said.

"Well, you must be getting hungry," she said.

"Yes, but can I just bounce something off you, call it, The Max Rosen Conjecture?" I said.

"Of course," she said.

"I've been trying to come up with ways to unlock that period, which is a complete blank; and one way I've been thinking about utilizes music from that period and alcohol as a relaxant," I said.

As I said that, she looked at me with a bemused look on her face which turned into a smile as she nodded her approval. I wanted to tell her that the music and alcohol had brought back memories from my childhood, some as long ago as fifty-six years ago and that one of them was when I was four years old, walking with her husband, my Uncle Joe on Church Avenue in Brooklyn. That it was so clear and vivid, I could remember his uniform, his metals and ribbons, his boots and the 82nd Airborne insignia on his cap.

"The Mozart Effect," she said.

"You mean they have a name for it?" I said.

"Max, we have a name for everything," she said. "I'm not an expert on it but some scientists suggest that song preceded speech in humans, which means that music was the original language of humans. In fact, the right side of the brain which has to do with feelings, imagery, and the unconscious, is activated by music. I also remember some articles in the literature by a group of psychoanalysts in London who utilized music as a means of helping patients who had major gaps in their memories of childhood recall lost or suppressed experiences."

"So, it wasn't a crazy idea after all," I said.

"Max, we have only scratched the surface, so to speak, when it comes to understanding the workings of the brain. That being said, there are a number of similarities of your memory loss with the epidemic of Post-Traumatic Stress Disorders suffered by combat veterans. Your symptoms seem to point to a disorder called, dissociative amnesia. This type of amnesia is usually the result of some traumatic event like the terror of war or as the victim of some crime," she said.

"How do they, I mean, can they bring back these memories?" I asked

"Max, what I'd like to do is consult with a colleague here in Great Neck. He, like myself, is semi-retired. This is of course, if you desire to bring back memories which maybe unpleasant and better off not revisited. Remember, you've lived very happily without any recollection of this period in your past. There maybe a reason why your mind has blocked any reference to that time period," she said.

"I'm afraid that it's too late to stop now. I've got to know what happened at Sackett Lake that summer. I just have to know," I said.

"Max, I'll call my colleague to try and arrange an appointment for you and, I must organize some dinner for us. Why don't you bring your things up to one of the bedrooms . . . I think the one at the head of the stairs is all made-up and please, you must call Vicky and tell her you're staying with me here in Great Neck," she said.

I guess that Norma wasn't accustomed to sitting so long, since I had to help her out of her chair. She gave me her hand as I helped her to her feet and thanked me as she crossed the room and headed for her office. I collected my bags and with a deep breath started up the spiral stairs to the bedroom Norma had offered to me. I remembered sleeping in this bedroom before.

It was large and airy overlooking the backyard and Norma's French flower garden. Norma always liked everything French, from the food, to the countryside, to the architecture, to the language, to the museums, to the people, and to mostly, the lights of Paris at night.

After unpacking and putting my clothes away, I called home only to get the answering machine. I left a message that I was at my Aunt Norma's and that I'd call back later. I thought about calling Vicky on her cell phone but decided not to bother her in case she was still at work. I wanted to ask her to look up dissociative amnesia on the Internet and tell me what it said about an individual's attempt to regain one's memories.

I loved eating at Norma's. I knew full well that Norma didn't prepare dinner any longer. Not that she was a bad cook, she was an excellent cook but rather, she had made many friends over the years and now that she was in her eighties, one of her friends in particular, a Mary Lou Prentiss, had her cook prepare and serve dinner for Norma at her home when she had company. It also acted as a great incentive for Norma's children and grandchildren to visit. Mrs. Prentiss's cook was a Mrs. Romalli, who up until a few years ago was the head chef of an exclusive club on Park Avenue in Manhattan. The story was that Mrs. Prentiss' late husband, Otto, was a member of the club or owned the club and that Mrs. Prentiss made Mrs. Romalli an offer she couldn't refuse. Norma once told me that her husband, my Uncle Joe, used to play tennis with Otto Prentiss everyday and that both men died within two weeks of each other. Mrs. Prentiss even suggested that Norma sell her home and move in with her. Mrs. Prentiss lived in a mansion in a section of Great Neck called Kings Point. The estate was situated on a promontory which jutted out into Long Island Sound. The mansion itself was actually brought over from Germany after World War II. Norma said that the Prentiss' honeymooned at the mansion in Germany before the War and that they fell in love with its grandeur. Years later, Otto purchased it and had it moved to Great Neck as a surprise anniversary gift for his wife.

Later that night, after a sumptuous dinner of Greek style stuffed leg of lamb, couscous, pickled beets, and a Bordeaux you could die for, Norma told me that she had made arrangements for me to see her colleague, Dr. Steven Levine, a psychiatrist, at 10:30 AM tomorrow. However, before seeing Dr. Levine, I had an 8 AM appointment at the North Shore Community Hospital to have an exam and some blood work. I couldn't imagine why it was necessary to have blood work to see a shrink unless it was to rule out some chemical imbalance which might inhibit my ability to remember the past.

I also had a nice talk with Vicky. She told me that she understood my desire to find out about the past and bring closure to my doubts and fears I was having about what happened or didn't happen at Sackett Lake. I also sensed she was relieved that I was staying with my Aunt Norma and not anywhere near Phyllis. Best of all was my conversation with my boys. Randy, my movie maven, told me about a sneak preview of a new Batman movie he was going to see. Kenny, my jock, told me of a new pitcher the Red Sox had just signed. All in all, it was a perfect ending to a perfect day.

# TWENTY EIGHT

Sleep didn't come easy. Afraid of oversleeping and no alarm clock in my room kept me up most of the night checking my wristwatch. It was now 6 AM and I decided I could no longer pretend that I could sleep. Norma had given me cursory instructions to the hospital. Up the hill to Northern Blvd, then left to the second set of lights, then right at the lights, and the hospital will be up the hill on the left.

"You can't miss it," she said "Go in the main entrance and take an elevator to the third floor and follow the signs to the Laboratory. They'll perform the tests."

So, there I was tiptoeing to the bathroom with a fresh set of clothing over my arm. Norma's bathtub had a sliding glass shower door that required a certain amount of finesse to close properly. I was never sure which side slid right or left. All I wanted to do was close the damn door as quietly as possible and not flood the bathroom floor. The memory of Phyllis' screeching at me for leaving water on the bathroom floor in Rutland caused me to take unusual precautions against a repetition of that embarrassing faux pas. After making sure the door was closed I turned on the hot water lever, or what I thought was the hot water lever, which is usually the one on the left, just a little bit. When it didn't seem to be getting warm, I turned on the right water lever a little bit and here too, it didn't get warm. So, while standing there as naked as a jaybird, I decided that the left water lever might need a boost in water pressure so I turned it up. Well, the first thing it did was belch, followed by a spitting action, then a rush of burning hot water shot out of the shower head hitting me directly in my beer belly. The shock of being scalded caused me to retreat to the opposite end of the shower while I nursed my wound. In the meanwhile, the hot water had turned the bathroom into a virtual steam room. Unable to reach the controls for fear of being scalded again, I made my way out of the shower and attempted to slide the door on the other side open enough to reach in and add some cold water to the mix. After pushing and pulling, the god dammed thing wouldn't budge. Finally, frustrated beyond no end, I stood on the toilet seat and draped a towel over the shower head, and then I reentered the shower and turned the cold faucet all the way. Voila, I said to myself, time to take a relaxing shower.

After mopping up the puddles and wringing out

the towels, I dressed into somewhat moist clothing and made my way back to my room, gathering up my money, wallet, car keys and eyeglasses. Then like a cat burglar, I made my way down the stairs to the front door, when I heard, "Max, would you like some breakfast?"

"Oh, Norma, did I wake you?" I said.

"No, I was up. I can make you some eggs if you like," she asked.

"Thanks but I probably shouldn't eat until after the tests," I said.

"You know, you're probably right. I forgot. Now, did I tell you where to go?" she said.

"Yes, it's just off Northern Blvd. I can find it," I said.

"And you'll see Steven . . . Dr. Levine at what time?" she asked.

"10:30," I said.

"You'll like him," she said as she opened the refrigerator door and took out a container of orange juice.

"Have a little juice," she said pouring me a glass. "It can't hurt you and it wouldn't affect the blood tests."

"You took a shower upstairs?" she asked.

"Yes, after I got the knack of the controls," I said.

"Max, forgive me I should have told you. I've been trying to get a plumber to fix it. I don't know, they have to replace the old type of faucet with a new type that automatically mixes the water. But in order to do it, they have to break open the wall. It's a major job . . . and very expensive. You'd think that they would be queuing up for the work but here in Great Neck, a plumber can make more money than a heart surgeon," she said.

"It was fine Norma," I lied.

"I'm happy that Dr. Levine can see you on such short notice. He's a brilliant psychiatrist and good friend," she said putting up water for tea. I finished my juice and put the glass in the sink. I kissed Norma goodbye and asked if I could take her out for dinner that evening. She said that she would let me know.

Since the hospital was merely a hop-skip-and-a-jump from Norma's I decided to check out Dr. Levine's house. Norma said that I turn right and go over the Long Island Railroad tracks and down Main Street until it ends, then right onto Bay Road and that Dr. Levine's house was at 717 Bay Road, on the left. I had no trouble finding Bay Road and the breathtaking array of beautiful homes on either side of the road. In some cases, the estates along the water were hidden from view behind high walls and locked iron gates. Others were nestled in the trees surrounded by magnificent gardens and shrubbery. Dr. Levine's house was a stone Tudor mansion facing Long Island Sound. Impressed with the grandeur, I continued around Bay Road until it snaked back around to Great Neck's shopping district. I also noticed that Bay Road was monitored by video cameras and had the eerie feeling that everyone and everything on Bay Road were being watched by unseen security forces. I guess it's a necessary evil for the trappings of wealth.

The hospital parking lot was surprisingly full by the time I got there forcing me to hike quite a bit to find the main entrance. When I arrived at the Laboratory on the third floor, they handed me the perfunctory application to fill out. However, I was shocked to discover that the tests were covered under my wife's existing health plan. It was probably because Dr. Levine ordered the tests and he was an MD. I wondered if my session with Dr. Levine would also be covered under her plan.

After I completed the questionnaire, a young woman led me into a room which had several small cubicles for drawing blood. She expertly withdrew two vials of blood and labeled each with stickers that I could clearly see the words; STAT and Steven Levine, MD on them. Then, I was brought into an adjoining room and asked to remove my shirt and lie on my back on an examination table. After a few moments, another technician in a white lab coat entered pushing a cart with an EKG machine on top. She gave me a big smile and asked me how I was and whether I ever had an EKG, to which I said I had. Then she proceeded to stick several leads to my chest and connect them to the machine. Slam, bang, thank-you-ma'am, I was through and out the door in ten minutes and on my way to the Fireside Diner on Northern Blvd for a hearty cholesterol clogging breakfast.

I arrived at Dr. Levine's house at precisely 10:30 AM and was greeted by an elderly woman in a nurse's uniform. I told her who I was and she led me into a small waiting room where I filled out another questionnaire. She told me that since the doctor would be administering certain drugs, I would have to read and sign a release but, before I did so, the doctor would discuss with me the risks. Drugs, I said to myself, what have I gotten myself into? Just then, before I had a chance to escape, the door opened, and in strode Dustin Hoffman or his exact double now in his eighties. He wore a light brown pair of wool slacks, a white shirt and light green paisley bow tie, brown tassel loafers, and a dark brown cashmere sports jacket. I rose from my seat as he approached offering me his hand. He took my hand with both of his hands since his right hand was permanently closed with arthritis.

Looking up at me with fierce green eyes he said, "So you're Norma's nephew. She's a wonderful woman."

"She says the same things about you," I said as he directed me into his office.

His office was everything you'd imagine a distinguished physician's office would look like. The parquet floor was covered with beautiful Persian carpets. The furniture was of the finest dark mahogany with several leather chairs and a couch. The walls were covered with diplomas from Harvard, Johns Hopkins, Massachusetts General Hospital and awards from psychiatric institutes and government agencies. There were books and photographs of his family all over the room plus one of him in a World War II uniform and another of him having dinner with Albert Einstein. His majestic desk was positioned so that he could swivel around in his high back chair and look out through a large bay window at the sailboats on Long Island Sound.

"Sit, sit," he said motioning me to a large leather arm chair. He then told me that, with my permission, he would like to record our session. He also advised me that everything I said would be confidential under the client-patient proviso of the law. He then turned on the tape recorder and I acknowledged that I agreed to the taping and that I understood my rights under the law. Then he asked me to make myself comfortable and tell him everything that happened leading up to my trip to Sackett Lake and ending with my arrival at my Aunt Norma's house yesterday. He, like Norma, did not interrupt my stream of consciousness and within a little over an hour, I was able to run through all the details of the past few days. He also asked me to produce the photographs and postcard of The Laurels for his inspection. Then he told me in exquisite detail the procedure he planned to use, the drugs and their risks, and how he planned to help me recall episodes from that period. To begin with, he told me that the drug of choice was Pentothal, and that it would be mixed with several others, which he called a 'cocktail'. That it would be administered through an IV drip which he would monitor and adjust when necessary. He said that the risks of using Pentothal were mainly respiratory in nature and that I would be wearing both cardiac and respiratory monitoring devices. He also reassured me that he has used Pentothal for over 50 years and knew full well the warning signs.

"Max, do you understand what I've told you up to this point?" he asked.

"Yes, I do," I replied.

"Do you have any questions at this point?" he asked.

"What do you mean by, warning signs?" I asked.

"Good question. What we want to do is avoid an over dosage of Pentothal and we do this by administering it slowly via an IV drip, thereby reducing the risk of respiratory depression," he said. "Other things that are characteristic of this drug are apnea, increase in pulse followed by a decrease in blood pressure . . . all of which shortly return to normal. But remember, your vital signs will be carefully monitored. That's why I had you undergo a comprehensive battery of tests before the administration of any drugs. The lab sent me your results by E-mail before you ever got out of the hospital parking lot," he said.

"Really?" I said.

"Isn't science wonderful?" he said with a chuckle. "Do you have any other questions?" he asked.

"No," I said.

"O.K., I'll have you sign a release to that effect when my nurse comes in to setup the IV. Now let's turn to outcomes; what we wish to accomplish during our session. I noted on your questionnaire that you have never been hypnotized. Is that correct?" he asked.

"Yes, I have never been hypnotized," I said.

"Good, in that event let me give you a brief explanation of what therapists like myself call, hypnotherapy. I like to think about it as using hypnotic techniques to bring about beneficial results which in your case, will help us uncover repressed memories.

Ultimately our goal will be to bring your subconscious mind into alignment with your conscious mind so that we can deal with the events of that period. O.K., are you with me?" he asked.

"Yes, I understand," I said with a little tremor in my voice.

"Good," he said as he rose and went over and opened the door.

"Barbara, please bring in a 2.5% Pentothal IV drip cocktail and cardio/respiratory monitors. Let's premedicate with 5cc of Nembutal to see how he reacts. Oh, and bring in his release form for signature," he said.

Then he came over to me and told me to remove my shirt so that the nurse could attach the leads. He asked me to turn off any electronic devices that I might have on my person or in my jacket. I reached into my pocket and produced my cell phone, which was on vibrate, noticed that I had a message, and turned it off.

Shortly, his nurse came in pushing a stainless steel cart outfitted with an elaborate IV drip and heart and respiratory monitors like you'd see in hospital operating rooms. She handed me a clip board with a Release Form and waited until I signed it. I signed on the dotted line and handed it back to her which she slipped into a drawer in the cart. She then put a rubber tube around my chest asking me if it was too tight or if it pinched me. I reassured her that I was a good soldier, which made her smile; she then glued several leads to my chest connecting them to the monitoring device. After testing the equipment, she handed me a robe to wear that didn't have a left hand sleeve. I stood and put it on then sat back in my chair. She instructed me to pull the lever on the right side of the chair so that it would recline fully. After reclining, she gently took my left hand and examined the top of my hand for a promising vein. She found a nice one just above my thumb and after cleaning it with an alcohol swab; she deftly inserted a butterfly needle into my vein and held it in place with a small strip of surgical tape. All the while Dr. Levine sat motionless watching us with his hands crossed over his chest. Satisfied that all was in place, he thanked his nurse and asked her to leave.

"Max, are you comfortable?" he asked.

"Yes, I am," I said.

"Do you like the movies?" he asked.

"Yes, I do," I said wondering if I was on Candid Camera.

"Many scientists compare the workings of the brain to a computer and that maybe true in some respects but I like to compare the workings of the brain, specifically memories, to a motion picture. Some memories are in color and some in black and white . . . but don't ask me, we don't know why. What we're going to do is rewind the film, so to speak, to the period you allegedly worked at The Laurels. Now I said allegedly because there's no proof, other than a postcard that you ever worked at the Laurels. It might have been merely a gesture on your part back then to reassure your parents that you had found work in the Catskills, when actually you hadn't...we'll see.

"O.K., I want you to relax and close your eyes and begin slowly counting down from 100," he said as he began the IV drip.

"100, 99, 98, 97, 96 . . ." I said as I felt a slight chill. "90, 89, 90, ah, ah . . ."

# TWENTY NINE

"Max, we're going to watch a movie, O.K.?" he said.

"O.K.," I said.

"Let's have some fun while we rewind the movie," he said.

"O.K.," I said.

"I want you to pretend you're sixteen-years old. Can you do that?" he asked.

"Yes, I can," I said.

"And when you speak, I want you to speak the way you did when you were sixteen. Can you do that?" he asked.

"Yap" I said.

"Good, you're doing just fine," he said.

"Now I want you to open your eyes," he said.

"I have a postcard I want you to look at. Here take it with your right hand," he said handing it to me.

"Do you recognize the place on the postcard?" he asked.

"Yap," I said.

"What's the name of the place?" he asked.

"The Laurels," I said.

"Where's it located?" he asked.

"The Catskills," I said.

"Good, very good. Now, you can hold on to the postcard but I want you to close your eyes again. Close your eyes," he said.

"You're doing very good, Max. I have good news for you; do you want to know what it is?" he asked.

"Yap," I said.

"Well we've rewound the movie back to the beginning of the summer, the summer you were sixteen years old. Isn't that wonderful?" he asked.

"Yap," I said.

"Now I'm going to start the movie projector and you tell me what you see, O.K.," he said.

"Yap," I said.

"You're on your way to the Catskills, how did you get there?" he asked.

"I hitched," I said.

"From where?" he asked.

"Brooklyn," I said.

"That was quite an adventure. Had you ever done that before?" he asked.

"Nope," I said.

"And you were dropped off where?" he asked.

"Monticello," I said.

"You're doing just fine Max. Now you're in Monticello, what did it look like? Describe it for me," he said.

"Nothing like I imagined," I said.

"What do you mean?" he asked.

"Like I says, there was nothing . . . no hotels, restaurants, no big stores, nothing. It looked like Tombstone or Dodge City in a cowboy movie," I said.

"And the people, how were they dressed?" he asked.

"Plain, real plain. They looked like farmers, yeah farmers. They drove old pickups with, like bales of hay in back. And the town had like hitching posts and water troughs for horses. I expected the stagecoach to arrive at any time, you know. They were like hayseeds. They all wore these shit-kickers too. And I remember they wore these western hats and they were always spitting tobacco juice. Man was it gross!" I said.

"Then what did you do?" he asked.

"Tried to bum some money off this guy," I said.

"And what happened?" he asked.

"Tight wad . . . told me to get a job," I said.

"Then what did you do?" he asked.

"Well, just as I was about to give him the finger, he took this toothpick out of his mouth and smiled. He had this big freakin gold tooth right here," I said as I touched my big tooth with my hand that had the IV attached.

"Max, you must lower your left hand and keep it steady on the armrest, O.K. Lower your arm," he said.

"O.K., O.K., don't get so hot under the collar," I said.

"Continue Max, you're doing just fine," he said.

"He told me there was this place, down the end of the block that gives out jobs . . . that's all," I said.

"Did you go there?" he asked.

"Yap," I said.

"And what happened?" he asked.

"Got a job," I said.

"Describe the place and the people for me," he asked.

"Just this guy, ah . . . like a little store at the end of Main Street,." I said.

"Give me a little more Max," he asked.

"Like I says, it was an old guy, the store was as big as a shoebox. It had an old desk, you know, the one that rolls up and has lots of little drawers. The walls had color posters from the hotels. They looked nice . . . you know, big places, with big pools and basketball and tennis courts . . . and golf courses . . . and lots of people having fun," I said.

"Then what happened?" he asked.

"Well, he's got these cards with jobs on them, you know . . . and he goes through these cards until he finds one and says, this one's for you Boychick," I said.

"He called you Boychick?" he asked.

"Yeah, cause I was from Brooklyn," I said.

"Was the place busy?" he asked.

"Sort of, there were other guys there looking for work. Some were musicians looking for a gig at a hotel. That's why I came to Monticello; my friend Larry was working in a band somewhere in the Catskills," I said.

"Did you find him?" he asked.

"Nope," I said.

"Max, let me ask you, weren't you too young to work in a hotel?" he asked.

"Told 'em I was eighteen," I said.

"He didn't question you?" he asked.

"He did, but I lied," I said.

"Then what happened?" he asked.

"I don't know, they came and got me," I said.

"Just you?" he asked.

"Nah, there was a bunch of guys. We all piled into this old station wagon, boy was it hot," I said.

"Did you all go to the same hotel?" he asked.

"Nah, they dropped guys off here and there. I was the last stop," I said.

"Where did they drop you off?" he asked.

"I told you before, The Laurels," I said.

"Oh, that's right Max; I forgot...the hotel in the postcard," he said.

"Yap," I said.

"Then what happened?" he asked.

"Saw Mr. H," I said.

"Before that, what was The Laurels like?" he asked.

"Oh, it was big. It was the biggest hotel I ever saw. They had all these buildings where the guests stayed; they were White with like orange colored roofs, and they were all over the place. Then there was this enormous main house, with this big lobby and lots of chairs and couches. I think the chairs and couches were red velour and the floors were like big tiles covered with all kinds of rugs. Then you went through this lobby and it led you to the dining room. The biggest dining room I've ever seen. It was the size of a city block . . . no kiddin'. And the tables were all round covered with white table cloths. Each table had eight chairs, real plush chairs, like in the lobby. And when I went into the dining room I saw this man sitting at a long table drawing circles on a big piece of paper. Funny, he used a shot glass to draw the circles with," I said.

"Who was he?" he asked.

"Mr. H. He was boss of the dining room," I said.

"And what happened?" he asked.

"Gave me a job, you know, as a busboy," I said.

"Max, you're doing great. Now I want you to open your eyes. Open your eyes, Max. Good, now take this picture with your right hand and tell me who it is. Tell me who it is, O.K. Max, take the picture," he said. I took the picture from Dr. Levine and looked at it. "It's Sam," I said.

"Good, now close your eyes. You can hold onto the picture. Hold the picture. Now, who is Sam?" he asked.

"Sam's my waiter," I said.

"Tell me more about you and Sam," he said.

"He's my waiter, I worked for him. He showed me the ropes. Taught me what to do. Setup tables for him. That's what a busboy does. Then take away the dishes and cleanup the mess," I said.

"Did you like the work?" he asked.

"It was O.K.," I said.

"Then you didn't like it," he said.

"No I didn't say that. It was that our station was at the other end of the dining room. I had to carry these heavy plastic tubs filled with dishes all the way to the kitchen. Man it was hard work. And in the beginning, our tables were on this balcony that had three steps . . . those freakin' steps were a killer," I said.

"What do you mean?" he asked.

"You tripped going up and tripped going down. One guy, I'll never forget it, was carrying this tray of goblets, a full tray . . . and they were heavy mothers, well, he tripped going down the stairs one night and those freakin' goblets became airborne and flew, no kiddin', twenty feet through the air and exploded all over the place. The poor bastard spent all night picking up glass," I said.

"Was that the only time you saw Sam?" he asked.

"No, we bunked together," I said.

"What was that like?" he asked.

"It was like a chicken coop, you know, all these guys jammed together," I said.

"Like an army barracks?" he asked.

"I don't know from barracks but Sam and I had this tiny room. Had to keep your things on the bed 'cause when it rained, the floor was under water. Then the toilets wouldn't work and we had to find places to take a crap. Funny, I remember Sam had keys to some of the rooms, you know, guest rooms; and we'd sneak in and take showers 'cause they had hot water and clean towels," I said.

"You liked Sam?" he asked.

"Sam was my friend, he watched my back," I said.

"Did you go out after work with Sam?" he asked.

"Yeah, all the time," I said.

"What did you do?" he asked.

"Cruise and pickup chicks," I said.

"He had a car?" he asked.

"Yeah, he had a cool car," I said.

"What type?" he asked.

"49' Hudson Hornet," I said.

"Did you like it?" he asked.

"It was a tank . . . couldn't go fast but it had class. It had these great curves and chrome, and really big headlights," I said.

"And you met girls?" he asked.

"Tons!" I said.

"Tell me about it?" he asked.

"We once picked up these girls from Ohio; they were sisters, just got off the boat. We had a lot of fun with them. They were on their way to some hotel to work. I don't remember the name but they were real good-lookers," I said.

"What happened?" he asked.

"While I took one for a walk, Sam got lucky with the sister," I said.

"How do you mean?" he asked.

"He banged her in the Hudson," I said.

"Were you jealous?" he asked.

"Nah, Sam was a ladies' man . . . he had a gift. He'd snap his fingers and they'd drop their drawers," I said.

"You looked up to Sam didn't you?" he asked.

"He was the brother I never had," I said.

"How big was your family? Did you have any brothers or sisters?" he asked.

"Nope, just me," I said.

"You were an only child?" he asked.

"Yap" I said.

"Did you resent it?" he asked.

"Nope" I said.

"Did you want brothers and sisters growing up?" he asked.

"Didn't turn out that way . . . nothing I could do about it," I said.

"Max, you're doing very good. Now, I'd like you to open your eyes. Open your eyes. Take this photo and look at it. Look at it and tell me who it is?" he asked.

"Who is this girl, Max?" he asked.

"It's my Daisy Mae," I said.

"Was that her real name?" he asked.

"Nope" I said.

"What was it, Max?" he asked.

"Judy," I said.

"What was Judy's last name?" he asked.

"I don't remember," I said.

"How did you meet Judy?" he asked.

"She came to The Laurels," I said.

"From where?" he asked.

"From camp," I said.

"What camp?" he asked.

"Camp Odetah," I said.

"Where was that?" he asked.

"Down the road," I said.

"Was it far?" he asked.

"Nope" I said.

"Was it a mile, a half mile, how far?" he asked.

"Not far," I said.

"Did she have a car?" he asked.

"Nope" I said.

"Then how did she get to The Laurels?" he asked.

"They walked," I said.

"There was more than one?" he asked.

"Yap," I said.

"How many?" he asked.

"She had a girlfriend," I said.

"What was her name?" he asked.

"Diane" I said.

"Was she at Camp Odetah also?" he asked.

"Yap" I said.

"And they walked over to The Laurels?" he asked.

"Sometimes" I said.

"And other times?" he asked.

"We'd pick 'em up," I said.

"In Sam's car?" he asked.

"Yap" I said.

"Did you ever drive?" he asked.

"Nope" I said.

"Why not?" he asked.

"Didn't know how," I said.

"Did you like Judy?" he asked.

"She was O.K.," I said.

"What did you like about her?" he asked.

"She was really built . . . you know, long blond hair, big tits, great ass . . . and put out," I said.

"What do you mean?" he asked.

"She was easy," I said.

"Did you have a lot of sexual experiences before Judy?" he asked.

"Nope" I said.

"What about Sam?" he asked.

"Chicks loved him, they wouldn't leave him alone. 'Specially, the old ones, they were crazy about him," I said.

"What old ones?" he asked.

"The ones from the bungalow colonies," I said.

"Tell me about the women from the bungalow colonies?" he asked.

"Nothing to tell you, the husbands left Sunday afternoon and ya banged 'em Sunday night," I said.

"Did you do this too?" he asked.

"Sometimes" I said.

"How often?" he asked.

"I don't know, lots of times," I said.

"With Sam?" he asked.

"Yeah," I said.

"Wasn't it always with Sam?" he asked.

"No, sometimes they drove over and picked me up," I said.

"Anyone special?" he asked.

"Carla," I said. .

"Who was she?" he asked.

"A lady from Queens," I said.

"And she was staying at a bungalow colony?" he asked.

"Yap" I said.

"How did you meet her?" he asked.

"I don't know, probably at The Laurels," I said.

"And you had sex with her?" he asked.

"Yap" I said.

"Often?" he asked.

"Yap" I said.

"Did you like her?" he asked.

"She was nice to me," I said.

"How?" he asked.

"I could talk to her," I said.

"About what?" he asked.

"About all kinds of things . . . and she was fun. She wanted to do things. She was a great dancer too. We'd go to the Raleigh Hotel and dance," I said.

"Where you a good dancer?" he asked.

"Nah, but she tried to teach me," I said.

"Why didn't you go to The Laurels to dance?" he asked.

"Sam always said, you don't shit where you eat," I said.

"What about Judy?" he asked.

"What about her?" I said.

"You had sex with her too?" he asked.

"Yap," I said.

"O.K., Max, you're doing just fine. I want you to just relax. Relax, Max. Now let's try something different. I'd like you to tell me one of your fondest memories of The Laurels?" he asked.

"That's easy," I said.

# THIRTY

"You know, we mostly worked a Friday night dinner through Sunday lunch schedule but every so often, we'd work a mid-week convention. Well, one week we had the furriers come up. Just picture this, we got the dining room all setup for their arrival at about 7 PM Friday night and then, the doors opened and in strolls a couple a hundred old men each with one or two gorgeous hookers on each arm. And get this, each gal had on a beautiful, full length mink coat. You're not going to believe this but when they got to their tables, each man pulled out a chair for their lady or ladies, whereupon each gal dropped their mink on the floor behind their chairs. We had to serve dinner tiptoeing between the minks. In any event, they were the nicest guests the hotel ever had, and a far cry from the Chief of Police Convention we hosted one week. All the cops did was get drunk, fight, and run out on their bills. During breakfast on the morning they were scheduled to leave, the Chairman of the organization made a plea to the attendees to 'please pay their bar bills and to return all the stuff they stole from the hotel.'

"And that was one of your fondest memories?" he asked.

"Yeah, and the night we played Kutcher's Hotel," I said.

"Tell me about it," he asked.

"Well, we used to play basketball against other hotels at night . . . you know, also during the mid-week break. We had a pretty good team, some of the guys played basketball for their college . . . let's see, one guy played for Columbia, and another played for Georgetown, and Sam played for Temple . . . the others I don't remember, but I played too. It was a rough and tumble game; you know, a lot of flying elbows. When you were near the basket, they'd pound you. That's why I learned to shoot from the outside, 'cause on the inside, they'd beat me up . . . really," I said.

"O.K., so this night we we're to play Kutcher's Hotel. I remember it was a hot night and really buggy. A crowd had gathered to watch the game and every seat in the bleachers was taken. I think that some people came from Kutcher's to watch their team. Well, this old bus arrives from Kutcher's and out comes, Red Auerback the coach of the Boston Celtics, Bob Cousey, Bill Russell, Bill Sharman, and the best of the best college players in the country. I'm telling you, it was the funniest game

I've ever been in. It was like, they were so amazing, we didn't know what to do. I think I just watched them. Did you ever see the Harlem Globetrotters? How they run circles around a hapless team . . . that was us. At one point, it was so lopsided; Russell sat in the bleachers laughing as Cousey dribbled around the court. After the game, we exchanged shirts and all went for a dip in the pool. I remember Auerback sitting at the edge of the pool dangling his legs in the water while puffing on his trademark cigar," I said.

"That's wonderful Max. It sounded like you were actually there. Those were good memories now go back and find me one of your worst memories," he asked.

"Do I have to?" I asked.

"Max, anything that happened back then was a long, long time ago . . . it's time to . . ." he began to say when I interrupted him.

"I killed her," I said.

"Who did you kill, Max?" he asked.

"My Daisy Mae," I said.

"Judy?" he asked.

"Yeah," I said.

"How did it happen?" he asked.

"I got her pregnant," I said.

"And . . . ," he asked.

"She got an abortion and died. I told you, it was my fault," I said.

"Max, it would help if you could give me more of the details . . . so that I can understand . . . so that I can help you," he said.

"No one can help me," I said.

"Let me be the judge, Max," he said.

"She said she missed her period and didn't want to see me anymore. That it was my fault that she got into trouble . . . and that I had to help her get an abortion," I said.

"Exactly what happened Max? You had unprotected sex with her?" he asked.

"Yeah," I said.

"And you were her only partner?" he asked.

"Yeah," I said.

"Now, did she have a pregnancy test?" he asked.

"I don't know, all she told me was that she was sick and missed her period . . . and that I had to do something," I said.

"When was this?" he asked.

"At the end of the summer . . . around Labor Day," I said.

"She was still working at the camp?" he asked.

"Yeah, that's why she got into such a panic . . . she had to go home," I said.

"Did anyone else know about her condition?" he asked.

"Just Sam," I said.

"What did he say?" he asked.

"He said there was a doctor in Port Jervis who performs abortions . . . and that they cost $400," I said.

"You said that Judy was sick, what were her symptoms?" he asked.

"What do you mean?" I asked.

"Exactly what did she tell you about her sickness?" he asked.

"You know, she was throwing up, real bad headaches, cramps . . . some kind of red-like rash . . . I don't know, she was pregnant," I said.

"O.K. and then what happened? You took her to the doctor?" he asked.

"No, I didn't have enough money," I said.

"Where did you get money?" he asked.

"My father sent me a couple of hundred by Western Union and Sam loaned me some," I said.

"Did you tell your parents?" he asked.

"Oh no, no, I made up some cock-in-bull story that I owed someone money," I said.

"Now that you had the money, what happened?" he asked.

"Sam took her to the doctor," I said.

"You didn't go with them?" he asked.

"She didn't want to see me no more," I said.

"So Sam took Judy to the doctor?" he asked.

"Yeah, to Port Jervis," I said.

"How far was Port Jervis from Sackett Lake?" he asked.

"I think about an hour. You had to take country roads all the way," I said.

"And then what happened?" he asked.

"It was nighttime and the place was deserted. I was getting worried when Sam didn't get back, when all of a sudden, he burst into the barracks and said Judy was in the car and she was throwing up. He was as white as a sheet. He told me she was crying in pain and wouldn't go to a hospital. He said that he parked the car in the woods behind the barracks and needed some aspirin for Judy. We looked all around the empty barracks but couldn't find any so he told me to run over to the main house and get some from the night clerk while he ran back to the car with some blankets and a wet towel for Judy. I ran up to the main house and it was eerily empty, except for Bruce the night watchman nursing a beer in one of the lounge chairs and Mike the night clerk sorting through papers. I got a fistful of aspirins from Mike and stopped in the kitchen and got a couple of bottles of club soda then high-tailed it back. I was running as fast as I could and didn't notice some water near the pool and slipped landing on a pair of chairs, knocking over a table, and skinning my elbow. I could have avoided injury if I used my hands but I didn't want to lose the aspirins and drinks. I got to my feet and began running again to the barracks. I had to find this path behind the barracks that led into the woods where Sam used to park the car. It was down at the end of an abandoned overgrown path. Sam said that it was the perfect place for his nocturnal romances since it couldn't be seen from Sackett Lake Road or the hotel grounds but it was so dark that night, I mean pitch black, I couldn't find the path. I was really getting panicky just wandering around in circles, tripping over fallen logs and up to my knees in thorns when I heard Sam call my name . . . Max . . .Max . . . and as I turned in the direction of the sound, I saw a light coming from the forest, it was the light from Sam's flashlight and it guided me to his car," I said.

"Just like what happened when you revisited The Laurels years later with your boys. Max, I know it's hard . . . but you're doing very good. What happened when you got to the car?" he asked.

"Sam was crying. I never saw him cry. He said she was dead. And he handed me the flashlight for me to see," I said.

"Where was she?" he asked.

"It was cold that night and as I aimed the light at the car, the bonnet was still warm from the trip back from Port Jervis and a white ghostly mist seemed to be rising from the car like smoke and as the breeze caught it, it swirled a trail of smoke around the car through one open window and out the other. When I looked in, she was like all curled up lying on the backseat with a blanket over her," I said.

"Did you touch the body?" he asked.

"No, I just looked at her through the window. All I could see was her blonde hair sticking out from beneath the blanket. You know, she had such pretty blonde hair," I said.

"Then what happened?" he asked.

"I got real dizzy and threw up next to the car," I said.

"What was Sam doing?" he asked.

"He was just walking around in the dark crying and talking to himself," I said.

"What did you do then?" he asked.

"We sat on the ground by the car for a long time in the dark without speaking to each other until Sam stood up and said that we had to make sure she was really dead. He went over to the car and opened the back door and motioned to me to come over and confirm that she was dead. I was petrified to do it but felt compelled because her death was my fault. So while Sam showed the light on the blanket covering Judy, I went around to the other side and opened the rear car door. Then I leaned over the blanket trying not to touch her and slowly pulled back the blanket covering her face when all of a sudden the shock of seeing her eyes staring up at me and her face contorted as if she were screaming caused me to jerk back and fall to the ground. Then I scrambled to my feet and began running blindly into the forest until my legs gave out from under me and I fell head first down an embankment into a pile of rocks. I recall someone pulling me by my ankles then lifting me from under my arms into a sitting position. It was Sam and he was shining the flashlight into my eyes. He asked me if I could walk, but I was numb. Then he lifted me over his shoulder and staggered up the incline, dropping me onto the ground by the car. I laid there on my back on the wet ground staring up at the trees, while Sam was doing something at the car. I heard the jingle of some keys, then a click and something opening, then a little while later something slam shut. Then Sam kneeled over and asked me again if I could walk. I said I could and he got me to my feet. We began to walk back to the hotel but my legs were like rubber and he had to carry me most of the way. I remember he put me in the front seat of one of the hotel's station wagons. Then Sam went into the hotel and came out with Bruce, the night watchman. They propped me up in the middle and drove me to the Monticello Hospital. When we arrived at the Emergency Room entrance, Sam ran in and got a wheelchair for me and pushed me into the reception area to see the doctor. I don't remember him too well but he said that he thought I had a severe concussion and had to see the neurologist in the morning. He said that I had a deep cut above my right eye that needed several stitches. Then he sewed me up and bandaged my head. My right eye was so swollen that I couldn't see out of it. Since it was late, they put me in a chair in one of the examination rooms with instructions to keep an icepack on my head until I saw the doctor. When I told the nurse that I had to use the bathroom, she brought me a bedpan to pee in. When she came back and it was empty, she showed me how to use it," I said.

"In the morning, Sam was back to check on me. I told him that I was sore but O.K., and that I wanted out of the hospital. He told me that I should wait until I saw the neurologist, but I insisted that I was O.K. He reluctantly agreed and said I should sit tight while he went to check on possible avenues of escape. He came back about fifteen minutes later with my suitcase and told me to put on a fresh set of clothes. I told him that nothing in my suitcase was considered fresh. Then he helped me take off my hospital garb and change into my street clothes. He said that the car was parked near a rear door. We waited until the coast was clear then Sam helped me down a flight of stairs and out into the parking lot. There, parked only a few feet away was the hotel's station wagon of which Sam still had keys to. He got me into the front seat and threw my suitcase in the back and we were off. He asked me if I was hungry but I said no, that I just wanted to get home. I told him to drop me on Route 17 and that I'd catch a ride to New York but he only laughed. He told me that no one in their right mind would stop for me the way I looked and he brought me to the Trailways Bus Stop in Monticello which was nothing more than a ticket office at the end of Main Street. When I told him that I was broke, he went inside and bought me a one way ticket to New York City and a small carton of orange juice. While we sat in the car waiting for the bus, he told me to just forget about last night and that he'd fix everything. I wasn't sure what he meant but the cold orange juice did taste great. When the bus finally came, he helped me up the steps and into a seat in the front of the bus. I remember thanking him and shaking his hand when he took out a couple of dollars and stuffed it into my hand saying I should use it for the subway. Then he nodded to me and made his way off the bus. As the driver closed the door, I looked out my window and saw Sam standing on the side of the road with his hands in his pockets. That was the last time I ever saw Sam."

# THIRTY ONE

"Max, Max, when I count to three, I want you to open your eyes. Do you understand my instructions?" he asked.

"Yes" I said.

"Max, you will remember our conversation and the events you related to me regarding Sackett Lake. Do you understand me?" he asked.

"Yes, I do," I said.

"Max, I'm going to count to three . . . one, two, three . . .open your eyes Max," he said.

When I opened my eyes, I was still seated in my chair with the IV and monitoring leads still attached to my body. Dr. Levine told me that since I had no trouble remembering the events at Sackett Lake under hypnosis, that with some prompting, I should have almost total recall of that period.

"What kind prompting do you mean?" I asked.

"That Journal you penned might help you recall other events, that is, if it can be restored," he said.

"I hope to know more today," I said.

"O.K., now here's your prescription for today. No driving for 12 to 24 hours. Drink at least eight glasses of water during that period and stay out of the sun. You have sunglasses?" he asked.

"Yeah, in my car," I said.

"O.K., where in your car?" he asked.

"I keep them in my glove compartment," I said.

With that, Dr. Levine rose and went over and opened his door asking his nurse, Barbara, to come in. He instructed her to remove the IV and monitoring leads and print out a copy of my vital signs for the file. Then he asked her to take my car keys and retrieve my sunglasses from my glove compartment for me. When she got back with my sunglasses he asked her to call Towne Taxi and arrange for someone to pick me up and to bring along another driver to ferry my car over to Aunt Norma's house.

"How do you feel Max?" he asked, coming over to me and pointing a small flashlight into my eyes.

"A little wobbly, I think," I said.

"Stand up and walk around for me," he said.

I gingerly got to my feet and walked around his office stopping to look out his bay window, then remembered his admonishment about sunlight and put on my sunglasses.

"You O.K.?" he asked.

"Yes, I am," I said returning to my chair.

"Remember, your eyes are still dilated . . . you've got to protect them from the sun. The water will help flush out the drugs, and if you have any problems, if you begin to hypo ventilate, have trouble breathing, or have heart palpitations, call me immediately. Now, let me give you some of my impressions based on our session. It is in all likelihood that the trauma of Judy's death coupled with your fall precipitated the dissociative amnesia. Since you were very lucid under hypnosis of the events associated with the trauma it indicates that there was probably little or no brain damage due to your concussion. Of course only a scan would tell us for sure, however, what we have been able to accomplish and in so short a period of time, has been to adjust, so to speak, those unconscious elements of the past with your conscious mind." Then using his thumb and index finger of each hand he made two separate circles. He said one circle represented the subconscious mind and the other the conscious mind. Then he moved the circles so that they overlapped each other. "See, they're now in phase, we've brought them into alignment and there's a connection to the subconscious memories of that period," he said.

"Now, what about the long term effects? You hold very strong guilt feelings regarding your alleged complicity in the death of this girl, which must be addressed. I suggest that when you return to Boston, you consider seeing a mental health professional. O.K., you understand me?" he asked.

"Yes, I understand you," I said shaking my head.

"Anything else?" he asked.

When I asked him about a bill, he told me that he would submit the office visit to my insurance company and whatever they didn't pay, I'd be responsible for. I thanked him for his help just as his nurse came in to tell us that the taxi had arrived.

The driver instructed me to get into the backseat of his taxi while his associate got behind the wheel of my car and followed us to Norma's house, caravan style. As they dropped me and my car off at Norma's house I had the impression that Towne Taxi had provided this unusual service for Dr. Levine before, since my driver avoided both eye contact and conversation during the ride back. Dr. Levine probably also gave a heads up to Norma that I'd be coming back since she opened her front door just as the taxi arrived.

I begged off lunch from Norma but did request a pitcher of ice water. Norma washed out a dusty old water pitcher and filled it with ice water for me to take to my room while I recovered from the effects of the drugs. After I went to the bathroom, I began washing my hands at the sink and glanced up at my reflection in the mirror to see for the first time in my life what dilated pupil's looked like. My irises were wide open and I had these big black holes in my eyes. It was so frightening, that I went back to my room and drank two glasses of ice water one after the other. Then I got into bed and put a pillow over my head.

I laid there for a while, thinking of what Dr. Levine said about using the Journal to recall events and decided to call Fritz, the conservator, to see if some of the pages where ready, when I remembered my cell phone was turned off and that the last time I looked, I had mail. I turned my cell phone on and while it searched for a strong signal, I retrieved my reading glasses from the pocket of my jacket. I activated the command to get my mail and found that I had missed several calls from Phyllis, one from Vicky, and one with a New York exchange I assumed was from Fritz. I decided to try to get Vicky first at her office and was pleased that she was free. I told her that I was O.K. and that, with the aid of hypnosis, I had almost complete recall of the events the summer I worked at The Laurels. She was happy there might be some closure to the nightmare and peppered me with questions which I deflected until such time we were together. She accepted my reasoning and asked when I'd be home. I told her that I had to spend the night at Norma's and that I'd probably leave tomorrow depending on the results from the conservator. When she questioned why I still had to decipher the Journal, I told her what Dr. Levine said about its possible use as an aid in my recall of events. I told her that I loved her and not to worry and that I'd call her tomorrow. Then I called Fritz, who was a little irritated that I hadn't called him immediately back. I told him my phone was off and that I just retrieved his message.

"Well, I thought you were in a hurry, so I worked all night on the book," he said.

"That's great," I said. "Have you been successful?" I asked.

"I have several pages for you. Bring me another $150 dollars and if you want more pages, bring me another deposit, same like yesterday, $200," he said. I told him that I'd be over first thing in the morning which surprised him.

"You can't come over now?" he blurted out.

"I can't, it's impossible . . . I'll see you tomorrow morning with the money," I said, which seemed to calm him down hearing I was going to show up with more cash. Then I called Phyllis on her cell phone.

"Phyllis, it's Max, I'm sorry for not getting . . ." I started to say when she interrupted me with, "Max, I can't talk now," she said almost in a whisper.

"Are you O.K.?" I said with concern.

"Yes, I'll call you back, now's really a bad time," she said and broke the connection. That was not the Phyllis I'd gotten to know and wondered what trouble she'd gotten herself into and whether it was because of me. How did we leave it? I asked myself. She was going to stay with a college friend in Manhattan. I wondered if something might have happened to her in New York City. A girl by herself in the City is sometimes the victim of violence, especially a young attractive woman driving a fire engine red BMW with Vermont plates. It says, 'Hello, steal me and ship me off to Belize'. I was tempted to call her back but resisted, deciding to wait for her call and that if she didn't call me by 10 PM tonight, I'd call her back. Feeling a little better after a nap, I joined Norma in her kitchen for a bowl of Ramen Noodles and a Caesar Salad.

I told her, without her asking, of my session with Dr. Levine and the details of Judy's death. As before, she listened carefully to my story without interrupting me then asked me the same questions

Dr. Levine asked me about; Judy's symptoms and when they first appeared. I reiterated what Judy had told me; that she had missed her period, she had a fever, vomiting, bad headaches, bad cramps, and some kind of reddish rash.

"Did you see the rash?" she asked.

"No, I didn't," I said.

"And when you returned from the Catskills, did you see a neurologist?" she asked.

"I don't recall what I did when I got back," I said.

"Do you remember if you had any headaches after your concussion?" she asked.

"I'm sorry, Norma, I don't recall anything when I got back. Maybe, it will come back now. Dr. Levine said that items, pictures from my past may help me recall events," I said.

I told her of my concern for Phyllis' safety and Norma reminded me that since Phyllis was able to speak to me on the phone, it indicted that she was probably all right but that calling her at 10 PM was also not a good idea. However, the call I received at 9:45 PM that night from Phyllis, put things into an entirely new perspective.

# THIRTY TWO

"Max, this is Phyllis," she said as I bolted upright in bed fumbling with the antenna on my cell phone.

"How are you?" I asked instinctively.

"I couldn't speak ...," she said, then after a slight pause, "I was, ah, with the District Attorney in Rutland."

What was this all about, I thought to myself.

"The District Attorney in Vermont?" I asked "What's going on?"

"Yes, but I can't go into any details at this point in time," she said, sounding lawyerish.

"I don't understand...," I started to say, when she interrupted me saying, "I want you to know that there has been a development in the Mary Ellen Mullen case . . . and, ah, Sam Bergman was not, I repeat not, involved in her death," she said.

"What do you mean?" I asked.

"Just that, Max; he was not involved," she said.

"Well, who was?" I asked.

"I . . . I can't disclose the facts of the case Max, and I'm telling you more than I should…you'll just have to trust me on this," she said.

"I'm confused," I said, pretending that I still thought Sam was a suspect.

"Are you still at your aunt's house in Great Neck?" she asked.

"Yes" I said.

"O.K., good. I'm driving back to New York City tomorrow morning for some meetings and would like to meet with you sometime," she said.

"When?" I asked.

"Not sure right now . . . probably, ah . . . sometime in the late afternoon," she said.

"You're really being evasive," I said.

"Max, I have to be," she said.

"You asked me to trust you . . . but what about you trusting me?" I said.

"It's not about trusting you . . ." she said angrily, "It's about a delicate legal matter which doesn't involve you, Max."

This was followed by a long period of silence while we both thought of what to say to each other . . . finally, she asked about my Journal, effectively changing the subject and whether Fritz had restored any of the pages. Not wanting to disclose my new found memory and the fact that I now knew Sam was not involved in Judy's death, I parried back at her with, "Look, Phyllis, I'd like to share this information with you but . . . you know, the information contained in the Journal is, well . . . confidential and on a need-to-know basis," I said.

"Yeah right," she said and hung up.

I looked at the LCD display on my phone which indicated that she had broken the connection after 2 minutes and 37 seconds. I could have sworn that we had spoken longer than that . . . and what was this 'legal matter' she alluded to? They caught Mary Ellen Mullen's killer? That was ludicrous; those Keystone Cops in Vermont couldn't catch a wet dream. What could she have learned in the space of 24 hours . . . . and that thing about the District Attorney . . . Hello? What's going on?

But then again, look at what I'd discovered about myself under hypnosis just a few hours ago. I now knew that this quest to find Sam, the so-called serial killer who deposited girls in the trucks of cars, was just a charade. That this fantasy I had created about Sam was probably an unconscious ploy on my part to shift the blame to someone else. That Sam was actually once a friend, a person who tried to help me out of a jam, a person who rescued me the night I ran wildly into the woods at the sight of Judy's dead body and ended up falling head first down an embankment into pile of rocks, who then took me to the hospital and later put me on a bus home . . . . I mean, what did he do to deserve my having Phyllis Cho sicced on him. Judy's death was my fault, not his. Sam wasn't the ogre I made him out to be, he did what he thought

was right at that time. What happened was a tragedy
. . . an innocent life was lost because of my fear and
stupidity. I should be thankful to him; he allowed
me to live forty-four years of my life without the
memories of that dreadful night. I also knew that this
so-called investigation I was undertaking with Phyllis
must cease. That this was no way to repay a friend, I
thought. I made up my mind that if he was still alive,
that I would go to him and ask his forgiveness for
getting him involved in my youthful transgressions. I
also owed it to Judy's family, if they too were still alive,
to bring closure to the whereabouts of Judy. That she
just didn't runaway like many other girls because she
was an unhappy teenager. That what happened was
not as a result of anything they did or didn't do. That I
was the guilty party . . . only me. I also thought of how
I'd have to prepare my family for the consequences of
my confession. Would they understand? Would they
be forgiving? And what would my boys think of me
now? They're young and imagine that their father
walks on water. It's probably the way of the world
though, we strive as children to please our parents so
that they may be proud of us and when our parents
are gone and we're a parent, we want our children
to be proud of us. I wanted desperately that things
would stay the same.

That my family would still love me and be proud
of me for who I was now and not judge me for my
actions as a sixteen year old, forty-four years ago. And
the more I thought about it, the more I compared it to

Pandora's Box. Maybe there were warning signs along the way that said, don't go there, walk away, the past is the past . . .Max, open at your own risk. But no, I didn't read the sign posts along the way, I didn't take my own good advice to let sleeping dogs lie and had to look in the Box. Now the ghosts of my past are all around to haunt me and bring dishonor and misery.

And as I lay there wrestling with the problem of what and what not to say to my family, I also rehashed the last few days in my mind trying to make some sense of it all. Finally coming to the conclusion that, although I didn't think of myself as a believer in predestination, something drove me back to Sackett Lake, to the deserted grounds of The Laurels Hotel, to the forest where the car was hidden and to Judy's remains in the trunk. And as I laid there staring up at the ceiling I once again felt an icy chill go through my body and I began to shake uncontrollably. I closed my eyes as tight as I could and turned over onto my side covering myself with a blanket hoping that this feeling would pass and . . . I was there, standing next to the car; it was pitch black and cold to the bone. The bottoms of my pants and shoes were soaking wet. I saw Sam; he was on the opposite side of the car flashing the light around the backseat. I went over and opened the car door. Sam was saying something to me, I saw his lips move but I couldn't hear what he was saying, all I saw was a smoky mist coming out of his mouth. He was pointing to the blanket.

He was motioning to me. I think he wanted me to

check Judy for a pulse. I said I would but he didn't hear me. Then I reached over with my hand to gasp the blanket and felt Judy's hair, it was flowing from underneath the blanket. Then, I bent over and slowly lifted the blanket, but her hair was stuck to the blanket covering her face, so I put my hand underneath to brush it back and I felt the icy cold of her face on my hand. Finally I grabbed the blanket in one hand and Judy's hair in my other hand and ripped them apart and in doing so, my face came a few inches from Judy's frozen face. Her eyes were wide open staring up at me and her mouth, her mouth was open as if she was screaming. Then I heard Sam say, "Is she dead? Is she dead? Oh God, is she dead?" Then, everything went black.

# THIRTY THREE

**D**eep breath, deep breath, I said to myself as I awoke and found myself sitting on the floor at the side of the bed. Was it a panic attack? I got up and started walking aimlessly around the room in circles. Deep breath, deep breath, I kept telling myself . . .could it be the drugs? He said something about hypo or was it hyperventilating. I don't remember and anyway, what's the difference, I can't catch my breath. Should I awaken Norma? No, I've got to deal with this myself. Get dressed and get out of the house. Skip, most certainly skip, the unpredictable shower. I put on yesterday's clothing, a bit ripe but still in season, gathered up my watch, wallet, cash, cell phone, and headed for the door before I realized I had forgotten my shoes. I turned back, picked them up, tucked them under my arm and slowly and very quietly made my way down the stairs to the front door. Try to control yourself; I told myself, you're almost there. No, don't stop now, I know you want to leave Norma a note, . . . just leave, you'll call her from the road. Oh shit, is the alarm on? I don't have the code. I went into the foyer and opened the closet door to check the control panel. It didn't indicate that it was on nor did it indicate it was off. It was a crap-shoot. If I opened the front door and all hell broke loose; sirens, bells, and whistles, it was probably on. So I went over to the front door and as I chanted an Indian mantra for good luck, I threw the dead-bolt, turned the door knob and deftly pulled the door open. To my surprise, the gods were with me this morning and I was able to leave Norma's like a professional second-story man. Except of course, that I had to squat on the front steps of the house in order to put my shoes on.

Then after a 3,000 calorie breakfast at the diner on Northern Blvd, I drove around Great Neck looking for a 24 hour ATM. Within 30 seconds, I spotted no less than four ATM's. Then I remembered, this is Great Neck, all they have are banks. All they do is hand out money. They probably print the stuff locally. There's rich and then there's Great Neck. These ATM's probably have no limit to how much you can withdraw. I was tempted when it asked you to punch in how much money you wanted to withdraw, to ask for $10,000 but decided on $ 300. I didn't have room in my wallet for all that money. And anyway, if I requested the $10,000, the ink might still be wet.

I knew that it was early but decided that I'd call

Fritz anyway. He was so hot and bothered the other day because I didn't show up to pickup my pages, that it might be poetic justice to wake him and tell him I was on my way over. But, when I called him, the old rascal was up and anxious for me to come over. He had found a way to separate multiple pages . . . and get this, I owed him only $200 more.

"A bargain," he said "Come, come, with the cash," he said.

When I arrived at Fritz' apartment house I was lucky to find a parking spot directly in front of the building. And after taking a few deep breaths of fresh air I entered the apartment house only to be greeted by the stench of either ammonia, or burning tires, or rotten eggs, or for that matter, all three which made my eyes water and my nose run. How can anyone stand living under these conditions, I asked myself as I raced to find Fritz' door. I've got to get in and get out, I told myself. Pay him, grab the pages and you're gone. No dancing around, no small talk about the old country, no more pages until I call, thanks, see you, bye.

Fritz, anticipating my prompt arrival opened the door after only one knock. He led me into his kitchen where scatted over the entire kitchen table were pages and pages from my Journal housed in plastic protective covers. From where I stood, the pages looked a little bluish but the script was perfectly legible. It was amusing how Fritz tried to position himself between me and the pages for fear that I might read them and decide not to pay him. He gave me one of his yellow-toothy grins as he requested payment before inspection. I felt like telling him that I wanted nothing more than to pay him off, grab my pages, and hightail it out of that stink pot. So, I pulled out $200 in cash and handed it to him and while he counted out the money, I went around the table and scooped up all the pages. Then, I made an unceremonious mad dash for the door. I thought he said something to me but I couldn't hear it, so I shouted, "I'll call you," as I ran out the door into the street. In any event, I had something now in my possession which represented the observations I made as a 16 year old some forty-four years ago. I couldn't wait to read it and see how brilliant I was as a teenager and how far I'd fallen since then.

As I sat in my car, I tried to organize the pages chronologically but except for the title page, none of the pages were numbered or carried any indication as to the date they were written. However, with my new found ability to recall some of the events of that period, these pages might help me recall the events that caused me to put my thoughts in a Journal. As I skimmed the pages, I was amazed as to how nice my handwriting was as a teenager . . . it was far better than the 'scribble-script' I use today. In fact, with the advent of computers, especially E-mail, I hardly write letters with a pen any longer.

Then it hit me, the title page, written across the top of the page in bold:

Monday, June 22, 1955

It was today . . . it was forty-four years ago to the day! I didn't believe it . . . it couldn't be a coincidence. It was freaky. Was this some type of an omen? I really don't believe in that shit, I told myself. Then the voice in my head said, if you're so smart, how do you explain it? I couldn't.

Monday, June 22, 1955

Hooray!!! Finally Free
Plenty of seats on the subway this morning. Thought school would never end. Cramming for finals all night wrecked me. Time for some fun. Heading for the Catskill's to make some money and meet up with Larry. Said there's lots of jobs and that he's going to work in a band. I hope that I can get some work at one of the hotels as a waiter or busboy. Anything.

This is great. I've never been so free in my life. When I got up this morning and saw that same pattern on the wall that the sun made through those dusty old Venetian blinds, the stripes that looked like jail bars, I knew there was no turning back. A clean break. I told them, sort of, that Larry went upstate and that I wanted to go also. They'll understand. Got to get off at 14th street and catch the train to the Bronx. The people on the train have such blank faces. Like zombies reading newspapers. Just rocking back and forth while the train screeches through the tunnels.

Wow! Everything just went black.

Nope, everyone's still here, staring off into space. I think that if I had to ride this subway everyday, I'd lose my mind. I don't think people should have to ride the subway.

We're coming into a station, let me catch the sign, it's Atlantic Avenue. Yeah, Dad brings the Pontiac to someone on Atlantic Avenue for service and we wait for it at some diner. Dad always tips the mechanic before he works on the car. He says you give them a little something before and they do a good job. Anyway, a few more stops and it's 14th street and closer to the Catskills and no more sleeping on the couch.

When they get home tonight they'll see the note I left and I'll be in the mountains. The cool, clean mountains. I've got a suitcase full of things. $6 in my wallet, and $28 hidden on me in case I get robbed. 14th street, time to get off.

It's amazing, I wrote those words when I was sixteen, years ago as I ran away from home on my big adventure. Little did I know then, that the next few weeks would change the course of my destiny for the next forty-four years.

# THIRTY FOUR

I had to get out of Brooklyn, I told myself. There are too many unresolved memories here. I started the car and just for an instant thought that I should go back and retrieve the balance of the Journal from Fritz, then decided against it and headed for Manhattan. Yeah, I'll head for Manhattan and find a quiet bistro in Greenwich Village to finish reading the Journal.

Larry, I spoke about Larry as the reason I was heading for the Catskill's, I remember Larry. He lived on the first floor in our tenement house on East 97th Street, in Brooklyn. As I remember, his father worked in a band. He would get all dressed up in a black tuxedo every night and go to work in Manhattan. He was a very, very nice man, a very soft spoken and gentle man. Larry always spoke about his father and his desire to be a musician too. In fact, Larry was a fabulous piano player . . . and he wanted to write music like George Gershwin. As I remember, I never met up with Larry the summer of '55. I wonder whatever happened to him.

I took the tunnel into Manhattan and headed for a little place I knew on West 11th Street. After circling the block for twenty minutes, I was happy to find a meter, with time on it no less, and just steps from Pacini's Bistro. I gave my name to the hostess and requested a quiet table in the back.

"Just one?" she asked with a smile.

"Just one," I replied.

"Follow me," she said. Who says New Yorkers are impolite? She brought me to a little table in the back and took my drink order after telling me that the Osso Buco was excellent. As I settled in to peruse the Journal, a handsome young man dressed all in black arrived at my table with a basket of freshly baked French bread and a saucer filled with olive oil, shaved garlic, and bits of red pepper and oregano. There's something wonderful about the aroma of fresh garlic. I suspect that little is really known about this fascinating species of the onion family. I immediately broke off a piece of warm bread and dunked it into the mixture . . . oh, was it delicious. A few moments later, the hostess returned carrying a large cold glass of Guinness Beer. As I sat back with the garlic bread in one hand and the cold Guinness in the other, I thought I died and went to heaven.

The next few pages in the Journal told of how I rode the subway train to the end of the line in the Bronx and hiked to the Henry Hutchinson Parkway.

There, I hitched rides from motorists heading north to different parts of the mountains, but the most poignant story was the last leg of my journey, the ride to Monticello:

Man, it took all day. It wasn't easy getting on and off the New York State Thruway. Didn't know ya couldn't hitch on it. The last guy, the truck driver, I can't remember his name, he spoke with a funny accent, anyway he was very nice. You know, you think you have it bad until you hear someone else's story. He couldn't be much older than me. He said he came north with his wife and baby for a better life and ended up in a two room, cold water, rat infested apartment in Red Hook. We joked about the size of the roaches. Were they a roach or were they a rat? I told him that the only way to tell the difference was to turn the light on at night.

The roaches ran like mad and the rats just froze and stared up at you. He said that he was hauling foodstuff from the Brooklyn docks to Middletown, which was just 20 miles from Monticello. He said Monticello was the heart of the Catskill's and that if I could wait until he unloaded, he'd run me into Monticello.

Let's see, what other tidbits to record in my journal. Oh, yes, to kill some time, I told him that I knew all about Red Hook. That I played on a YMCA basketball team and that one night we went to Red Hook High School for a game. Even as I told him the story, I got goose bumps just thinking about it. We had such a good team. A couple of our players were colored and when the crowd saw them, they started chanting, "Coons, coons . . . coons, go home". I told him that the game became very physical with elbows flying, pushing and shoving and the more they played dirty, the wider the score became. By halftime we were killing them and the crowd became angrier and angrier. I forget the score maybe 40 to 18, well at halftime, our coach, he was this big Irish guy we all loved, told us to follow him. He took us down the hall to a door that said, 'Principal's Office' and ushered us all inside. Then he told us we couldn't go back to the gym and that we had to make a run for it. He opened one of the windows and told us to jump and run for the subway. When we asked him about our stuff in the locker room, he said, forget it. Luckily, it was a short drop to the street because when we didn't return to the gym the crowd piled out onto the street looking for us. I told him we ran like hell to the subway, down the stairs, hopped the turnstiles, jumped on a train and played basketball all the way to Flatbush Avenue.

When we got to the warehouse in Middletown, he backed the truck into a loading dock and told me to wait in the cab. I offered to help him unload but he said it wasn't allowed, some union thing. Then he took me to Monticello. I wish I could remember his name. He was a nice guy. Made me think, his family, he said everyone worked in the mines. 'Way under the ground digging for coal. That some got sick from the coal. That's got to be worse than living in the city. When we said goodbye, we shook hands and wished each other well.

When the waiter came back to take my order, I was almost speechless from reading my observations as a teenager. The empathy I seemed to feel for that boy, the truck driver was a hint as to who I was back then.

"The Osso Buco, please," I told the waiter, "And another Guinness." After the waiter went off into the kitchen to put my order in, he came back curious as to what I was reading. He must have thought it was some type of old manuscript because he told me that he had just graduated from NYU and was working as a waiter until he got his big break in the theater. That he'd been to several auditions and was waiting for a call-back. I wished him good luck in his quest and I told him that the pages I was examining were actually written by me forty-four years ago in the form of a Journal and that I was reading them now for the first time. "Man that's so cool," he said as he went to check on my order.

As I sat here trying to organize the Journal chronologically, I noticed that my entries became shorter as the summer progressed. Maybe I was just too busy or possibly too tired at the end of the day to memorialize my comments and impressions. But decidedly, the pages revealed that I went from a wide-eyed optimist in the beginning of the summer to a battered and frightened teenager by the end of the summer of 1955.

Although many pages were missing from the Journal, what had been restored gave me a glimpse of what my first impression of The Laurels was:

Dropped me off at the front gate and saw this great big place. It was like a giant Howard Johnson's. The buildings were all white and the roofs were all orange. There were lots of trees and grass with cement paths and flowers on either side. They smelled real nice but some had bees so you had to be careful to not get stung. The main house had the biggest lobby you've ever seen with all these chairs and couches and rugs all over the place. I asked this guy, I think he was a bellhop, where Mr. H was. I told him that I had a note for him.

He showed me to these doors and said Mr. H was in the dining room. Well, when I pushed open the door, I went into the largest dining room I had ever seen. It was even bigger than Lundy's in Sheepshead Bay and that was the biggest restaurant in Brooklyn. It had these tables all over the place and they were big and round and each had these big gold chairs around them. The waiters were setting up for lunch with baskets of rolls and buckets filled with pickles and half sour tomatoes and they made the red cloth napkins into the shape of a bird and put them on each plate. Everyone was just running around carrying trays filled with things. I almost got run over looking for Mr. H until someone pointed him out to me. He was a tall thin man with jet black hair combed straight back. He wore a black pair of pants, like from a tuxedo, and a white shirt with the collar opened and the sleeves rolled up. He reminded me of a movie actor but I can't remember who. He was standing in front of a large table with a big roll of paper spread all over it. When I walked over, he was making circles on the paper using a shot glass. It was a chart of the dining room.

Well, getting the job was easier than I expected. I gave him the note from the man at the agency in Monticello and he just read it quickly and tucked it underneath the chart and told me to go find Manny. That's all he said. I don't even think he looked at me for more than a second, but I got the job. I didn't have to lie about my age or anything. I couldn't find Manny, so I wandered around for a while, scouting out the area until I came to these two funny guys. They were like Mutt & Jeff. I think one was a waiter and the other a busboy. They both wore black pants and a white shirt with a small black bowtie. Well, one was tall and very thin and the other was very, very short and fat. Every time one of them said something, the other would repeat it. I asked them if they saw Manny and the tall one says to the short one, did you see Manny and the short one says, did you see Manny? Then they both said no.

When I told them that I was just hired, the short one said, got to get your linens and the tall one nodded in agreement and said, got to get your linens. I swear it went on for ten minutes like that. I did everything I could to control myself from laughing. Anyway, they gave me directions to the Green Building where they kept the bed linens. When I found the place, no one was there so I helped myself to a blanket and two sheets. But as I was leaving I was stopped by this lady, who reminded me of Miss Hartman, my 8th grade teacher at PS 165. She could have been her sister. We called her heartless Hartman. She was a very mean woman who enjoyed punishing students and everyone, even the principal, was afraid of her. Well I had to put everything back while the witch told me to keep my freakin' hands off the stuff. That no one was allowed to take anything without her O.K. I think to punish me, she gave me the thinnest, oldest, rotten blanket she could find.

The Journal also gave an amusing comparison of

my grandfather's chicken farm in New Jersey and the staff barracked at The Laurels:

It looks like the chicken coop grandpa had in New Jersey. And it smells like it too. I remember when I was little and my father took me to the farm. I used to get the eggs. I would crawl underneath the shed they kept the feed in. Sometimes chickens would escape from their coops and lay eggs underneath the shed. I would find 5 or 6 eggs, still warm. It was nice on the farm even though we would go for only a day or two. It was in the country and at night, the sky was so bright with stars it was like you could bump your head on them.

Later, the Journal helped me to recall the first of which would be many faux pas at The Laurels ... and one of the barracks' unwritten laws. I shared a room with Sam that had just enough space for two twin army cots. The space between the cots could not have been more than three feet. And in lieu of a window, there was a 2' X 2' opening in the wall which was covered by a torn insect screen that allowed all manner of creepy, crawly things into our room, especially at night. Well after a sumptuous luncheon of gruel, I hastened to the head in the rear of the barracks to purge my body of the poisons and when finished, I flushed the toilet to the ungodly screams of Hans ... the, "If-I-get-my-fuckin'-hands-on- you-I'll-kill-you," Hans.

I mean, who knew you shouldn't flush the toilet when someone's in the shower? Well, I had this stark naked crazy guy chasing me out the barracks until Sam tackled him and convinced him to spare my life.

Then there was this entry about running away from home:

> Got up enough courage to call home. Mom was real pissed at me on the phone for taking off as I did. She said I should come home. I lied to her that I was with Larry and we were both working at The Laurels. She said that Dad was very disappointed in me too. It made me feel real bad laying that Jewish guilt trip on me.

# THIRTY FIVE

T he great thing about my parking spot by the restaurant was that I could periodically feed the meter. That's because I knew Manhattan's Meter Maids had the uncanny ability of stopping at your vehicle just as the time on the meter runs out. Then, quicker than you can say, "I have a friend at City Hall," they're lifting your windshield wiper and sticking a $100 parking ticket under it. You can scream, stand on your head, and tell them what they can do with the ticket until you are blue in the face, all to no avail. They are the masters of, 'anger management,' and can not be dissuaded from their lawful duties. And anyway, I was now working on my third Guinness and needed all the sustenance I could muster to finish reading the last few Journal entries. I had occasionally peaked ahead at the cryptic notes and wasn't sure I wanted to be sober when I read them; however, there were some amusing war stories with Sam:

Sam took me to this place for pizza off Main Street. He said the pizza was good, "New York Style" and that it was a watering hole for bungalow colony wives looking for action. He said the husbands leave Sunday afternoon for home and the hottest broads start canvassing the town at 9 o'clock at night for studs.

I asked him about his disappearance from the nightclub Saturday night and he told me he went to this girl's room to make-out but her roommate kept interrupting them. He said he was on and off and on and off. She'd knock, then go away, then bang on the door and go away, then do it all over again. Sam says you have to have your own place. He said that he's going to buy an old jalopy and park it in the woods just to get laid.

At 9:30 a bunch of gals came in and started playing the jukebox. One was real nice looking. Built like a brick shithouse. She kept looking over at us until Sam got up and sat down with them. Sam's got brass balls. He came back in a little while and said it was time to head back to the ranch. I asked him what happened and he said she gave him her phone number. He said you can't fuck around with them in public and you can never take the chance of being caught with them at their bungalow colony. Too many eyes and ears.

Since my typical shift as a busboy was

Friday night dinner through Sunday lunch, by the time Sunday night comes around, it was usually dead at The Laurels. This is when Sam introduced me to, 'The Friendly Sunday Night Poker Game.'

Sam said it was just a nickel and dime game. How much could I lose? After all, back in Brooklyn, I used to play poker with my friends. Maybe not for money, usually comic books or playing cards but I thought that this might be a way of being one-of-the-boys. So, I squeezed into Bob's room near the showers and put a five dollar bill on the table and asked if anyone had change. There were six guys in the game counting me and we sat around a small cocktail table someone borrowed from the pool patio. We all anted up a nickel and after drawing cards we'd all bet. I had no idea of what I was doing and I was soon in pots with $5 or $10. Needless to say, I lost everything. All the tips I had made that weekend, $78, gone in less than 30 minutes. Sam offered to loan me some money but another guy was waiting for my seat and I was glad to get out of that smoke filled room into some fresh air.

Later Sam confessed that those guys are pros and that I might want to stay away from those friendly games if I wanted to go home with some money at the end of the summer. Sam said that anyway, he had an investment for me. That he saw a car parked at a bungalow colony on Sackett Lake Road with a 'For Sale' sign on it and he wanted me to go with him to check it out. We got Uri, the bell hop, to drop us off on his way into town. It looked real nice. It was a big white 49' Hudson with shiny chrome bumpers. Sam got the key from the owner and we drove back to The Laurels to give it a good look-see. It seemed like it was in good condition, except that the tires were sort of bald but it rode O.K. so Sam said, "Let's buy it." We brought the car back and Sam convinced the owner that he'd make payments every week until the $300 was paid off. Sam said that I owed him $150 and that I could pay him out of my tips every Sunday.

It was great, now we had wheels!

Then it seems as if Fritz skipped parts of the Journal, possibly out of necessity, and went to another section of the Journal, the part when Judy comes into my life:

What a day this has been.

I don't feel so bad now. For a while, I wasn't sure she'd go out with me. But she did and now I'm on top of the world. This must be how love feels.

I got up enough courage to call her; I had to do it from the payphone in the lobby with all these people listening and then I had to wait and wait until they could find her. I asked her if she wanted to come over to The Laurels and I held my breath. She said sure, but that she had to wait until the parents had picked up all of her campers. She said she would catch a ride to The Laurels at 4 PM.

I was so happy, I ran around and around The Laurels looking to tell Sam the good news, but he said it was a bad idea. He said that if she was as nice as I let on, bringing her back to The Laurels would attract all the wolves. Sam's funny the way he says things sometimes. He said that female counselors were considered a delicacy and that I might have to carry a whip and a chair to keep the animals at bay. Sam's amazing; he knows just what to do and say. He's like a brother.

Just as I was about to say something to the waiter about whether they had found a suitable calf for my Osso Buco, he came to the table with a mouth watering portion of veal shank braised in an aromatic vegetable stock surrounded by a saffron risotto.

"Another Guinness?" he asked.

"Not right now," I replied, "But possibly more French bread?" I asked thinking of how good it would taste dipped in the gravy.

"Certainly," he said.

As he went back to the kitchen to fetch more bread, I put my reading glasses back on to see what advice, my mentor gave me:

Sam said to call her back and tell her we'd pick her up in front of the Camp Odetah sign on Lake Road. So I called her and she said okey doke. I was really excited. I wanted Sam to meet her. And was he really impressed. When we drove up and saw her standing on the side of the road barefoot in cutoff jeans and this little white top tied in a knot at her waist, he said "hubba, hubba . . . she's Daisy Mae."

Well, Judy sat between Sam and me and we had so much fun driving around the lake. It was so good to just feel her next to me. She has such an earthy laugh too. I mean she just oozed beauty. Sam dropped us off at this boat rental place and Judy and I took turns rowing around and splashing each other with the oars. She said she was a junior at Far Rockaway High School and that this was her first real job. I could have rowed all day but Sam came back and beeped his horn. I promised to show Judy around The Laurels next time. When we dropped her off at her camp I threw my arms around her and gave her a big hug and told her I'd see her soon. All I know is that I hated to say goodbye.

"It must be exciting . . . you know, to read what you wrote years ago," said the waiter as he returned with another full basket of warm French bread.

"It is to a point," I said. "Most of it is pages and pages of teenage war stories and coming of age episodes . . .some . . . ," then I caught myself and decided not to say any more about the Journal. After the waiter had gone, I couldn't wait to dig into my meal but what I had said so glibly in the spur of the moment and to a complete stranger, a kid old enough to be my son bothered me. Was it just the alcohol speaking or was this quest for the truth just a form of adult voyeurism? So, I decided then and there to accomplish two things today; first, to call Phyllis and tell her that there was nothing of interest in the Journal and that I was heading home and second, to slowly finish my Osso Buco.

By the time I got out of the restaurant and strolled over to my car, there sticking out from under the windshield wiper was a bright orange parking ticket. I guess that I was so enthralled by the meal . . . and the Guinness, I had forgotten to feed the meter too. Well, I told myself, I had accomplished one of the things on my list, now I had to say good bye to Phyllis. So with the courage only found after finishing four pints of Guinness, I rang Phyllis's cell phone number.

"Phyllis, this is Max, are you in New York?" I asked as she answered on the first ring.

"Max, oh Max, did you catch the news?" she asked sounding out of breath.

"What news?" I asked.

"About Archer," she replied.

"No, what about Archer . . . are we talking about the old guy in the nursing home?" I asked.

"Yes, that Archer," she said "Are you sitting down?" she asked.

"I'm in my car and I . . . ," I started to say before she interrupted saying.

"Max, Archer's confessed to killing Mary Ellen Mullen," she said.

"What? Did you say he killed Mary Ellen Mullen?" I asked.

"Max, it's been all over the news here in New England and probably New York by this time. He's been arraigned here in Rutland and has pled guilty," she said.

"I would have never believed it, that old codger killer her . . . and we just saw him the other day," I said.

"Yes and that means you're part of the story," she said.

"Part of what story?" I asked.

"Max, it's too long to go into on the phone. I'm leaving Rutland for New York in about twenty minutes and would like to meet you around 6 PM," she said.

"That's why I was calling you," I said.

"Good, when I arrive I'll give you an exact time and place for our meeting," she said.

"No, I mean . . . I haven't got the stomach for all this mystery," I said.

"Max, it's a little too late for that now, you're in it whether you want to or not," she said.

"Phyllis, why do I have to be involved . . . I've got my own problems to deal with," I said

"Max, I know, but this is 'Pulitzer', this is 'America on Trial TV', this is my ticket out of Palookaville. And anyway, I'm sure you'd like to see your old friend Sam, wouldn't you?" she said.

"What about Sam?" I asked.

"Oh, now you're interested? I thought you just said you had a stomach ache from all this mystery," she said sarcastically and when I didn't answer, she shot back, "Are you in or out, Max?"

"You've found Sam?" I asked softly.

"I didn't hear you, Max; what was that?" she said rubbing it in.

"I said, did you locate Sam?" I said much louder.

"Yes, I know where he is and what he's having for dinner tonight," she said proudly.

"Well, where is he?" I asked.

"In or out, Max?" she barked.

"In" I said reluctantly.

"I didn't hear you Max," she said.

"In, I'm in," I said.

# THIRTY SIX

After tearing out a few pages of hotel listings from a Manhattan Yellow Pages Directory I found hanging on a chain in a phone booth, I retreated to my car and called what I considered to be reasonably priced hotels. Luckily, I was able secure a room at the Marriott on 3rd Avenue and 52nd Street for under $150, which is considered a major coup since comparable rooms in the City were in the $275 to $500 range. Then I called Norma and told her that I was staying in Manhattan and that I appreciated all that she'd done for me. She was a little concerned, being that I snuck out of her house in the morning but when I explained that I had to retrieve pages from my Journal in Brooklyn, she sorta understood or claimed she did. Although in retrospect, I felt she wanted to tell me something but . . . maybe not over the phone. It wasn't what she said or didn't say; it was the uncomfortable pauses that seemed to hang there during our conversation. Like, was it my turn or hers to speak?

I made my way uptown from Greenwich Village while rehearsing a few possible scenarios that I could use during my meeting with Phyllis. I had to figure out a way of separating Sam Bergman from the Mary Ellen Mullen murder case. If what Phyllis had said was true, and Mr. Archer was the perpetrator then Sam was in essence a red herring. I had to convince her that mentioning Sam would only confuse the authorities and the public. I might say, 'Actually, what good would it serve? It will only confuse the listener or reader . . . best to edit him out.' I also had to devise a way of extricating myself from the story too. My problem was that I didn't have enough information. Why would Archer confess?

When I arrived at the Marriott I was so happy to get rid of my car, I tossed the keys to the doorman saying, "She's all yours." He gave me a ticket to give to the receptionist at the front desk to be validated and advised me to call down at least a half hour before I needed my car. After the receptionist swiped my credit card I was given a keycard to room 1917, on the 19th floor, which turned out to be a spacious room with two queen-sized beds, a desk, an entertainment center with a large screen TV, and a new fangled shower curtain which bowed out giving the shower a more spacious feel. A card on the bed boasted that Marriott had refurbished all the rooms and that if I wanted clean sheets on subsequent days, I should leave the card on my pillow. I pitied the long term guests who might neglect to place the card on their pillows since they would be sleeping on the same unwashed linens for months.

That being said, the view from my window of the 59th Street Bridge spanning the East River was very nostalgic. Many, many years earlier I would travel from Long Island across the 59th Street Bridge on my way to work on Madison Avenue. Those were the days when working at an advertising agency was fun. It was a time when some of the most creative minds in business and the arts worked on Madison Avenue. Later, when the MBA's took over, the ad agencies became merely a shill for big business.

After propping up several pillows against the headboard, I hopped in bed to search TV news stations for information on what transpired in Rutland. I checked ABC, CBS, NBC, FOX, CNN, and none had anything on the murder investigation in Rutland. This meant that either I missed it or it would be shown at a later time or most likely, it wasn't worthy of primetime coverage. After all, most people don't even know where Rutland is or for that matter, Vermont. So, I called down to the first desk inquiring if the hotel had computers with access to the Internet and was told that there were computers on the 12th floor for guests to use and that I could log onto the Internet with my room cardkey. The girl also advised me that the cost for a 12 hour period on the Internet was $15 and that it would be automatically charged to my room.

I wrote my room number down on a slip of paper

and slipped it into my wallet, put the "Do Not Disturb" sign on my door knob, and took the elevator down to the 12th floor. The girl said something about a Business Center so I followed the signs to the end of the hallway to a door with a brass plate on it which said, "Business Center for Guests Only." Oh, I felt so important as I slid my cardkey into the lock and saw the green light go on signifying that I was allowed entry. The room sported several conference tables with office chairs around them, a fax machine, copiers, a wet bar, and both Apple and IBM compatible PC's each at their own attractive workstation. In front of each computer was instructions as how to use your cardkey to access the Internet and in the space of only a few minutes, I was logged on and surfing the web for anything on Archer's case, when . . . Bingo, posted on the Rutland Free Press web page, Front Page, Headline:

### "Reporter Solves Cold Case"

Staff Reporter Phyllis Cho is instrumental in solving the Mary Ellen Mullen cold case. Miss Mullen, was a Mount Lawrence School student who was found dead in the trunk of her car in 1962. Detectives from the Special Crime Unit of the Vermont State Police arrested Mr. John Archer, Sr. at the Franklin Nursing Home in Gatesville early yesterday. Mr. Archer is being held under guard at Maryweather General Hospital in Rutland. In an interview with Ms. Cho before his arrest, Mr. Archer admitted that his actions or lack of action caused Miss Mullen's death. Mr. Archer claimed that Miss Mullen came to his garage where there was an argument about a recent repair which got out of hand. Mr. Archer claims that he may have accidentally pushed Miss Mullen backwards causing her to fall into the well of his grease pit to her death.

Assistant Attorney General Robert Pearce announced that Mr. Archer will be arraigned this afternoon in his hospital room on manslaughter charges. Mr. Archer is the owner of; Mountain Auto on Champlain Street and resides at, 15 Blue Hill Lane, Rutland.

I continued to search the web for more on the case but found they all led back to this particular article. What I couldn't figure out was why Archer felt compelled to confess after all this time and why to Phyllis. I knew she was aggressive but what could she have found out? Maybe she went back to the nursing home with a case of Marlboro's and Jack Daniels'. After all, he'd have to be really shit-faced to confess to murder.

Then, while I was there, I decided to check my E-mail . . . bad idea, it said I had 154 unread messages in my inbox and 399 messages in my bulk mail box. After whipping through all the offers for sexual enhancement, lotteries that I had won, offers from Nigerian officials to help them deposit $30 million dollars in my bank account for a 20% commission, cookbooks, PayPal notices, Delta Airline deals, and countless other bogus offers, I deleted them all with two clicks. Just as I was shutting down and logging off, my cell phone rang. Glancing at the caller ID, I saw it was from my home telephone number.

"Hello," I said.

"Hello, Daddy?" he said.

"Yes, is this my big boy?" I said.

"Daddy, it's Kenny," he said.

"Oh, I miss you, how are you . . . what's up?" I said.

"Daddy, you know what? I got a part in this play," he said.

"That's wonderful," I said.

"You know what, it's a big part. I got pages and pages to read," he said.

"Really, I'm so proud of you," I said "When can I see it?" I said.

"Not sure . . . will you be home soon?" he asked.

"Of course, I wouldn't miss it for the world. Did you know I miss you?" I said longingly.

"I miss you too . . . gotta go," he said.

"Wait, is Mommy home?" I asked.

"Yap, do you want to talk to her?" he asked.

"Yes, please," I said, then tried to think quickly of what to say to her. Sure, just tell her that I was staying at a hotel in Manhattan and that I had a date with Phyllis tonight. I don't think so.

"Max, how are you?" she asked.

"I'm fine honey. Kenny tells me he's got a part in a play. That's great," I said.

"Oh, he's so excited; he's calling everyone he knows," she said.

"What's Randy up to?" I said trying to keep it light and airy.

"Randy had an accident at school. Didn't I tell you?" she asked.

"No, what happened?" I asked.

"He just tripped in the hallway at school. They took him to South Shore Hospital and he's got a broken arm," she said.

"He just tripped?" I asked.

"That's what he says. He's in a cast for, I don't know, six weeks," she said.

"Oh poor muffin, six weeks. Can I talk to him?" I said.

"Hold on, I'll get him," she said as she walked with the portable phone to find Randy.

"Daddy, I broke my arm," he said.

"Mommy told me, does it hurt?" I asked.

"No, but I have this big cast on. It's very heavy and I can't take it off for six weeks," he said.

"Oh, my poor boy. I know how you feel," I said, pretending that I once broke my arm. "Daddy broke his arm too when he was your age. I couldn't play ball or do lots of things for months. But you know what, it mended and everything turned out all right. Also, it gave me a good opportunity to use my other hand and soon, I became ambidextrous. Do you know what that is?" I asked.

"No, what?" he said.

"That's when you learn to use both hands equally. You learn to write with both hands, pitch with both hands, and catch with both hands. You know, in a way, you're lucky. Now you can develop an important skill not many boys have an opportunity to learn," I said.

"Really?" he said.

"Would I make up stories?" I said.

"Yap, you would," he said.

"Well, this is on the up and up," I said.

"O.K., Daddy," he said.

And just hearing the word, 'Daddy', brought me to the realization that I would do anything to protect them from the shame and ridicule their father faced if his actions were brought to light.

"I miss you muffin," I said.

"I miss you too Daddy," he said.

"Kiss, kiss," I said.

"Kiss, kiss," he said and hung up.

When I got back to my room, I spread the Journal pages on the bed and culled out the ones that dealt with Judy. I wanted to mentally go back to Sackett Lake and read my comments and observations in light of my new found memory.

# THIRTY SEVEN

Where's those pictures? I said to myself fumbling through my rucksack for the glassine containing the precious pictures of Max, Judy and the postcard of The Laurels Country Club that started this odyssey. When I found them, I took the photo of Judy out and leaning back against the headboard of my bed and looked into the eyes of my first love. There memorialized forever was the stark beauty of youth. A young girl who would never experience the thrill of romance, childbirth, a career, travel, and God knows what destiny had in store for her. I placed her picture back into the glassine and haphazardly picked up one of the Journal pages:

> Sam was right!!!
> I should never have brought Judy to The Laurels nightclub. The guys were all over her. She couldn't even go to the john without one of

them trying to pick her up. I don't blame them though, she's so beautiful. The trouble is; she's sort of a tease too . . . I think she encourages them.

It really hurts. I don't know what to do.

What would Sam do?

After reading those heart soaking comments, I put the paper down and closed my eyes and tried to will myself back to The Laurels, to the nightclub on the lake, to the Latin music, to the couples strolling arm in arm around the hotel grounds, . . . and I was there, walking down a path leading to the lake. I saw the lights . . . the lights reflecting at night on the still waters of Sackett Lake. They were the lights from Camp Odetah and the bungalow colonies on the opposite side of the lake. And as I got closer to the shore I could hear the clatter of the peepers and harmony of the bull frogs. When I looked up, the sky was a brilliant canopy of stars; and all around were the momentary flash of fireflies. Then I saw her, she was wearing a thin white summer dress with little roses on it. She was walking in and out of the water while carrying her sandals in her hand. As I caught up with her, I put my arms around her and pulled her close to me as I put my lips on her warm bare shoulder and gave her a kiss. She laughed and threw her head back pressing her body closer into mine. As I turned her around, we embraced and pressed our bodies together and I felt the moisture of her skin against my body and then her lips on mine in a long passionate kiss. Then we walked hand in hand along the shore stopping to wet our feet and embrace, until the heat we both felt drove us to find a spot in the high grass to make love.

Then, things seemed to change between us. Although there were gaps in the Journal, I had a sense, a foreboding, that our all too brief love affair had run its course. I wonder if I knew, at that time, of the coming crisis in Judy's life. One of the entries in the Journal alluded to a problem:

> No chance for a medal.
> Spoke with Judy on the phone today and she seemed distant. She said she couldn't see me today and when I asked about tomorrow, she said I should call her. I'm worried she found someone new and is just trying to duck me. I don't know if it's something I did or didn't do. The last time we made love, it was like I was trying out for the Olympics . . . maybe I didn't make the team.

In retrospect, I probably picked up that lingo from Sam. He had an uncanny knack of making even the most frightful situations laughable. He reminded me of the comedian Oscar Levant who had an amazing gift of coming out with irreverent and then again, the most humorous remarks to catastrophes. But then, in my eyes, the eyes of an impressionable teenager, Sam was fearless. Like the time Bob was looking for him:

Both gone.

Called Judy three times today and they said she's not there.

Where could she be? She had complained about this rash but she wouldn't show me. Is she sick or what?

Sam's gone too. He had something to do in Philly. Something about school???

Bob was looking for him. Said I should tell him that he wants his money. He was angry.

I'd better warn Sam.

Then, I could picture Sam and I sitting in the back of the dining room after working a grueling Saturday night dinner after all the guests had left. Our black vests thrown on the floor, our soiled white shirts opened at the collar, our sleeves rolled up, our little clip-on bowties resting in our coffee cups, our hair soaking wet with perspiration eating a plateful of steaks which we had smuggled out of the kitchen under the ever vigilant eyes of Mr. Spitz, the Steward. However, the next few pages confirmed my worst fears:

I'm in deep shit.

Manny came to get me this afternoon to tell me I had an important phone call in the lobby. That a Judy Freeman was on the line and that I shouldn't have my girlfriends call me during working hours.

Judy sounded scared. She said that she had to see me. That there was a problem but wouldn't tell me over the phone, that I had to meet her by the boathouse at 4:30 PM.

When I got to the boathouse Judy was already there. She looked real pale, like white. I never saw her so nervous. She said that she was sick with bad cramps and she missed her period and thought she was pregnant. Then she squatted and put her hand down on the ground to keep from falling. I didn't know what to say for a long moment but I knew we had to go to a hospital. When she started to cry, I went to my knees and tried to hold her in my arms to tell her I'd take care of her but she only pushed me away saying, "It's your fault, it's your fault." I told her that I was going to get Sam and we'd take her to the hospital but she screamed at me. She said I did this on purpose. That I got her pregnant on purpose. I swore to her that I didn't, that I loved her and would take care of her forever. She only cried and ran back towards the camp.

After reading how much pain I had brought upon that poor girl, I had to get out of my room and get some fresh air. I grabbed the cash on the desk, my wallet and my hotel keycard and took the elevator down to the lobby and out the revolving door onto Third Avenue. The street was filled with people either heading home or out for dinner at one of the many restaurants in the area. I remembered that a popular watering hole on Third Avenue was just a few blocks away, P.J. Clark's. It was a classic Irish pub with an intimate little dining room in the back. It was the kind of place that if you had a Harp Beer in 1959 and left for 40 years, when you returned they'd say hello and place a glass of Harp Beer in front of you. Clark's was busy with smartly dressed young men and women shoulder to shoulder around the small bar. I realized that any thoughts of grabbing a stout and sandwich at the bar were dashed and I decided to find another place to quench my thirst and hunger. With dozens of restaurants within walking distance I headed down 55th Street until I found a quiet looking Indian restaurant between 2nd and 3rd Avenue. I asked the waiter to help me pick out some of the favorites, emphasizing that I didn't want it too hot and he brought me out an assortment of chicken, rice, and beans in a mild curry sauce. It was delicious but somewhat hot. I guess they can't make it any other way and still be considered authentic Indian cuisine. However, just as the check came, my cell phone rang announcing Phyllis was calling.

"Hello, Phyllis?" I said.

"Max, where are you?" she barked.

"I'm at an Indian restaurant on East 55th Street," I said.

"Good, you're just cross town from me. Take a taxi to 646 Avenue of the Americas. When you get there tell the guard you have an appointment with Mr.

Richfield on the 45th Floor," she said.

"Who's Richfield?" I asked.

"Max, we spoke about this before. You did say you're in, didn't you?" she snapped back.

"Yes, but I'd like to know who I'll be meeting with," I shot back with the after taste of curry in my mouth.

"Just be there . . . 646 Avenue of the Americas, Mr. Richfield, 45th floor . . .got it?" she said.

"Got it," I said sheepishly.

She was right; it was within walking distance of the restaurant. It was one of those steel and glass Goliaths which reached up into the stratosphere. It said, 'he who enters these portals must be rich and important and in that order'. It was built for the sole reason to impress people. As I entered the massive lobby, I could only imagine that when I actually met Richfield, that he'll be seated on a throne. After all, anything else would be so, pedestrian.

"Can I help you?" said the uniformed guard standing behind a massive black marble counter. On his hip was holstered a 9mm Glock semiautomatic pistol and off to his right was another guard, also carrying a weapon, guarding the elevator bank. Above him were several video surveillance cameras recording everyone and everything that came in and out of the building and when, down to the microsecond.

"I'm here to see Mr. Richfield on . . ." Now what floor was he on? All these security precautions confused me. "Ah, the 45th Floor," I blurted out.

"Your name please?" he asked.

"Max Rosen," I said.

"Just one moment," he said as he punched my name into his secret database.

"Everything O.K.?" I asked.

"Yes, thank you for your patience. Please fill out this card and I'll direct you to Mr. Richfield," he said, sliding over to me a small card and pen. The card asked for my name, home address, company I was with, who I wanted to see, and nature of my business. After I filled it out, he gave me a badge allowing access to the 45th floor. He told me to wear the badge at all times in the building and to please return it and sign out when leaving. As I walked over to the elevators that ran between the 40th floor and 50th floor, another guard nodded to me and pushed the elevator button for me. He told me that when I exited the elevator that there would be a receptionist who would direct me to the party I was to see. Wow, I was impressed. They were so polite and courteous; they must think I'm important. Fooled them.

# THIRTY EIGHT

Once the doors closed the elevator raced to the 45th floor so smoothly and effortlessly that I had no sense that I was actually moving until a few seconds later, the doors opened with a soft but polite . . . bing. As I came out of the elevator, the first thing I saw was a secretary seated at large stainless steel desk. On the wall above her head was a sign in two-foot silver block letters which stated that this was the home of America on Trial TV. My first reaction, as I realized where Phyllis had asked me to meet her, was an equal dose of fear and anger: fear that America on Trial TV's brand of, 'gotcha television' would expose me to ridicule and anger that I was so stupid as to agree to meet her at a place of her choosing without any knowledge of what I was getting myself into. So, I decided that I might use this occasion to my own advantage . . . two can play the same game, I told myself.

"Are you Mr. Rosen?" the smartly dressed secretary asked me knowing full well that I was the party who had just cleared security in the lobby. I felt like responding, no . . . I'm Bond, James Bond . . . but figured she wouldn't be impressed.

"Yes," I said.

"One moment please," she said as she picked up her phone.

"Listen, if you're calling Richfield, tell him I wish to speak with Phyllis Cho . . .in private before our meeting," I said deliberately leaving out the mister.

"Certainly," she said seemingly somewhat confused. I guessed that Richfield was so important; an audience was considered a privilege. After repeating my message verbatim to Richfield she advised me that, "Miss Cho, would be right out," and several moments later, a fuming Phyllis stalked into the reception area. Well, I said to myself, let the games begin.

"What the hell are you trying to pull, Max?" she said by way of a greeting.

"Let's go over here," I said motioning with my head to an area away from the receptionist.

"Look, if you're doing this to make me look bad . . . ," she started to say when I grabbed her arm and brought her to me and whispered, "The place is bugged, don't say anything you don't want recorded on videotape."

She swiped my hand off her and still as angry as a cat taking a shower, looked suspiciously around the room. Not seeing anything, she faced me defiantly with her hands on her hips and said, "What the fuck are you talking about . . . are you on drugs, Max?"

"No, this place is like Fort Knox, you can't see all the hardware. It's buried in the walls," I whispered in her ear.

I saw the light go on in her head as she reexamined her surroundings.

"Tell Richfield that we'll be right back," I said pushing the down elevator button.

"Are you nuts? Do you know who he is?" she said.

"I know, he's a god but either we talk somewhere outside of this joint or I walk," I said forcefully.

I could see her wheels turning. She was searching for something to threaten me with but on such short notice couldn't think of anything, so she walked briskly over to the secretary and told her to please tell Mr. Richfield that she would be back in ten minutes. As it turned out, this was perfect timing as the elevator doors opened right on cue.

During the ride down to the lobby, Phyllis stood frozen, her arms folded across her chest, staring straight ahead at her reflection in the elevator doors. I could see she had on her signature tight fitting red outfit with white high heels which accentuated her lovely legs. I bet she positioned herself in Richfield's office to take full advantage of her lovely thighs when she crossed her legs . . . the old 'Sharon Stone Technique'.

After signing out and returning our badges, Phyllis told the guard, who had probably been alerted, that we would be back in ten minutes. The guard thanked her and said he'd hold our badges for when we returned. Then, high heels clicking on the marble floor, I followed Phyllis through the revolving doors and out onto the Avenue of the Americas.

"Did you know this street was once called Sixth Avenue?" I said.

"Cut it out Max, what do you want?" she said angrily.

"I want Sam's address," I said.

"Not unless I go with you," she said matter-of-factly.

"Then you're on your own. baby," I replied.

"Why are you doing this, Max? This ... this meeting is important to me," she said walking in a tight little circle around me.

"But not to me. This is nothing more than ambush television and the worst kind of journalism," I replied tying to appeal to her sense of professionalism.

"Max, that's bullshit. A story is a story is a story. We're all whores today looking for headlines and exposure. We're only giving them what they want," she said.

"But if it destroys someone's life, then what?" I asked.

"That's not my problem. I just report the news ... I don't create it," she said glancing at her watch.

"Really, what about this thing with Archer? How did that come about?" I asked.

"Look, we have to get back to our meeting. I'll go through everything with you after we see Richfield, O.K.?" she said leading me back towards the building entrance.

"Wait, what does Richfield want from me?" I asked hesitating at the revolving door.

"He's the Executive Producer of America on Trial TV. I've briefed him on the Archer case and he asked to meet you," she said.

"What about Sackett Lake . . . what have you told him about it?" I asked.

"I only mentioned that we were drawn to Archer while investigating another similar case in New York," she said.

"Did you specifically mention Sackett Lake to him or any of his cohorts?" I said almost saying, cronies in lieu of cohorts.

"No, I figured that it was my ace in the hole, so to speak," she said.

"Phyllis, I don't see how you can separate the two cases when I came to Rutland specifically looking for information on Sam Bergman," I said.

"Sam, I mean Max, I must get back before he gets suspicious especially since he told me that he has a dinner engagement tonight that he must attend. Look, I promise we'll be in and out and right after that, I'll explain what really happened in Rutland and where Sam is, O.K.?" she said slapping at the revolving door.

The guard in the lobby gave us back our badges and within a few minutes we were being shown into Mr. Richfield's corner office. I also realized why they designed the building with glass walls, the view of New York City at night, and especially LaGuardia Airport just across the East River, were breathtaking. When we entered, Richfield was seated behind a large rectangular desk made of inch thick glass supported by what resembled, chrome saw horses. It was really quite attractive. On top of the desk were several folders and a rich looking leather writing pad next to a very fancy, space-aged looking, portable telephone. Upon seeing us, Richfield rose and came around his desk to shake my hand and welcome back Phyllis. He was an attractive man probably between 45 to 50 years of age, slim, with thinning black hair, and dressed in a pair of pleated grey designer wool trousers, light blue shirt, yellow silk tie, and comfortable looking brown leather loafers. He had a good, firm handshake, which he used to size me up. He motioned us to a seating area which had two light brown glove leather chairs and a matching couch. In front of the couch was a glass cocktail table with a silver serving tray with a sterling silver decanter of coffee, three coffee cups, a bowl with packets of sugar and Sweet-n-Low and two small silver servers of cream and milk.

"You have a beautiful office," I said, opening with a complement.

"Thank you, I appreciate your coming on such short notice to meet with me," he said.

As I settled into one of the chairs, I was tempted to ask Richfield where he got the furniture and how much it cost but decided that the old axiom of, "if you have to ask how much it cost, you probably can't afford it," applied.

"Would you care for some coffee or some other type of drink?" he said. We both declined and he continued, "I understand from Miss Cho," he said glancing at

Phyllis, "that as a result of your inquiry into the death of Mary Ellen Mullen, a case that has been open for some 37 years, a John Archer, Sr. of Rutland, Vermont has confessed to the crime."

After Phyllis and I looked at each other, we both nodded in agreement which brought a smile to Richfield. I surmised that he was probably bringing me up to speed on material he and Phyllis had already covered.

"And, correct me if I'm wrong, in an interview conducted by Miss Cho at the Franklin Nursing Home, Mr. Archer confessed to the crime on audio tape and later signed a confession to that effect. That he was arrested by Vermont State Police at the nursing home, arraigned in Rutland and pled guilty. Am I correct to this point?" he asked.

"Yes, that's correct," said Phyllis.

"Good, I also understand that there were several other collateral issues which transpired which may or may not affect the presentation of this case to the public on America on Trial TV.

We'll just have to see how this all plays out over the next several weeks before we consider producing the program," he said.

I sensed that this timetable didn't fit well with Phyllis' hope of instant stardom but guessed they were just being cautious. Now, if I could only get out of this place . . . I thought running my hand over the rich leather arm of the chair. I bet this chair cost more than my car, I mused to myself.

"Mr. Rosen," he said fixing his dark brown eyes on me, "I understand that you were investigating a possible crime which happened in New York and that the trail led you to Rutland, is that correct?" he asked looking right through me.

"Yes, that's essentially correct." I said, not wanting to elaborate.

"Fine, is this case still open to the best of your knowledge?" he asked

Hmmm, this guy didn't just drop off a turnip truck. I sensed I was dealing with Columbia Law School, Class of 1976, stint as Assistant District Attorney in the borough of Manhattan, White Shoe law firm on Wall Street . . . this guy was definitely a few grade levels above me.

"I believe so, however, it's still in the preliminary stages . . . just following what leads I have," I said trying to sound intelligent.

"Let me just ask you this, was there some connection or similarities between these two cases?" he asked.

I realized then, that in essence, Phyllis had told Richfield more than she alluded to in our conversation on Sixth Avenue. The giveaway was the word, "similarities," because Richfield knew that in both cases, the bodies were placed in car trunks. I decided that the best response was one of seemingly complete openness.

"Yes, in both cases the bodies or in New York, the skeletal remains, were found in the trunk of a passenger car," I said, which didn't bring any noticeable response that I could tell from Richfield.

"Do you have any theories regarding your case that you would like to share with me at this point-in-time?" he asked.

"I wouldn't like to speculate at this time, there are too many loose ends," I said.

"O.K.; then let me ask you this. If we decide to do an America on Trial TV production of the Mary Ellen Mullen case, are you willing to be an on-air guest?" he asked.

"When you say, 'on-air guest', are you implying that a fee will not be paid for my performance?" I shot back, which brought a slight, unbecoming smirk to his face. I guess he sensed he wasn't dealing with a complete moron.

"I'm sure a fair honorarium can be negotiated for the complete rights for your appearances on America on Trial TV and/or our affiliates," he said with a knowing smile.

"I'm sure we can negotiate a fair and reasonable honorarium for my appearance on America on Trial TV," I said omitting the reference to, "affiliates," also with a smile.

"Fine, and one last thing, we're planning on bringing America on Trial TV to the next level, that of assisting public and private entities in solving cold cases. Therefore, would you consider our assistance in solving the crime in New York?" he asked me to Phyllis' complete surprise.

"What do you mean?" she blurted out.

"We have amassed a strong investigative team here

at America on Trial TV that can be used to solve cold cases. By working together, we can cover much more ground in a shorter period of time and at the same time, avoid unnecessary duplication," he said.

This proposal, which came out of left field, was a complete surprise to both Phyllis and me. He was asking if we wanted his help. It was a wonderful idea and although I had no intention of getting America on Trial TV involved in the tragedy in New York, I couldn't just turn him down in good conscience. And since I had already gotten his hackles up with the honorarium business, I thought it best to play along with him at this point.

"I'm sure we'd welcome your cooperation if it would help solve the case," I said looking at Phyllis, who to my surprise sat there speechless.

"Excellent" he said getting to his feet. "Now you must excuse me. I must run to another engagement." Then he went over to his desk, lifted a chrome handset from its cradle and asked his secretary to come to his office.

"Max, before you leave, would you be kind enough to give my secretary your home address, phone number, you know . . . so we can get in touch with you . . . O.K.," he said. "And Phyllis, once again my congratulations on solving the Mary Ellen Mullen cold case, we'll talk more," he said with a reassuring smile as his secretary appeared. Then a strange thing happened. As I was shaking his hand, he moved his body close to me until his face was just inches from my face and he stared into my eyes. Although it was for only a fleeting moment, he was cautioning me that he was the Alpha dog and that he'd bite my head off if I gave him any trouble. I understood him perfectly and tucked my tail between my legs and left.

# THIRTY NINE

"**D**o you want to get a drink?" I asked her as we exited the building onto Sixth Avenue or as it is now called, The Avenue of the Americas. When she didn't answer, I touched her arm and asked her if she was all right.

"What?" she said coming out of some deep thought.

"A drink?" I asked.

"No, yes . . . a drink sounds fine," she replied.

Then it hit me, she thought that solving the Mary Ellen Mullen case would propel her into the limelight. That it would be her fifteen minutes of fame. Unfortunately, it doesn't always end up as you had expected. They say that New York City has eight million stories, if so; chances are Phyllis' story will only be lost in the crowd.

So I took her arm in mine and gently steered her towards an old haunt that held memories of my hellion days on Madison Avenue. The restaurant was called the Baccara and it was one of New York's hidden gems. When you enter the Baccara, you're whisked back in time to the elegant world of the Great Gatsby. From the exquisitely upholstered intimate booths, to the turn-of-the-century lighting, it was a place where old and new money mixed to the syncopation of food, music, and laughter. It was New York City circa 1920 in all its raucous beauty. It was also a restaurant where a reservation was a must . . . although in special circumstances a crisp, newly minted $100 bill will get you a booth for two.

"Where are we?" she asked looking around.

"The Baccara," I said.

"Have you ever been here?" she asked.

"A long time ago," I said as a waiter came out of the darkness to take our drink order.

As Phyllis pondered what to drink, I ordered a vodka martini . . . upon which, Phyllis lit up and said, "Make that two!"

"Well, when were you here last?" she asked.

"It's a long story," I said.

"You show me yours . . . and I'll show you mine," she said while nervously making groves in the tablecloth with her fork.

"What do you mean?" I said as the waiter returned with our drinks.

"Too embarrassed to tell me?" she said taking a sip of her martini . . . when I didn't respond she said, "Look I'm not going to print it!"

"Why don't you first tell me what happened with

Archer . . . why did he confess?" I asked taking a well deserved swig of my martini. Oh, wow, that was strong I said to myself as the potent concoction cleared my adenoids.

"Let's do a little quid pro quo," she suggested . . . "and you go first."

"O.K.," I said fishing for the olive in my martini. "It was a long time ago, I was a just out of college and working as a junior something at a big Madison Avenue advertising agency and looking to rent an apartment closer to work. So, I placed an ad in the Times which read something like:

'Young exec desires,
1 bedroom, furnished
Apt., East Side, call:'

"Well, I gave my office number and extension at work and the day the ad ran, I got this phone call from a woman who said she had the perfect apartment for me. When I asked for details, she said that if I was interested I should come to; 12 Sutton Place South at 6 PM tonight and ask for Mrs. Robinson. At lunch when I told my boss, Artie, about the strange phone call, he laughed. He said it was just a lark, that Sutton Place South was the world of the super rich. Wondering if Artie was right, I got hold of a Manhattan phone book and skimmed through every 'Robinson' in the book and there weren't any at, 12 Sutton Place South."

"Someone was pulling your leg at work?" she asked finishing her martini.

"Well, I didn't know what to think. If I actually showed up at 12 Sutton Place South and it turned out to be a prank, I'd feel pretty stupid but then again, if it was real . . . I might miss a golden opportunity."

"So you went," she said asking the waiter for another round of martinis.

"When I got out of the cab at the building, I was certain it was a fluke. The building looked like a fancy hotel with a doorman, a concierge, elevator operators . . . the works. So what do you do when faced with all that pomp and circumstance? Act as if you own the place! I strode in to the lobby and told the receptionist to call Mrs. Robinson and tell her Mr. Rosen was here to see her. Then I waited for them to throw me out."

"Did they?" she asked dipping her finger in her second martini.

"They didn't. They called up to her and confirmed my appointment and escorted me to the elevator telling the operator to bring me to Mrs. Robinson in 1525. During the elevator ride up I worried that I might have made a big mistake. This place was way, way, way beyond my price range. I remember I nervously knocked at her door while tucking in my shirt and fixing my tie. After what seemed like an eternity, the door was opened by a stunning blonde with short cropped hair who I guessed was in her 50's. She was wearing a short black dress that curved around her ample figure and heels that brought out the best of her shapely legs." I said pausing to take a sip of my martini and gather my thoughts.

"Oh, this sounds interesting. Are you sure I can't use it in my newspaper. I wouldn't use your real name," she said in jest. I could see that the lack of food combined with the alcohol was beginning to get to her and decided to edit my story considerably.

"O.K., she showed me the apartment . . . which was probably done by an interior decorator. Everything was top drawer, the finest; certainly money wasn't a problem. Meanwhile, all I was doing was biding my time until she told me the price . . . at which time I was prepared to tell her it was out of my price range, when she asked if I liked the apartment. I told her I loved it but . . . then to my complete surprise she said, very matter-of-factly, O.K. let's discuss it over dinner. Flabbergasted, and in a bit of a daze, I followed her down the elevator out onto the street where we caught a taxi to guess where?"

"The Baccara," she said, as we clinked glasses in honor of her correct answer.

"Yes, the Baccara. We had a wonderful dinner and spent hours telling each other our life stories. I felt very relaxed telling her things about myself that I hadn't told anyone else. She was a very intelligent and sensitive woman. She told me that she owned an airline freight company which was based in Egypt and that their main source of revenue was carrying a narcotic-like leaf from Yemen to London each week. She said that the leaf was called, 'khat' and that workers chewed the leaf for relaxation."

"You mean she was smuggling drugs?" she said slurring her words.

"No, everyone knew what was going on. Her planes arrived at Heathrow Airport once or twice a week at 4:00 AM and were met by lorries that would carry the cargo to places like, Liverpool and Manchester for distribution and sale," I said.

"Funny, I've never heard of it," she said.

"Neither had I until then," I said "Now what about Archer?" I said, finishing my martini?

"Is that all? What about the apartment? How much did it cost?" she begged.

"O.K. after we mutually poured our hearts out to each other and after a couple of warm glasses of Courvoisier, I felt her hand slowly creep between my thighs. Then I leaned over and gave her a long passionate kiss," I said.

"And, and . . . ?" she asked.

"And we never discussed what it would cost after that. Let's say she made me an offer I couldn't refuse," I said.

"What a story!" she said genuinely impressed.

"Now Archer," I urged sensing time was of the essence in her condition.

"I wish mine was as romantic as yours but, here goes," she said.

She told me that while she was in New York, she was contacted by her editor that her home had been burglarized and that the perpetrator, a John Archer, Jr. had been caught red-handed leaving her house with some of her jewelry and her laptop computer. He told her Archer was being held at the Rutland

Police Station pending his arraignment the next day before a judge.

"That's Billy Archer's brother?" I asked.

"Yes, his younger brother," she said.

"How come he was never mentioned as a suspect?" I asked.

"Because he was only 12 years old at the time of Mary Ellen's death," she said.

"That's why you had to return so suddenly to Rutland the other day," I said.

"Yes, and when I got to the police station, Archer had lawyered up. So, I went to see his father at the nursing home to get his take and guess what? When I signed the Visitor's Log at the nursing home guess whose name was there from the previous day?. . . .yap, John Archer, Jr.," she said asking the waiter for another martini. I could see that like the Titanic, Phyllis was going to sink beneath the waves in a little while and that I'd have to act swiftly before she became too inebriated to finish her story.

"So that old reprobate put him up to it?" I asked.

"Yeah, seems like the story we ran in the paper spooked the old guy and he called his son and told him to drop everything he was doing and get his ass down to the nursing home," she said rocking back and forth in her seat.

"What was he looking for at your house?" I asked.

"Anything that would incrimal, incrimmal his father . . . ," she tried to say.

"Incriminate," I said correcting her.

"Yes . . . but wait, let me tell you what happened when I met with Archer, Sr. at the nursing home. He knew that his son had been arrested by the time I got there. You know you're allowed one phone call when you're arrested . . . well like a good boy, he called his Daddy. So I said to him, 'Got your boy to do your dirty work, Archer?' and he said, 'what do you mean?' and I told him that I knew Junior visited him the day of the burglary and that Junior was going to spend the next few years in a state penititary, penit . . . "

"Penitentiary," I said trying to help her.

"Then, it all came out, that he put Junior up to it and that he was sorry and all that . . . that Junior had a wife and three kids and that he, Archer, had a secret, a terrible secret he'd tell me," she said.

"That he killed Mary Ellen Mullen?" I asked.

"Yap," she said.

"But, why?" I asked.

"He said it was an accident. That Mary Ellen had come to the garage to complain about an oil leak . . . a simple oil leak. He said that he told her that it might be the oil filter seal had gone bad or maybe it was something serious, like it was coming from the engine block. He claims she started screaming at him, that she used profanity, that she told him that he and his son Billy were a bunch of incompetent idiots. He said that he couldn't reason with her and that he told her, 'to get the hell out of his garage,' but she followed him around. He claimed that he was trying to avoid her when he tripped over a muffler pipe and knocked her backwards into the grease-pit. That when he ran down the stairs into the well of the grease-pit to help her, she was already dead. He said he panicked and put her into the trunk of her car and drove it out of town, leaving it on the side of the road," she said.

"Then it was just an unfortunate accident?" I asked.

"That's what he said," she said.

"And the part about the plastic bag over her head, what did he say about that?" I asked.

"Said he did it in the spur of the moment . . . that he couldn't look her in the face so he put a black plastic garbage bag over her head," she said.

"And Junior, what about him?" I asked.

"Claims Junior wasn't there," she said.

"Do you believe him? I asked.

"What's to believe, he was only twelve," she said playing with her glass.

I could see that Phyllis was having trouble focusing and that I'd have to move fast before her eyes closed and her head hit the table ending our little chat.

"And the confession?" I asked.

"Made him a deal. If he confessed, I'd drop the burglary charges against Junior," she said.

"Could you do that? He was caught red-handed," I asked.

"Not really but I told I would . . . and he believed me, anyway I had him between a rock and a . . . and a," she stopped to think of what the next word was.

"Hard place," I said helping her finish her thought.

"I had him on tape too . . . but he didn't care, the

jig was up. I even had him sign a confession which I printed out on the nursing home's computer," she said proud of herself.

"And what about Junior?" I asked.

"Oh, he was a good-old-boy. Did everything his Daddy told him to do and when Senior told him, 'find out what she knows', he took my computer. Said he took the jewelry to make it look like a burglary. He's harmless . . . never been in trouble," she said drifting in and out of consciousness.

I knew that I'd have to get her back to wherever she was staying so I motioned to the waiter to bring me the check.

"We going?" she said staring at me with one eye open.

"Yeah, just let me pay the tab," I said.

"Spoke with the DA in Rutland to reduce the charges against Junior to a misnomeaner, I mean, misno . . ." she tried to finish when I helped her.

"Misdemeanor" I said.

"Yes, that's it . . . just a misdo . . ." she said slurring her words and teetering for a fall. I signed the credit card receipt and asked the waiter to call us a taxi. Then I moved closer to Phyllis in order to help her to her feet when she pushed me away saying, "Stop, stop . . . I have something for you," as she opened her purse and gave me her business card. I turned the card over to see that she had written; Sam Bergman, 'The Dacha on Lake Ariel,' PA. Then, just like in the movies, she fell into my arms.

# FORTY

Oh . . . I awoke with a splitting headache. I felt as if someone had shoved a hot poker into my right eye. I really can't drink like that, what the hell was I thinking? I don't drink vodka. As I looked around my hotel room, I noticed a trail of the clothes I wore the night before on the floor, starting at the door and ending up beside the bed. I must have pealed them off before I collapsed on the bed.

Then I slowly got out of bed and using the furniture and the wall as support, made my way into the bathroom to splash some water on my face. It felt so good, I decided to skip the rinse and take a shower. I fumbled with the controls turning the lever first to the right then back some to the left until I got the water temperature to lukewarm. Then I got in the tub and stood under the shower head letting the spray hit me right in the eye. I found a tiny packet of soap and washed my body trying not to bend down too far for fear I'd lose my balance and topple out of the shower. I also opened three itsy bitsy plastic containers, one was probably a shampoo and the two were probably a cream rinse and a mouthwash. However, in my precarious condition and without my eyeglasses, I couldn't tell which was which so I mixed them all together in the palm of my hand and washed my hair trying not to get any of it in my damaged right eye. In case I had actually washed my hair with mouthwash, at least I'd know my hair would smell nice.

Somewhat refreshed, I dried myself with a fluffy white towel and slowly made it back into the room and opened the curtains. It was a bit bright out there and I looked back from the window to see what time it was on the bedside clock, 11:30. Wow, that was quite a nap, I told myself. I thought of calling Phyllis to see how she was but decided that she was probably in no condition to receive calls until, well . . . much, much later.

I took the towel which I had tied around my waist and rubbed my face with it trying to clear the cobwebs from my mind. Why do I instinctively put a towel around me when I'm all alone? Do I think the chair will get a bad impression of me if I sit in it naked? We have so many idiotic phobias I thought as I sat on the edge of my bed and tried to play back what happened after Phyllis and I left the Baccara restaurant last night. I remembered someone from the restaurant helped me get Phyllis into a taxi and that, thank heavens, she sobered up long enough to tell the cabbie where she was staying. It turned out to be a relative of hers who lived in a brownstone on West 72nd Street. It was a short ride from the restaurant and after I paid the cabbie, I helped Phyllis up the stairs to the front door. Well, you should have seen the look on this woman's face when she opened her front door and saw Phyllis, half in the bag, and this old guy propping her up against the wall. "Oh, come right in; are you the serial killer Phyllis told me about? Just put her anywhere . . . care for some tea?" Not exactly...she took one look at me and grabbed Phyllis by the arm pulling her inside and slammed the door. To make matters worse, I had paid the cabbie but had neglected to tell him to wait. So, I had to make my way over to Central Park West to flag a taxi downtown, which is not an easy task with people on every street corner trying to do the same thing.

Desperately in need of coffee, I slipped into a pair of slacks and threw a polo shirt on. Then I searched my pants pockets for Phyllis' business card with Sam's address and my hotel keycard. I found the business card crumpled up with some cash in the front right pocket of the trousers on the floor and the keycard on the floor near the door. I slipped into my loafers grabbed my wallet with the paper that had my room number on it and glanced at my reflection in the mirror above the desk only to see an old disheveled man, with one eye almost closed and his body slightly tilted to the right. When the headache returned in force, I went into the bathroom and held a facecloth under cold water. Then I applied the facecloth directly over my bad eye and made my way out of the room in the direction of the elevators . . . I hoped. When I got off on the 12th floor of the Marriott it was busy with suits filling or refilling their coffee cups. As I got in line to get coffee, they glanced at me disapprovingly when they saw the facecloth over my injured eye. I was very tempted to say to them, "you should have seen the other guy," but didn't. I wanted to grab a hot cup of coffee and use the Internet for directions to Lake Ariel, Pennsylvania.

With a cup of coffee in one hand, I made my way down the hall to the Business Center and after gaining entry with my keycard I eased myself into a chair at one of the empty computer workstations. After I swiped the keycard into the reader to gain access to the web I was politely informed that I was free to explore the Internet at my leisure. The first thing I did was lookup what a 'dacha' was. Yahoo said that a dacha was an aristocratic Russian country house. I should have known it . . . . Sam was a Russian scholar. Then I checked MapQuest for the best route to Lake Ariel, Pennsylvania and found that it was only 110 miles away from my hotel which translated to a 2 hour and 23 minutes drive time. But when I looked closely at the map, I sat back shaking my head in amazement because Lake Ariel was also only 65 miles from Sackett Lake. Of all the places in the world to end up, Sam was in the Poconos just an hour southwest of Sackett Lake. I printed directions to Lake Ariel and logged off the web. As I rode the elevator up and headed back to my room, my heart was pounding with the anticipation of finally seeing Sam; he was just 2 ½ hours away. I cleaned out the bathroom collecting my toothbrush, toothpaste, and razor and deposited them in my toiletries bag. Then I hurriedly went around picking up my clothing from the floor and stuffed it into my rucksack. Remembering what the doorman said about collecting my car, I called down to the concierge and told him I was checking out and requested my car be brought around. In a final check of the room, I found an errant sock hiding under the bed which I stuffed in a compartment on the side of the rucksack.

After one last quick peek in the bathroom, I was down the hall in a flash at the elevators trying to decide if the next one down was the elevator on the right or the one on the left. I mentally picked the elevator on the right and . . . Bing, I was correct, as the elevator door on the right opened. At last, I thought, I was starting out on the right foot; this would be a day to remember.

When I got to the lobby, I stopped at the concierge and thanked him for his assistance. He was an older guy, about my age and probably didn't pull down too much as a concierge so I left him a generous tip. He directed me to the front desk to collect my receipt for the valet and I was soon out the revolving doors and in my Volvo en route down the West Side Highway to the Holland Tunnel to New Jersey and then due west to the Pocono Mountains. By the time I made my way through the Holland Tunnel into New Jersey, I was famished. Luckily, my route took me down a stretch with a large selection of fast food joints and interesting looking diners. Using an age old trucker theory, 'the ones with the most cars and trucks have the best grub," I chose a diner surrounded by cars and trucks. I didn't know if the place was good but it was certainly busy. I found a spot at the counter and tried to get the eye of the waitress by acting as if I was going to faint unless I got some food fast but she'd seen it all and wasn't impressed by my theatrics. She was a bleached blonde, probably in her mid 50's, dressed in a white uniform with a dainty little apron tied around her waist. Her demeanor was, tell me what you want, don't try to substitute something from the menu, and do you want ice cream on your pie? When I advised her that I was very hungry, she said, "Really? I would have never guessed." We both laughed and I ordered the, Lumberjack Special, which came with juice, eggs, ham, bacon, sausage, home fries, pancakes, and a carafe of hot coffee. When she stopped by later to see how I was doing and saw that I was licking the plate, she asked me, "Do you want a slice of pie?"

I said in my best Humphrey Bogart impression, "maybe on the way back, beautiful."

As I adjusted the seatbelt in my car, I checked my watch, it was 2:30 PM which meant that if I didn't stop and went straight through, I'd be at Sam's around 4:30 PM. So I took a deep breath and pulled out from the diner parking lot and headed west for the New Jersey Turnpike to Route 280 west towards the Dover/ Delaware Water Gap and Lake Ariel.

On my mind was should I call Sam before I show up on his doorstep, or should I just surprise him? What would I say? 'Hi I'm Max, I used to work with you at the Laurels 44 years ago . . . and I want to tell you how terribly sorry I am for having gotten you involved in the death of Judy Freeman, AKA 'Daisy Mae'... and by the way, the cops think I might have killed her because I found her remains in your car, you know the Hudson you parked in the woods at Sackett Lake'. I'm sure he wouldn't throw his arms around me and say, 'Hey, glad to see you.' Then, what was I doing heading to the Poconos? There was only one answer, I had to. Because seeing Sam will bring me full circle in my quest for closure and whatever we say to each other will be for our ears only.

The ride took much longer than I had predicted when large portions of the route were backed up due to construction. I think that no matter where I go, the roads are in a constant state of repair. I remember telling Vicky during a trip from Boston to New York recently that there was a stretch of road on the Connecticut Turnpike just outside of New Haven that's been under construction for over 40 years. Naturally, she thought I was exaggerating but it was true.

Finally, at a little after 6 PM, I could see Lake Ariel through the trees. There weren't many homes on the lakeside and I had no trouble spotting a large white estate on the far side of the lake. As I got closer, I saw that some of the upper floors had large balconies facing the lake and that below them there was a path from the terrace directly down to a boathouse and dock. This was either Sam's place or a very nice looking hotel, I thought. It took me about fifteen minutes to circumnavigate the lake, finally ending up on a tree lined stone driveway which wound its way through manicured grounds down to a large circular courtyard. In the center of the courtyard was a majestic stone fountain with figures that might have been inspired by the Trivoli Fountain in Rome. As I inspected the buildings architecture from my car, it was reminiscent of a European hotel, grand but not pretentious. Parked next to the fountain was a White Lexus SUV with Delaware plates. It's amusing how every wealthy person in our country is connected in some way to the State of Delaware. I parked my Volvo a few yards behind the SUV and gathered up the relics that I brought with me, the postcard of the Laurels Country Club, the photo of Sam while a student at Temple University, and the photo of Judy Freeman. Then I sat there for a full ten seconds and took several deep breaths before I quietly opened my car door and walked over to the front door.

The door had an attractive brass knocker which I lifted a few inches letting it fall hitting its sound plate. When there was no response, I repeated it, this time allowing the knocker to fall from a little higher position. Just as I was wondering if anyone was home, I heard the door begin to slowly open and I held my breath.

# FORTY ONE

The door was opened by a pleasant looking middle aged woman wearing a crisp white uniform. I told her that I was Max Rosen and asked her, a little nervously; if I could see Sam Bergman. She smiled and directed me to a study off the foyer to wait while she checked to see if 'Mr. Bergman' could see me. The study was a large rectangular room with a high ceiling. On one of the walls hung a medieval tapestry of hunters and their dogs chasing a white unicorn. The marble floor was covered with Persian carpets and the furniture reminded me of my visit to a Venetian Palace. The couch and side chairs were richly decorated in gold leaf and upholstered in red velvet. The assorted tables were of intricately carved dark woods which characterized classical Mediterranean designed furniture. Then I saw it, mounted on a small platform on the far wall illuminated by a small spotlight. It was an icon; a jewel encrusted Russian icon, an icon that may have once hung on the wall at the Tsar's Palace in Saint Petersburg. As I stood there appreciating the beautiful work of art, my mind strayed back to the day I saw similar icons in Mrs. Swanson's home in Rutland. Just that this one was probably the 'Real-McCoy.'

A few moments later, a very attractive woman wearing a cream colored jersey outfit that clung to her like a silk glove entered the study. She had long jet black hair that swirled around her head as she walked and I sensed that she was of eastern European decent after hearing her speak. She asked me the nature of my business and I told her that I was an old friend of Sam's. That Sam and I worked some 44 years ago together at the Laurels Country Club on Sackett Lake and that I was here just to say hello. She looked a little concerned but nevertheless said she would ask Sam if it was O.K. When she returned a few minutes later she introduced herself, she said her name was Tatyana and that she was Sam's wife. She told me that Sam had a stroke six weeks ago and was confined to a wheelchair and that when I speak to him, to do it slowly and that although he may not respond, he does hear and understand everything you say.

Then she gracefully led me through a magnificently furnished living room which was decorated in a similar style, whose ceiling was over three stories high, out through a set of French doors onto a large stone terrace. There seated in a motorized wheelchair by a teak patio table shaded by a large cloth umbrella was Sam. He was wearing a pair of wraparound dark sunglasses, a beige Ralph Lauren sports shirt opened at the neck, a pair of faded blue jeans, and his bare feet were resting on the wheelchairs foot supports.

His face was gaunt with a white pallor and the stoke had left a twisted expression of anger on the right side of his face. His once dark brown wavy hair had turned a silvery grey and his right arm rested in a sling which hung from around his neck.

As we approached the table, he sat motionless facing the lake only a hundred yards away. His wife introduced me and gestured with her hand for me to sit facing Sam. Then she asked me if I cared for a refreshment and I requested a beer confident that in a place like this, they probably had a well stocked bar somewhere on the premises. As she strolled away, I got a glimpse of one gorgeous woman. She had the kind of classical beauty you couldn't put a number on, she could be 60 but would look 30 forever. I knew that Sam was a ladies' man back then but, you can't find a woman like that in a box of Cracker Jacks. She was definitely not a starter wife.   But besides her beauty I could sense that there was a fire in her and that if I did anything to harm Sam, she would cut my heart out.

I couldn't even imagine what a place like this would cost …probably millions. And his wife Tatyana, a ravishing beauty, well Sam must have done something right in the last 44 years.

"Sam, do you know who I am?" I said slowly, but he merely sat there staring at me through those dark sunglasses.

"Sam, I'm Max Rosen from Brooklyn; we worked together at the Laurels Country Club back in 1955. Do you remember me?" I said without any response.

Tatyana returned with a bottle of Michelob for me and what looked like a tall glass of ice tea with a straw in it for Sam. Then she stopped for an instant to say something to me, then seemed to change her mind and returned through the French doors into the house. I poured myself a glass of beer and took a quick taste while I took out the postcard of the Laurels and photos of Sam and Judy. I placed the postcard of the Laurels in front of him saying, "Sam, this is a postcard of The Laurels." Then for the first time, Sam reacted, he looked down at the photo and picked it up and studied it for a few seconds before returning it to the table. When he didn't say anything, I placed the photo of him taken when he attended Temple University on the table. Again, he picked up the picture, studied it for a few seconds and put it back down. Finally, I placed the photo of Judy on the table next to him and this time he looked at the picture for a longer time, turning it over to read the inscription, 'My Daisy Mae', when suddenly he started moving his head from side to side in a jerking motion. Then he looked up at me and in a guttural sound from way inside his throat he said, "She's in the boot . . . she's in the boot." I was so shocked by his outburst that I looked around quickly to see if anyone, besides me, had heard him.

"Yes Sam, its Judy", I said, as it all poured out, all the doubts and recriminations and guilt all in one furious outburst.

"Sam, please forgive me . . . I'm sorry about getting you involved. It was all my fault she's dead. I was stupid, I had no idea of what I was doing, I was just plain selfish. I got her pregnant then begged you to bail me out. . . to take her for an abortion," I said choking on my words.

"What?" he said, taking off his glasses and glaring at me through bloodshot eyes.

"I killed her, Sam," I said hitting the table with my hand and knocking over my bottle of beer.

"She wasn't pregnant," he said as I tried to cleanup my spill. Did he say she wasn't pregnant?

"What do you mean?" I asked.

"Listen to me, Max, she . . . was . . . not . . . pregnant," he said slowly enunciating each word as if English was my second language.

"But the abortion . . . you took her to the doctor in Port Jervis, remember?" I said.

"No abortion," he shouted.

I sat there dumbfounded trying to process what he said. Judy wasn't pregnant?

"She had a thing in her, the doctor removed a napkin, a tampon . . . you know what I mean. She probably forgot and had it in her for weeks," he said wiping his mouth with the back of his hand.

I couldn't believe what I was hearing. Judy wasn't pregnant . . . she only thought she was?

"Judy died of a staph infection, 20 years later they started calling it, Toxic Shock Syndrome," he said moving his wheelchair closer to me.

"She died of Toxic Shock Syndrome?" I said.

"Yeah, Judy was a victim of a deadly staph infection that killed hundreds maybe thousands of young women. Max, even with the best drugs today, women are still victims of this disease and die every day," he said with some difficulty. After that revelation, we both sat quietly looking at each other for several minutes not knowing what to say. Sam put his glasses back on and moved his wheelchair away from me, glancing back at the house. I looked around the terrace and then back at the house and caught a glimpse of Tatyana standing by the French doors watching us. I turned to Sam and said, "You have a nice place here," to which he merely acknowledged my remark with a nod of his head.

"Sam, I owe you a complete explanation for my visit," I said.

"Why?" he said, picking up his glass.

"Just listen to me," I said, and gave him a brief synopsis of the events of the last few days. I told him of my fear that he might be dragged into the fracas by the authorities in New York. All the while he sat there calmly looking out at the sailboats on the lake.

"Sam, the car, the Hudson … can they trace it back to you?" I asked.

Without looking at me he shook his head and said, "No."

"But the VIN number, can't they get your name off the registration?" I asked.

"Nope, it was never registered in my name," he said with a slight cough.

I had the sense that Sam was getting tired as he seemed to begin breathing with some difficulty and just as I looked up, Tatyana and the nurse were there at his side with an aerosol inhaler which the nurse placed in his hand. Then Tatyana faced me and in no uncertain words told me to leave. She collected the photos from the table and thrust them at me as she told the nurse to see me to the door. What she really wanted to say was, 'throw him out of my house.'

When I got back in my car, I sat there for a long moment going over in my mind what just transpired. Sam told me that Judy was not pregnant. That she had died of a terrible infection that killed hundreds of young women. Now looking back, I guess that's what Norma and Dr. Levine suspected when I described Judy's symptoms. But why didn't they say something to me? But then again, maybe ethics prevented them from speculating on Judy's death. I didn't know whether to feel good or bad. The doubt and uncertainty of the last several days had been exhausting. Now I had a great desire to put all those nightmares back into Pandora's Box. But before I could, I had one more favor to ask of my favorite investigative reporter. I needed her help to bring closure to the story of a girl named 'Daisy Mae.'

# Epilogue

7:29 AM, Monday, June 24, 1999
Far Rockaway, New York

After what seemed like an eternity, I eased my head forward to peek out at the street. It was empty. The police car was gone. With that, I relaxed and breathed a sigh of relief. I decided that it was too early to approach the house so I drove over to a Dunkin' Donut shop. After getting the key from a blurry eyed, flour-coated kid, I used the bathroom to cleanup. Then I sat at the counter and ordered a cup of coffee. As the boy put the coffee down in front of me he looked up as a car drove up and parked out front with its engine running and headlights shining through the window. It was as if the headlight's beams were pointed directly at my back.

Without saying a word, the boy started spooning sugar into a paper cup and pouring coffee into it. He then scurried over to the doughnut case and threw three jelly doughnuts into a bag as a policeman came through the door. The boy followed his stride, coffee and doughnuts in hand as the policeman moved behind me and eased himself into the stool next to me.

Glancing at the boy, he said, "just put it down here, Gregory". As the policeman reached over to pull the coffee closer to him, I noticed his shoulder patch read, Town of Far Rockaway Police Department in white lettering on a blue background. He eased open the lid and motioned to the boy to come over.

"Pour a little out like a good boy, will ya, Gregory" he said in a soft voice. As Gregory collected the coffee cup, the policeman turned slightly towards me and in the same low voice asked, "That Volvo wagon in the lot yours?" I looked up from my coffee cup and felt that my nose was running. I wiped it with a napkin and with a sniffle, replied, "Yeah", glancing his way for the first time. He was, I guess, in his mid 40's. He was wearing all the latest police accoutrements; shoulder radio, handcuffs, mace, gun and bullet clips, the picture of the modern policeman even though he'd outgrown the uniform around the midriff.

"Funny," he said accepting the coffee back from the boy with a nod. "I thought I saw it parked on Pearl Street, a little while ago."

All kinds of thoughts raced through my mind. Does he know who I am? I'm in New York State, is there anything he can arrest me for? I decided that the best course was not assuming anything. Just keep calm, I told myself.

"I'm . . . I'm early," I replied.

"Looks like you slept in the car," he said sipping his coffee.

I didn't know what to say. Keep calm I said to myself, keep calm.

"You from around here?" he asked putting his cup down on a napkin to absorb a few drops of coffee from the bottom of the cup.

"No," I replied. "Boston."

"You a Red Sox fan?" he asked.

"Not really," I replied "My boys are," I continued wondering where this was all going. He suspects me of something I thought but he's only fishing I concluded or I'd be in the back of his cruiser by now. "Not doing too well this year ... losing three straight to the Yankees last week," he said. I nodded my head. Then thought what if that were a test? I don't know what's been going on with the Red Sox. Maybe I should tell him I don't follow the scores. But then, he reached into his pocket and took out a billfold. He pealed a crisp dollar bill from it and placed it on the counter. He then, in a single motion, rose from the stool with his coffee in one hand and doughnuts in the other and moved towards the door. There he hesitated for a moment and turning, took a step towards me and said, "You know this is a small town and we frown upon people who sleep in their cars . . . especially on lonely residential streets. You get my drift?"

I could only stare back at him like a deer caught in the headlights of an oncoming car. Then he turned and slowly left. I turned my stool back to face the wall staring at the police car's headlights reflecting against the wall in front of me. It seemed that he was taking an inordinate amount of time sitting in his cruiser. Was he calling my description into his station? Was he checking on my car? Finally, the lights began to move as he backed the cruiser out and turned towards the exit onto the highway. I turned to watch the car slowly move away and could have sworn I saw him looking back at me through his rearview mirror.

I sat in the doughnut shop until the morning regulars started arriving. Office people collecting their goodies to go and construction workers jammed into booths wolfing down doughnuts and coffee.

When I thought the time was right, I returned to Pearl Street. I parked in the same spot as before and noticed that the rain had stopped and the sun was breaking through the clouds. I thought to myself that, this has been an incredibly long week ... and whatever might happen, from here on, was set in motion many, many years ago . . . a lifetime ago.

As I approached the front door, I noticed a hand lettered slate sign hanging from the door. It said, 'Welcome'. After ringing the doorbell a few times and listening for a response from within, I decided to knock on the door and was about to, when it suddenly opened. The old woman who came to the door was dressed in a pink chiffon bathrobe and matching bedroom slippers. She had a sweat round face with gray hair.

We stood there looking at each other until she said, "Yes, can I help you?"

I didn't know how to begin. I'd rehearsed it in my mind, what I'd say but the words wouldn't come out. There was something in her eyes that looked familiar. Was she the right one? I could be wrong. It's been so long. I tried to say something because she started nodding her head up and down, wanting me to say something. Then it just came out without my thinking.

I said, "Mrs. Freeman, you had a daughter . . . Judy."

With that, upon hearing that name, the old woman seemed to freeze for an instant. She rocked back against the door jam and I could see her silently say the words, 'Judy, Judy, Judy.'

I nodded and repeated the name, "Judy." Then I said, looking into her eyes, "A long, long time ago," but couldn't continue. My whole body began to tremble and as I stood there weeping in front of her, I said over and over again, "I'm sorry. I'm so sorry."

With that, the old lady stepped towards me and with both hands on my arm escorted me into her home. Only stopping for just an instant to look up and say, "Come in . . . I've been expecting you."

She led me into a small living room where the morning light streamed through sheer white curtains. As I looked around, the sun's rays seemed to dance off miniature glass figurines which were scattered around the room. It was a quaint little room reminiscent of my grandmother's in Brooklyn. When I was little, I'd sit on the floor by her feet watching her crochet elaborate tablecloths, napkins, and doilies of every kind and description. When someone was sick in the family; Doctor Dissick would show up with his little black bag and a pocketful of lollypops. In those days, grandma would pay for his services by presenting him with something she'd made. I think that over the years, Doctor Dissick had collected enough linens to open a department store. It also seems that Mrs. Freeman had a penchant for some of those same items since, every surface, every table and chair was covered with doilies. Up against one of the walls was an old dark brown upright piano whose veneer was peeling back from its base. On top of the piano, were several photographs housed in silver frames. Going over to the piano, Mrs. Freeman gingerly removed an 8 X 10 color photograph of a young girl with ribbons in her long blonde hair smiling at the camera. It was Judy. If there were ever any doubts in my mind, that photograph settled the issue. She brought the photograph over to me and motioned for me to sit on the couch with her. As we sat together on the couch, she began tracing the outline of Judy's face with her finger as she spoke." She was such a beauty," she said holding up the photograph and looking into her daughters sparkling blue eyes.

"Yes, yes ... she was," I said staring at the photograph.

I realized that Mrs. Freeman was experiencing difficulty, so I gave her time to catch her breath before asking her, "Are you all right, should I come back another time?"

"No, no," she said. "I've been waiting all this time to

meet you . . . I never gave up hope," she said smiling at the photograph. Then she took a deep breath and began to tell me that some years after Judy's disappearance, that she received an anonymous letter from someone who said she was Judy's friend, a person who said she was her confidant at Camp Odetah. She said that Judy had fallen in love with a boy and that they were going to run away together. As I looked over at Mrs. Freeman, I sensed that this was not the right time to tell her the circumstances of Judy's death and that I should make a graceful exit and return another time.

"Mrs. Freeman," I began, "I want you to know that I loved your daughter with all my heart and soul and ...", I said, as she slowly rose from the couch and walked over to the piano. There she stopped for a moment to kiss her little girls photograph before replacing it in its place of honor. After collecting herself, she once again took a seat on the couch next to me. Then, she reached over and took my hand in hers and looking at me with misty eyes asked me, "Are you the boy from long ago who stole my little girl? Are you ... are you the one the letter spoke about ... are you, Sam?"

After enjoying Phil Sills' *Ghosts of Sackett Lake*, may we suggest other titles from our catalog we think you may enjoy?

## *Coco Colored Boy* by T.J. Gouin

Ted Medina is not crazy! He is a normal 55 year old man. So, why did his doctor recommend he see a psychiatrist? There is nothing wrong with him except that he seems to be losing his friends, he's bored at work and about to lose his job, he is not able to play with his grandchildren, and his wife and doctor believe he needs help.

A compelling story of personal conflict and racial prejudice, *Coco Colored Boy* relates the story of that impact on a boy part Mexican growing up in Southern California in the 50's and 60's. T.J. Gouin writes this story with a voice sprinkled generously with humor transporting readers back in time to a nostalgically authentic description of life in mid-century California from a child's point of view.

------------------------------------------

You may order online at www.bluewaterpress.com/coco or by mail:

BluewaterPress LLC
52 Tuscan Way Ste 202-309
Saint Augustine FL 32092

Name: _____

Address: _____

City, State, Zip: _____

Phone number: _____

Email Address: _____

(All information kept in the strictest confidence)

Please send me T.J. Gouin's *Coco Colored Boy*. Cost is $15.95 per copy. Shipping & handling is $3.95 per book for one copy, $6.95 for up to seven of any titles, and $1.15 per book for any combination of more than seven.

Number of books _____ x $15.95 = _____

Shipping and handling = _____

FL residents, please add sales tax for county of residence = _____

Total remitted = _____

We gladly accept payment of your choice: check, money order, or credit card.

## The Truth Lies in the Dark
### by Kristin Callender

What if you found out that everything you thought you knew was a lie? That the people you loved and trusted kept a life changing secret from you? These are a few of the questions Amanda Martineau must answer in The Truth Lies in the Dark.

As a child Amanda survived a plane crash that killed her parents and left her with no memory of her life before the accident. Raised by her grandparents, she only knows what they have told her about her past and her family. But her reoccurring nightmares tell her something different. They leave her feeling like a stranger in her own mind. Then an unfinished letter written by her grandfather thrusts her deeper into confusion.

-----------------------------------------

You may order online at www.bluewaterpress.com/truth or by mail:

BluewaterPress LLC
52 Tuscan Way Ste 202-309
Saint Augustine FL 32092

Name: _____

Address: _____

City, State, Zip: _____

Phone number: _____

Email Address: _____
(All information kept in the strictest confidence)

Please send me Kristin Callender's *The Truth Lies in the Dark*. Cost is $15.95 per copy. Shipping & handling is $3.95 per book for one copy, $6.95 for up to seven of any titles, and $1.15 per book for any combination of more than seven.

Number of books _____ x $15.95 = _____

Shipping and handling = _____

FL residents, please add sales tax for county of residence = _____

Total remitted = _____

We gladly accept payment of your choice: check, money order, or credit card.

## The Path of Our Destiny
### by Calvin Louis Fudge

Growing up is never easy, and Calvin Louis Fudge has written knowingly in The Path of Our Destiny of the pains of twelve-year-old Hunt Hews' living with a mother dying of cancer and an alcoholic father. Set in small town El Dorado, Arkansas beginning in the 1950s, Hunt tells his story of a difficult adolescence, made bearable only with the help of an understanding teacher, Mr. Ash and his wife.

Hunt meets temptations in junior high school as he deals with the problems of coming of age: first love, his first sexual experience, and losing his parents. Through all his troubles, business problems, and frustrations of love, Hunt never forgets his roots in his first real home in El Dorado.

You may order online at www.bluewaterpress.com/destiny or by mail:

BluewaterPress LLC
52 Tuscan Way Ste 202-309
Saint Augustine FL 32092

Name: _____

Address: _____

City, State, Zip: _____

Phone number: _____

Email Address: _____

(All information kept in the strictest confidence)

Please send me Calvin Louis Fudge's *The Path of Our Destiny*. Cost is $16.95 per copy. Shipping & handling is $3.95 per book for one copy, $6.95 for up to seven of any titles, and $1.15 per book for any combination of more than seven.

Number of books _____ x $16.95 = _____

Shipping and handling = _____

FL residents, please add sales tax for county of residence = _____

Total remitted = _____

We gladly accept payment of your choice: check, money order, or credit card.

Made in the USA
Lexington, KY
01 July 2010